THE HOUSES
OF CHILDREN

THE HOUSES OF CHILDREN

COLLECTED STORIES

Coleman Dowell

With a Postscript by
BRADFORD MORROW

Weidenfeld & Nicolson

NEW YORK

Published by Weidenfeld & Nicolson, New York
A Division of Wheatland Corporation
10 East 53rd Street
New York, NY 10022

Grateful acknowledgment is made for permission to quote from "In the
Mood," composed by Joe Garland. Copyright MCMXXXIX, MCMLX
Shapiro, Bernstein & Co., Inc., New York. Copyright renewed. Used
by permission.

"Wool Tea," "Writings on a Cave Wall," "The Great Godalmighty Bird,"
"Cancer," "City Sundays," and "The Silver Swanne" originally ap-
peared in *Conjunctions*. "Singing in the Clump," "My Father Was a River,"
"Ham's Gift," "The Moon, the Owl, My Sister," "I Envy You Your
Great Adventure," and "If Beggars Were Horses" originally appeared
in *New Directions in Prose and Poetry*. "In the Mood" first appeared in *The
Review of Contemporary Fiction*. Some of these stories also appeared in
Ambit.

"The Silver Swanne" was also published in a limited edition by
The Grenfell Press.

"Mrs. Hackett" appeared in somewhat different form as part of the
novel *Mrs. October Was Here*. Copyright © 1974 by Coleman Dowell.

Library of Congress Cataloging-in-Publication Data

Dowell, Coleman.
The houses of children.

I. Title.
PS3554.O932H68   1987   813'.54   86-15678
ISBN 1-55584-043-4

Manufactured in the United States of America

Designed by Irving Perkins Associates

First Edition 1987

10 9 8 7 6 5 4 3 2 1

CONTENTS

THE
HOUSES
OF CHILDREN

WOOL TEA

The Kid's brother wore heavy silk shirts, striped, cream on cream, shirts so heavy they dripped from your hands like hot taffy. He favored suits that were blue or gray with fine pinstripes, and soft moldable hats called fedoras, though sometimes he wore a hard hat (potty-shaped, The Kid had thought when he was younger) called a derby, and he carried canes with golden heads. His shoes were nearly covered by gray spats that buttoned up the sides. The covered shoes certainly put The Kid in mind of the tea cozy that kept the teapot warm in the afternoons, but his brother did not like to have this resemblance pointed out. The Kid assumed that it was because somebody might call him Tea Foot. His brother was a great one for nicknames; he called The Kid not only that but some names that had had to have a stop put to them. The Kid heard that order delivered in his father's voice, egged on by his mother, who used the word mortified in reference to the names. But his brother, the nicknamer, had turned pale once when a nickname was tried out on him.

The day this happened, The Kid and his brother and one of the brother's associates—which was all the brother called the man—were driving in the brother's Model A, but not so fast that The Kid, in the rumble seat, could not hear through the glassless back window what was being said. A lot of talk was weird-sounding but he became interested when the associate, who played the saxophone professionally in a dance band, said that he was an amateur compared to The Kid's brother when it came to smoking, and he called The Kid's brother a Tea Head.

The Kid saw his brother's neck and his ears turn white, and then he heard his brother threaten his associate with violence and heard him say, And you know I'm not just whistling Dixie. Then he called the associate some of the troublesome nicknames.

Thinking it over, The Kid decided his brother's reaction was due to what their mother called an excess of pride, a charge she leveled at her oldest son whenever she reached, as she often did with him, the very end of her rope. For one thing, she deplored the age difference between her two sons and blamed herself for waiting eight years, saying that there was no way a sixteen-year-old scalawag and heartbreaker could be a fitting companion for an eight-year-old innocent. And she said in a scared-sounding voice that it was the innocence she was most worried about. She said she would not have that tampered with for all the world, not if she had to give up her place in heaven, because a child should be allowed to be a child in the little time given. She said she had one example too many of somebody that grew up too fast and they all might pay the price someday. And so forth. Though after she said that about one example too many she said to The Kid's brother, You know I don't really mean that. I love you.

The Kid listened through walls to his mother's lectures and was as unaffected by them as his brother was. The Kid's antidote was to do something disapproved of, like going to spy on the first cousins across the street who were engaged to be married and were a scandal to the neighborhood; he had seen them kissing and more than that, hands everywhere like the way women put their hands in his brother's lap all the time, but he had not told anybody, about the cousins who had grown up together kissing, or about women feeling around in his brother's lap, some of them his mother's friends. The Kid's brother's cure for the lectures was to put more brilliantine on his hair and splash on some toilet water and go out and pick a fight with a girl his own age. These fights were often witnessed by the The Kid, who thought that the ammunition was pretty small stuff: calling each other High Brow and Low Brow over and over and saying Oh Yeah a lot. All the girls flirted with The Kid's brother, wanting to be asked for a ride in his Model A that had the painted slogans on it, like All You Girls Who Smoke Throw Your Butts in Here. But they were never asked as far as The Kid knew.

Willie T was the name of The Kid's brother's secret girlfriend. When they met, The Kid thought her name was Wool Tea because that was the way she said it. Her voice gave him a curious kind of pleasure. It was so hoarse that it was like she had a bad sore throat all the time, so that in her company there was always a memory of pain. But the important effect was that her voice made The Kid remember being coddled in bed and given terrific things like ice cream and custards, that would go down easy. The best memory was of being hugged a lot because unless he was sick there wasn't much affection coming his way. He knew that to ask for it at his age was to risk being called a sissy and so he did not ask. But he never minded when he felt a sickness coming on and knew it was going to lay him up for a while. Actually what he thought about a lot when he was laid up was Willie T.

When they first met he had wondered about the man's name, but Willie T wasn't anything like a man. And when he was laid up with a fever he thought about how she looked. Her hair, for instance, was as thick as a Labrador's pelt, tan hair that shone, and turned under at its heavy ends in a big deep roll. Her eyelashes were like Garbo's, his brother said, and her skin was like Dietrich's. In fact his brother sang a song, looking at Willie T in a silly way, that said, I didn't want Dietrich, I didn't want Garbo, I just wanted you. Willie T was as tall as The Kid's brother when they were both wearing boots and breeches, and taller when she wore shoes with heels and floppy-legged pajamas. Then, according to The Kid's brother, she looked like Lombard. But The Kid liked her best in what she was wearing when they first met at the creek, which was pants and a checked shirt and rubber hip boots, and a big black felt hat that made you think of the Gold Rush, which The Kid was studying about in school.

The Kid could not understand why Willie T had to be a secret girlfriend. For a time he thought she might be his brother's and his own first cousin, and that suspicion led him to say the name Willie T out of the blue one night at supper just to get the general family reaction. It was a lot more than he could have bargained for. His father turned bright red and his brother's face went white and then almost black, which was his color when he beat up somebody once while The Kid watched, scared. He was scared at having said her name but he forced himself to take notice of all reactions and saw that his mother was looking puzzled but like she might suspect something, the way she turned her head from his brother to his father and back again. It was like she was asking what was the matter with them. The Kid's father answered, saying he had got a goddamned fishbone sideways in his goddamned throat and almost croaked at the goddamned table. He was very belligerent about it. The Kid's brother's color turned back to normal while their father was yelling and then he explained that he had been scared by his father's struggle with the bone across the table. But both The Kid and his mother, exchanging looks, knew that both guys were answering a question that had never been put, in too positive a manner. The Kid could see his mother storing up something before they all got back to the business of eating the goddamned fish.

Later when the three guys were playing catch in the backyard The Kid's brother threw a ball and hit The Kid in the temple and knocked him out. As everything was going black he heard his father saying to his brother, You did that on purpose. So The Kid knew he had been punished for saying Willie T at supper though his brother never said one word about it afterwards. But the episode, which left The Kid with a duck egg on his temple and a headache that came and went for about a week, was enough to teach him that in addition to being beautiful and fragrant and exciting to be with, Willie T could also be dangerous, or could cause odd and dangerous things to happen to men.

He thought that was maybe why his brother did not play golf with Willie T. The Kid thought she would have looked really keen in the golfing skirt and long jersey with a belt and the shoes with flaps. He would have liked to watch her swing the driver and then turn and select a mashie from the bag slung on his shoulders. He would have caddied for her for nothing and wouldn't have minded the blisters the way he did when he caddied for his brother, in spite of the fifty cents he got. The Kid would have liked seeing Willie T at the Club House. He could imagine her sitting with him and his brother after the eighteen holes, at the table under the umbrella, looking down the hilly green, with a long fizzing drink silver-colored in her hand. He could imagine her at the Sunday dinners at home, but she was never asked. She would have fit right into the gatherings that were sometimes so big that the sliding doors had to be opened between the dining room and the sun parlor and the table opened all the way out so that its two ends were in different rooms. Everybody in town but Willie T came to those gatherings sooner or later. Cousins, school friends, obscure old people who mumbled. Once a couple of people came up to his mother and asked how much they owed her. They had followed the crowd in and sat down and ate, everybody thinking they had come with somebody else, they themselves thinking his mother's private dining room was a boarding house. Because they were respectable it became a favorite story of his mother's for a long time, though The Kid had wondered, laughing a lot, how it would have been if they had been a couple of the bums who slept in the graveyard, everybody there thinking everybody else had brought them.

One of the relatives who showed up now and then was, next to Willie T, The Kid's favorite person in the world, he guessed. This was a sister of his father's, a woman who was called most eccentric by just about the whole town. She was no longer young, as they said, but they talked about how hard this was to tell, especially after a long trip she took when The Kid was six. What had puzzled and interested The Kid was how when she got back from her trip she was missing splotches that had been on her face, and the skin that had hung under her neck was gone also. Her lips were tight and something she said a lot after her return was Don't try to make me laugh it would be cruel. The Kid knew that she dyed her hair for he had caught her at it, being helped by one of her Negro friends. There were basins and cotton and bottles all around and his aunt's hair was a real mess, white in places, dark in others, reddish in others. She cried out, Caught, sounding happy, and she and Miss Mary her friend and helper had laughed to beat the band, hooted and hollered, his aunt with helpless and pained-looking tight lips.

That day she said to The Kid, Lovey, it won't do to find out all the secrets of women at too young an age. You'd have nothing to keep you going and growing and she said to Miss Mary in a different voice, That's all it is with men you know. Just curiosity. Once they find out everything, they can drop us like hot potatoes.

Miss Mary nodded, but her face was not in agreement at all. The Kid thought that Miss Mary knew something his aunt didn't know about men and was protecting her from it.

The day he found them dyeing her hair he had been looking for them for a long time. After his aunt's husband, his Uncle Judge by marriage, had left her and run off with a young Negro girl, she had boarded up the house in the country, where people said she had buried money all over the place in tin cans, and bought an old empty college on the edge of town and moved in there. Except it was not what could be called moved, like it had happened and been got over with. Because she never stopped moving. Every day or so, no more than that, her people, all Negro women, some of them as muscular as men, moved her, always after dark, from one building to another and set up her bedroom and a kitchen and sleeping quarters for themselves.

The college covered several acres; some said thirty and some said as many as eighty; and there were many buildings on it, seminaries, because the college had been a religious school. In addition to these buildings there were what had been dormitories, and a sort of village called Gladys Court where women, exclusively, had lived. Gladys Court was like a fortress and could be locked and when his aunt was in there you had to give up trying to visit with her. But any time you went looking for her was a real challenge and no Negro person met on the grounds was willing to be any help and could not be bribed. The Kid had tried it with candy and his mother, exasperated and mad, had tried it with money. Once the building was found it was still a game to find his aunt because corridors were often blockaded with stacks of boxes that made dead ends like the old maze in the garden at his aunt's boarded-up house. And promising-looking doors turned out to be locked or were closed off on the other side by big chiffoniers and wardrobes and high painted screens. Just moving all that stuff around must have been as hard as ditch digging and only women to do it. But his aunt would not have a man anywhere near her and told him that in his case she made the only exception, except when she went visiting and had to put up with husbands and sons.

When at last his aunt was found it was generally on her bed, lying high up under the lacy canopy on stacks of cushions and pillows, always wearing something unusual and pale-colored, filmy or stiff, what they called chiffon or organdy. She liked big sleeves like butterflies and wore wide ribbons in her hair that had bows on them too. One woman who didn't like her said about her, It's little girl's day every day. But The Kid thought she looked like the pictures of princesses in his old kid books.

He would often be invited up on the high bed and they would have food and drink, nearly always interesting if not very good, something he would never get at home. He had had oysters up there, a pretty nasty experience, and goose liver with black fragments in it that his aunt said were rooted for in France by pigs and specially trained hounds. Seeing that he did not like the truffles she picked the pieces out with a spoon and ate them. He had drunk wine up there. He had had verbena tea and Madeira cake up there. After the first moments of strangeness the room became just his aunt's room, that was all, the way it had always been since he had known her, with its preposterously big bed, and not a dormitory or fortress on a deserted college campus, and he would settle in for a good talk that must always, but always, be about off-the-record things; she did not like small talk. What they generally talked about was what a son of a bitch his uncle by marriage had been, and the way he had knocked up god knew how many black girls, which was not how The Kid remembered him but he let it pass.

So it was on the big canopied bed with his aunt, surrounded by Negro women, everybody drinking something and eating, that he asked his aunt about Willie T.

Do you mean you know her? his aunt asked, giving him all her attention as the Negroes did.

Well, we've been fishing together, he said, making it just the once in case he had already gone too far. He tried very hard to understand the quality of their attention without seeming to study them. He imagined that he was his Labrador, sniffing something on the other side of a fence, and it helped. First of all, his aunt did not say Who is Willie T, which meant that she either knew her or had heard of her. None of the other women said Who? either and he was glad Willie T was not a secret to them. He let himself wonder for a minute if she had been on the big bed, having food and drink. But there was something else going on, something funny, and he felt cautious about it.

Fishing, his aunt said to the women. That's a euphemism, or would be under other circumstances.

There was a pause and then Miss Mary said to the others, Means a prissy word for something that ain't. The Kid heard them all sigh together.

His aunt said to him, I'm sorry, lovey, that's what we called in the theatre an aside. Now what else do you know about Willie T? Would you tell us how you have come to know her?

But The Kid was on his guard and not just because his brother could kill him for snitching if he found out. He was on guard for Willie T.

His aunt said, Well I don't imagine the mystery is all that great, ladies, not with a Don Juan in the family. I've heard that he has been consorting and I do mean seriously since he was twelve. And every one of the women went tee hee. To The Kid it sounded like they were poking fun at his aunt, maybe at her big words.

He said to her, rudely for him, What was that word?

What word?

The big one. A prissy word for something that ain't.

Isn't, she said, then, Oh. And told him, giving all the syllables: You fem is um. He thanked her and left soon after.

He wished he knew where Willie T lived. He would have gone

and spent the afternoon with her. He bet anything that her room was not closed in with tall curtains like his aunt's but was full of dappled light like the creek bank where they met. And he was sick of you fem is ums.

The day he met Willie T he and his brother drove to The Creek, which was really a river, in the Model A and soon afterwards this beautiful woman drove up in a yellow Buick and got out and hawked and spit like a man and laughed at The Kid's brother who took hold of her and they talked some kind of private language and then The Kid was remembered and she said, I'm Wool Tea, and The Kid was hooked on his first lady.

He was no more than seven at the time so he had known her for over a year. In all that time he had probably not thought about anything else as much as he thought about her. He did not know why exactly because there were many reasons. One was that he never knew when she would show up and where so there was always surprise in meeting her again and his reaction was like being scared by somebody jumping out at him, his heart beat so fast. One thing he had come to believe was that she would never show up at his house, and another was that he would never see her in public. So when his brother would grab him and say, Let's go fishing, or Let's spend the night up on The Hill, his heart would start up just in case Willie T might be there. Then he began to think that the reason it was all so secret was because his brother was afraid another guy would take her, or something, though his brother could have any girl or woman he wanted, that's what everybody said. When The Kid was six his brother had had a bad time with pleurisy. One of the cures was to lie on the sun without any clothes on like a new baby. He did this in the long stretch of ground called the Back Lot and they rigged up lines and hung quilts and sheets over them to make a private place for his brother. But The Kid heard everybody talking about the way women and girls too would sneak onto the lot and peep through the screens at his naked brother. Stuff like that The Kid had been hearing all his life and in the past year it had started to disgust him just a little. He didn't know why, just that it did not feel right when you thought about it. There was the schoolteacher who came to The Kid's mother and asked for a pair of his brother's pants to wear to a picnic. The Kid's mother had gone all mottled-looking. They were on the front porch in the facing swings and he watched the two women when his mother said to Miss Louise in a peculiar voice, You've got brothers. Why do you want my son's clothes? And then Miss Louise had turned red and said her brothers were all bigger than her, which was not so, and she said it mad and ran out to her car, a little Chevy, and drove off grinding the gears so much The Kid wanted to give her a driving lesson. His mother's mouth was just one line, then she said, like she wanted to slap somebody, Even a school-teacher. The Kid didn't say, Even a schoolteacher what? He didn't want to know.

A couple of days after his abrupt leave-taking of his aunt and her friends he and his brother met Willie T at The Creek. He wanted to tell her the reaction her name had brought about, wanted to ask her if she had in fact been to his aunt's house because all of them had acted like they knew her. But caution made him weigh his words, a caution new in his life since he had been knocked out by the baseball his brother threw, and he decided to keep mum.

The three of them sat on the bank of The Creek, their poles baited and dug into the mossy ground that seemed, even after a month of drouth, to be newly wet so that the handles of the poles were not only dug in deep but were supported underneath by rocks to hold them steady. There was comfort for The Kid in the thought of the deep mossy wetness. The worst things in his life always seemed to happen when everything was dry and there was a hot wind blowing. He liked rainy days so much he wondered if he might be part tadpole.

The Kid's brother and Willie T began to smoke one of their hand-rolled cigarettes, made with the tobacco that was much more disturbing to the nose than Camels or the Bull Durham that The Kid had smoked a couple of times. The smoke, drifting The Kid's way, made him drowsy but it also made him feel as if he was running a high temperature and was drunk on rock and rye, like the time he had whooping cough. Then, like now, his legs had seemed to be as big as houses. The things he looked at wavered like heat over asphalt. All the sounds of the day came to his ears twice. It was like the echo that lived in the stone quarry had moved along to The Creek. He could not decide if the way he felt was good or just plain lousy. When he had had the whooping cough and was given the tablespoons of rock and rye and got drunk on top of his fever, his mother had been beside him and that made all the difference. What he knew for sure lying on The Creek's bank was that he wanted to apologize to his mother, but he didn't know what for.

All of a sudden Willie T grabbed him saying, Keed ol Keed and pulled him over between her and his brother. Then laughing loud and long she pulled him onto her lap which separated and let him down onto the ground so that he was between her legs. His brother was laughing too, so hard that it sounded like he couldn't ever stop. The Kid was lying on Willie T, his face on her breast which was as fragrant as a bush of sweetbrier. He heard his brother say, Go on. I dare you. You can blame it on ree fur madness.

And Willie T made a hooting sound and called out in a very loud voice, Ree fur madness. And the two of them laughed like crazy people were supposed to.

The Kid felt Willie T doing something beneath him and then, though it was like a dream, he felt his raw skin against her raw skin and then it was exactly as if her body parted in some way and let him down. He had a sense of making connections with things that came in little pieces out of his mind. He felt Willie T's tongue and heard his brother's crazy laughter. Other pieces of his mind floated by like fish and he made grabs at them but they wiggled away and then he floated after them wondering if he was feeling good or bad.

When they were getting ready to leave he heard Willie T say to his brother, I think I've sinned. And his brother said, Go to church on Sunday. All the way home his brother kept looking at him. It was for his brother's sake that The Kid sat at supper and ate, because all he wanted to do was go to bed and sleep.

It took The Kid four days to feel like really getting around again, though he felt he was pretty successful in hiding his long tiredness from his mother. The day when he felt like raising heck was a Sunday. That day his aunt showed up for the noon meal. The gathering was especially large, probably because people had got wind of the ice cream being made on the screened-in back porch, two freezers, vanilla and peach.

His aunt came with four of her Negro friends, Miss Mary and three other ladies, and there was a lot of undertow even though they were dressed to kill. The Kid heard his mother say to his aunt in a low voice, Are they supposed to sit with us. It was not a question. He tried to figure out what it was and again it was like the meaning was on the other side of a fence. He was sniffing for it when his aunt replied in a cool voice, Two card tables will do for the five of us. You can have West set them up back by the hydrangeas.

His mother said his aunt's name, just, Evie, with a sharp sound. His aunt, still cool and easy, said, Don't worry, Callie, we'll be at the head of the table after all. And so the tables were set up in front of the tubs of blue hydrangeas in the bay windows and made very pretty with a lacy cloth over a starched one and a jar of flowers in the middle. The Kid saw that the English bone china was set out just on that table, and the heaviest silver that was generally used at only the most serious dinner parties.

During dinner, which was remarkably good even for an ice cream Sunday, The Kid's aunt said from her table, just the way The Kid had said it, loud and clear, the name Willie T. The Kid could not look everywhere at once but he did see his mother jump as though Sarah, her peke, had touched her leg under the table. And there his father was, reacting the way he had before, with a big red face. But all of this had to be seen in a hurry because The Kid's brother jumped up and away from the table so fast and hard that he knocked his chair over and did not set it up but kept on going. Then in the silence The Kid watched his mother surveying the tables, the big one and the one where his aunt sat with her women, very slowly, and from the faces she surveyed he believed she was reading as you read from a book, and was learning a sad and hard lesson.

After the coconut cake and the fresh ice cream, vanilla for him, and another glass of iced tea which for once his mother did not object to his having because it made him pee, The Kid left the gathering, which was beginning to spread out onto the lawn, people carrying cushions and folding chairs and the youngest carrying the funnies, and went in search of his brother.

He walked slowly because of being so full and because of the bright August heat that filled the rooms in spite of the shades being pulled halfway down. He had some idea of where to look because he had listened carefully after his brother left the table but there had been no sound of a door slam from any quarter of the house. This probably meant that his brother was still indoors.

The Kid trailed up one staircase after another, sleepy, feet dragging. At such times when he was looking for a person or a missing animal he got the impression that their house was actually a world, an endless world like eternity that turned in on itself and spiraled around and around, some parts of it freezing and some parts of it burning and in some parts the possibility of great joy. Once when he was little and could only count to ten he had set off on a journey to count the rooms in the house, but after he had counted to ten twice he was lost and sleepy and had his nap in a strange room, and woke up afraid because the voices calling him were so far away.

He walked through the secret hum of window fans, looked through gloom and across stretches of floor so bright they were like sheets of still water in the dog days. He looked on three floors, in all the rooms and onto all the balconies that circled the house. He looked under and over and through things, getting sleepier all the time.

He did not find his brother, but on the fourth floor in his brother's private place, which still had the rings in the ceiling from which the trapeze had hung until his brother fell from it on his neck and nearly died, he found, not hidden away but lying out as if somebody had just left it there, a picture of Willie T. It was her face and he guessed it had to be her body for that reason, but he had never seen her undressed all the way and she was undressed all the way in the picture.

In the same box that the picture had come out of there was a balloon in a kind of wrapper that said on it Trojans. He did not know how to feel about Willie T's picture. He did not know if it was right for his brother to have such a picture, nor why Willie

T would let somebody aim a camera at her when she was like that. He did not know why she sat that way and stuck her chest out like she was posing rather than as if she had been caught naked the way he had caught his aunt having her hair dyed. But he was too worn out by the heat and the food and the search to let it get his goat.

He cracked his jaws with yawns, tried out sofas and beds and daybeds and window seats and the floor for his nap that would not settle on him the way it usually did, slowly like dust, like what was called motes in rays of sunshine, accumulating on him until he could feel it like a light summer blanket and pull it up over him and sleep and dream.

Why had Willie T put on so much lipstick and kissed her own picture. The impression was of her own mouth, the right size and shape and the crinkles were like the crinkles in her soft red mouth that was also big and laughed a lot. The lipstick was smeared on the picture like it was on her face sometimes when she and his brother came back from walking or lying down for a nap in her Buick while The Kid napped in the rumble seat of the Model A. In his mind The Kid saw his brother kissing the lipstick mouth. When he did that he was kissing Willie T's naked body. Then it was The Kid who kissed the lips.

They woke him up later on. He thought at first that it was nighttime but then heard the racket of the wind at the shutters and the passing rain like curtains being drawn, swishing curtains of rain on the sides of the house and the copper roof overhead, and then cutting through it he heard again the voices that had woken him, far away and hollow like the voices that had called him when he had tried to count the rooms and had fallen asleep, back when he was a child.

He had learned that the hollow cistern effect was because of what was called the phenomena of the house, a result of the way the staircases had been built. You could whisper on the fourth floor and be heard in the cellar if you stood in just exactly the right places. Another of the phenomena was the way a certain window would hold an image after particularly heavy lightning. You could sit there and watch the images slowly fade, once of a tree and once of a bird, and they said once the whole landscape had lingered on the panes for several hours. When it stormed in the night he would lie awake wondering what was happening in that room, what was appearing and disappearing on the windowpanes, but would not have gone in there to find out for anything in the world.

The voices rose and fell, fell and rose in the rhythms of a serious quarrel. By concentrating on them he could identify them as his mother, father, and brother. Slowly he came awake and walked softly to the stairwell, not wanting his footsteps to cover any word that was said. All at once he hit one of the right places and the voices came in as clear as if everybody stood in front of big round microphones broadcasting The Big Broadcast of 1933.

His brother said, I'd rather dance with Willie T than sleep with the Queen of Sheba.

His mother said, If only you *had* slept with the Queen of Sheba.

His father said, Well, it's done. It's not fatal.

His mother cried out, Fatal. It is so fatal. It can be fatal. How can you forget your cousin Lucille. I'll never forget the way she looked.

His father said, Hush. Don't go on. These are not the Middle Ages. That was a long time ago. Can be is not is, shug.

His mother said, Looked like a ninety-year-old woman and her only thirty. Oh my god.

Then it sounded like she turned on his father really mad. She cried out, Why are you sounding like you're taking his side.

His father said, Because I am taking his side. It's done now. We can't undo that part. The giving.

And his voice disappeared under The Kid's mother's outcry. *That part of it. Oh dear god. Willie T's gift to my son.*

His brother said very low, I'll get out. Don't worry.

His mother said, Where to? To Miss Willie T, the town—

Shut up. Was that his father or his brother? He heard the silence then heard somebody starting up the stairs to where he hung over the railing. So it had been him that yelled out. He was afraid, up on the fourth floor with the phenomena, and didn't know what they would do to him for telling them to shut up.

When they got to him they all tried to touch him, everybody trying to pat him or something, and that gave him the courage to look at them. Was his brother different? No, he decided, but he had been crying. Did his mother look different? She had been crying too but she did not look like the stranger who had been yelling downstairs. Did his father, then, look different? Yes. His father was as old-looking as Aunt Evie before she went on that long trip and came back young, and he was a lot younger than his sister, younger even than The Kid was younger than his brother. But on second look The Kid thought that his Tea Head brother didn't seem all that much older than him, with the tears on his face and the way he looked at their father. He wanted to ask his brother, What did Willie T give you besides the picture? But he knew he must not mention the picture, ever.

After supper they told him that his brother would be going away for a cure. They said he was having a flare-up of the pleurisy. Before he could stop himself The Kid asked, Did Willie T cause the flare-up? He wondered if that was what his mother had called The Gift.

His brother looked at him all of a sudden with his face crinkling and he said, Oh my god, twice.

The Kid's mother and father asked The Kid's brother, over and over, What? What? But The Kid's brother closed up like a creek clam.

That night The Kid dreamed that he went to find Willie T, that he found her house and stood knocking then pounding on her door, calling out to her, asking her, What did you give my brother? And then demanding through the thick closed door, Give me what you gave my brother. Give it to me.

SINGING IN THE
CLUMP

"Awake/And smell the fragrance of/A June morning/It's past dawning/And oh the sky/Is blue above/And you're in love . . ." Fatty was singing at the top of his falsetto in the tangled field, hidden by the clump of ivy-hung scrub trees from the gaze of nearby farmhands. Startled birds, after a time, sang along. The birds were not startled by his voice in the grove—he was there almost as continually as they that summer—but by the unfamiliar tune: Fatty was writing a new song after a week during which he had performed his latest number, "Who's Venus Compared to You?" to the point where the birds had come to accept it as the identifying call of his species. "There's a fatty," they could have said, recognizing the featured afterbeat. The melodic line of the new call was long, ascending, the nightingale's rhapsody inverted. The words, riding the surface of its streamlike flow, were carried far afield.

"Fatty?" asked his sister in the kitchen, pausing at the foot of the stairs, having wandered down for second breakfast while bedticking spilled airing from upstairs windows and plumped pillows sat around in chairs like pasty old ladies napping. The mother held up an assenting forefinger from which dough flaked. The girl pantomimed a question—"Where?" "In the clump," said the mother, bright-eyed and waiting as if her daughter's year away at school were expected to imbue her further remarks with pertinency if not wisdom. The girl poured coffee, scrounged a piece of bacon from the warmer, and sat, forgetful of both, staring vacantly out the window as though smitten blind by the glare of roses. Musingly she said, "That little bitch freak. I could have slapped her." "Don't let your daddy hear you talking like that," said the mother, sinking her fist up to the wristbone in dough. "Huh," went the girl, "did you see his face? He would have wrung her cheeks for a penny." Resentment marred her smooth face briefly. "I didn't think *that* would still be going on, at Fatty's age." "Why, yes," said the mother in a reasonable voice. "Yes, it is." She leaned her weight on the imbedded hand, the tendons in the scrawny brown arm standing out. She rested that way for a time. The vacancy of her expression matched her daughter's. The still summer morning transmitted unflawed into the cool kitchen Fatty's song and the accompanying twitter of birds. "It wasn't her face he wanted to slap," she said. The girl glared briefly then sighed, dropping her eyes to her mother's hands. "Mama," she said, determinedly amused, "that dough's pulling you in like quicksand. When they come home and ask where you are, I'll just point to that pile of dough." Fatty's chorus ended; the quiet trembled as though on the point of finding its own voice, then subsided. "Pretty," said the mother, yearning. "Pretty!" mocked the girl, hating herself for hating. "Your two feet sticking out of that dough, pretty!" "Don't be a torment," said the mother. The girl bridled halfheartedly. "Oh yes, I'm the thorn in your side; always have been, haven't I." "My sides are fine," said the mother smartly. "No thorns that I know about." As Fatty began a new chorus on cue the girl lifted an ironic eyebrow but her mother headed her off with a request. "Tell me about boarding school," she said, adding, in the girlish tone that never stirred her daughter to confidences as she always hoped it would. "We haven't had a *minute* since you got home. I'm *dying* to hear!" The girl thought, Oh Mama, don't; but knew she couldn't ever say it aloud, or admit to anyone how much her mother's gushing always embarrassed her, the same as if her mother were a man. When her mother spoke that way it was as unnatural-sounding as Fatty when he aped her, as he frequently did—had done, at least. "Well," she began, thinking, Oh God, this summer; not even one day of it gone. Her mother took a deep breath, thankful for the narrative begun, and attacked the dough with the heels of both hands, her taloned fingers reaching for the puffed-up white hills before them, drawing the hills into the valleys, causing sinkholes to appear in mountains and peaks to rise from craters as she dealt summarily with the one world surely in her grasp.

"Dad-blame it," said the Father, on his way to the barn with a broken harness, hearing the beginning notes of another of the expected daylong encores of Fatty's song. Everything seemed to be conspiring to get his goat: the drought, having to take on more hands, now this delay with the broken harness. He didn't know what made him yank on the harness like that; Old Bess hadn't been doing a thing but standing there, head down, waiting to pull the slide to the creek for another load of water. She had yanked back in surprise, feeling his disapproval traveling to her, and their opposing forces had met and clashed at the weakest point and sundered the leather. Anxiety at the sudden parting of the bond between mare and master had caused her bowels to move. It was just then—he snorted in disgust at the memory—that Fatty's words about "the fragrance of a June morning" had exploded the field into back-pounding, foot-stomping anarchy. Even the old hands who ought to know better had gone wild, choking and doubling over. It was their excess that bothered the father. He admitted that the situation was good for a laugh: the prissy words and Old Bess's down-home urge. God knew the men laughed with less provocation all the time; it didn't take much to set them off. It was just the feeling that they were letting off steam that had built up in them from some other fire and would have busted if the chance hadn't come along to let it off. It was just the dad-blamed feeling that they were laughing at him: nobody had slapped him on the back. It was far from the first time that it seemed to him he was separated from the others by something a man couldn't see. And the times when he tried to get through with a story, a tall tale or a joke, somehow always turned out to be the worst times. Straddling barbed wire he thought about the time he'd told a storeful of men and boys about the way Fatty got up in the mornings and went straight to the pump organ in his underwear, and played and sang until he was ordered to get dressed. He told them so that they could see for themselves that he could laugh about his son, too; that having a son like Fatty didn't make him feel like an outsider. But all he'd got for his efforts was the worst kind of snicker. He'd puzzled about it afterward, admittedly a bit sheepishly because of the idea they might have got that he was trying to ally himself against his son, which was not so; he was simply trying to present himself as the balanced man he was. He wondered if his failure to make his point was due to a wrong choice of word, or words, not that there was such a great choice; in his world words were like the farm equipment and the people themselves: they had to do extra duty because the supply was limited. Still, reaction was not something you could count on anyway, in man or beast. Old Bess yanking her head, snapping the harness. He'd been party to it, of course, because the first yank had been his. Ah ha, he thought, pushing the pasture gate open, that's it: they'd heard what that little old foreign girl said about Fatty last night. No wonder they were fit to bust. Which told him all he needed to know, because the only one who could have spread the story was the girl's grandfather. His frustration stung like a wasp. He would not be in a position to retaliate until threshing season, and he was not a good bider-of-time. The gate squealed, and he made a note to bring the oilcan back with him. If he forgot, his wife would be after him, saying it set her teeth on edge every time she went through to the pasture. Mountains out of molehills, he thought gloomily, entering the tack room and setting to work on the harness. He thought further, cloudily, that molehills produced mountains in country places as regularly as cows calved, but if you followed the mountain to its source, you could at least identify the source as a molehill.

Hody and Chigger, on their way to fish and swim in the farthest pond they knew, crouching down the grassy lane so their heads wouldn't show above the runty sumac, stopped at the sound of Fatty's song and straightened up for a minute as if they'd been found out. Hody started to laugh, recognizing the voice. He managed a guffaw before he stopped, sensing caution in the way Chigger stood, and the need for caution. Chigger had Indian blood that tempered his body like a knifeblade, and some ways he stood and looked you couldn't tell whether the blade was folding or unfolding. Chigger wasn't stronger than anybody else, and he could be licked, except when his Indian blood— "knifeblood," Hody thought of it as—was up. Then nobody could lick him, not grown men or anything. It made him a good friend and a dangerous enemy, and he was Hody's idol, though like everybody else Hody did not know the secret of what it took to rile up Chigger's knifeblood. He had seen men and boys try to get Chigger mad for the hell of it, without succeeding; then a word, or a look, or nothing, and Chigger was ready to take on bear cats. Seeing the way Chigger stood listening, Hody was certain that his knifeblood was up and, what was more, was aimed against everything and everybody except old Fatty, singing in the clump. Standing in the lane they could see the clump but not Fatty. The voice shot out of the clump like arrows, sharp and swift; you could almost see the ivy move on the trees as the voice pushed past, nicking the leaves that were in the way. Hody, thinking about Fatty and Chigger and the end of their friendship, and wondering how he could stand it if he lost Chigger, felt suddenly pierced with the pinging arrow words, felt himself bristling with them, porcupinelike, standing bleeding in the overgrown lane. He stared at Chigger, wondering if he was bleeding too. Chigger stood turned sideways, his chest like a shield from which the arrows deflected and entered Hody, standing a step behind and to the left of him. Once Hody realized, he took the arrows meekly and let his hide do penance for his mouth's mistake.

She swung on the gate, not counting the *backs,* counting only the *forths; forth* and *forth* and *forth* she swung, imagining the gate was taking her to the moon. She had brought a tree along with her for shade and color in the white journey. Above her the leaves hung motionless, tiny and separate as peepholes punched in a white sky to allow glimpses of the green sky that lay beyond. The tree was in full bloom, but it was easy to imagine the creamy racemes, swinging of their own weight, as clouds, or clusters of air fruit. For a moment she concentrated on the idea of a forest-sky beyond the white one, and a grassy sun, but before the idea could effect change she rejected it as merely bizarre rather than appealing. She could not allow her need of escape to interfere with the physical setup of the solar system. Someone else, en route to somewhere out there, flew too close beside her. They, whoever they might be, had a phonograph aboard and the song repeated and repeated something about a June morning. She thought how difficult it was to find quiet even in space, but it seemed that, song or no song, she was still to have her noisy guilt to stand between her and the peaceful stars. She thought hope-fully, but not quickly enough, that the song was pretty, for ear-lier thoughts caught up with her . . . but thoughts were, after all, the first heavier-than-aircraft to fly. She made a mental note of the observation, proving that she could at least keep the rude, clamorous earlier thoughts waiting, then opened that door abruptly, countering remark with remark. Very well. She had not meant to be unkind. As a scientist she merely made obser-vations. Sometimes, out of a sense of social obligation, she ob-served aloud. When she drew comparisons it was again a social consideration: comparisons are the quickest way to make oneself understood. In her notebook she could have notated it thus, simply: Fatty $= \female$; or, needing words, she could have written, "Fatty resembles that grouping of Homo sapiens bearing organs in which are organized large nonmotile gametes, requiring fer-tilization by smaller motile gametes." But on her grandfather's farm the result of such a precise statement would have been alienation and quite possibly an ego-unsettling paddling, since the purpose of her literal farming out for the summer was to encourage a more—to use her father's meager word—"normal" way of expressing herself; to, as he had put it to her grand-father, "bring her down to earth, for God's sake." And here she was on her way to the moon because she had expressed herself "normally" about Fatty, to Fatty's parents and Fatty himself and to the sister, with whom she had hoped to be friends. As she had really hoped to be friends with Fatty, too, though perhaps her urge there had not been altogether altruistic. She had never known anyone like Fatty and had wished to study him, but certainly not to hurt him. And now the summer was shot to hell on its second day out because she had thought that *intention* determined a word's weight with regard to its potential to wound. "Hallooooo there," she called, rocket to rocket, hoping to hear an answering voice, one which was reassuringly scientific, unemotional. God knew how long she might have to stay up here, eating locusts.

"*All* the boys have the month of June to unwind in," said the mother. "At least all the younger ones do. *You* know that." The oven was making its presence felt in the kitchen. Flies droned like emery wheels at the windows, a sound hot enough to melt the screens. The sun, in one leap, had made it to the tin roof of the kitchen and curled up there, too comfortable to move on to the other side of the big trees. The daughter pared potatoes and asked questions, sounding as if her year away at school had afflicted her with amnesia for the matters and customs of home. "You don't have to snap," she said mildly, head bent over the sink. The posture caused her still-unfamiliar grown-up face to be cloaked in twin falls of hair and exposed to the mother's prolonged gaze the tender little-girl nape. "Excuse me," said the mother briskly, "it's the heat talking." As her daughter's head swung around she turned somewhat hurriedly back to the biscuit board, leaning into her final attempt to make some meaningful change in the doughy world by stretching its horizons as far as they would go. "Excuse *me*," said the daughter, wondering and touched by something in her mother's tone. "I really had forgotten that." She pondered for a moment. "Of course; that's it, Mama, where on earth is Chigger?" She had to repeat the question. "They had a spat," said the mother, and began to hum. "Spat!" said the girl, chagrined and vaguely frightened by some implication now in the room. "Good Lord, you don't spat with the only friend you've got in the whole world!" "There are worse things, Sis," said the mother and hummed away. After a time the girl said, "Mama," sounding as though she had cut herself on the paring knife. The mother thought, She has guessed; she has seen; and knew a weary kind of relief. "I don't know what to do," she began tentatively. "I just don't know." She stopped, then turned swiftly, engaging her daughter's eyes. "I guess you may as well hear it, Sis. You're old enough, I guess, to—" She couldn't decide between "forgive" and "understand." The girl said, "*Old* enough?" Her head was reeling as if she were hung by her heels over running water, grabbing at fleeting shapes beneath the surface. "Mama, has Fatty—I mean, is there something else—besides—" Shadowy words glimpsed in medical contexts slide beneath the surface, causing her to shiver in the heated kitchen. She wanted to shout out, suddenly, "What *is* Fatty?" but was terrified that her mother would tell her, using one of those words. The mother felt regret at being so misunderstood, and a lonely satisfaction. She talked rapidly lest her ordinarily sharp-eared daughter hear the difference in her tone and put two and two together, as the mother thought she had done. It was fitting that only Fatty had seen, her summer-singing son, and consoled her with ironic love words, whose irony he trusted her to hear and understand. It was their unspoken secret against the others, against the silence. "His daddy," she began, putting the man in his place; then to keep him out of the kitchen she said, "*Your* daddy: it's like he's said to himself that Fatty could just catch up with him, if he wanted to know him, without once stopping to think that *he's* going ahead at the same clip and anyway paying no attention to other turnings along the way and that's to my mind where he's missed out because there's many a turning." I'm getting there, she thought, whether I want to or not. She cut biscuits rapidly, twisting them out of the dough like period marks with which later to punctuate and make separate for herself the autobiographical parts. "Nor will he go back and look. I'm not saying he could find it, it's just he won't try. Once something's mislaid, it's *lost* to him, and of no value; his pride demands that. And still he blames others for the loss, just the way he'd blame the person that found it and claimed it for his own." She thought, That's too close for anybody's comfort, and brought it back around to Fatty again with cunning indirection. "He counted too much on Chigger, and when Chigger couldn't do what he couldn't do, your daddy blamed him. Still does. But, my gracious, Chigger's finding his own way. How can he point out the way to Fatty, can you tell me that?" "But, Mama, what did Chigger say?" asked the girl. "Well, he wanted to grow up—" The mother tried to leave it there, hating to distort, but the girl was persistent: "And Fatty didn't? Is that what he said?" "No," said the mother, "Chigger didn't say that. I said it. But that's all it is with our Fatty. Just— that's all." Thinking, Not our Fatty, *mine,* she loaded biscuits on pans, squatted before the open oven door, letting the heat lap at her as though it were welcome to her. To her relieved-looking daughter she said, willfully autobiographical, "The trouble with some farmers is, they spend too much time with plants," and waited for the heat to draw from her like sweat the application of the remark to her son. She stood up and closed the oven door gently. "With plants, whatever's planted, that's what comes up. But people aren't like that, Sis." The girl saw tears in her mother's eyes and was grateful to recall that her mother was not demonstrative. She felt that she couldn't bear it if her mother came toward her with open arms, pressing confidences upon her. Whatever was responsible for the tears, the girl knew for certain that it had little to do with Fatty, and she suddenly wanted to think about her brother. It seemed important to do so. The mother, too, discovered that, with all her heartbreak at being alone again within herself, and the brevity of the time when she had not been alone, for some reason she wanted to think about her son. In her covering-up talk about him she had made him sound like an outcast; perhaps, after all, he was. If so, there were two of them, one to sing and one to listen. She thought, If it turns out that he really is an outcast, then I will have to take my turn, singing in the clump. But she did not know how to go on examining what her son was or wasn't. He was too young to be a definite, lasting thing; in his youth he was as fluid as water. She thought, Suppose nothing is until it's admitted to be; suppose sin without recognition is not sin, nor love, love; suppose that to save my son from being an outcast later on I would have to deny what I had in the two Aprils, that by not admitting what it was— sin *and* love—it would not have been! Then *he* would not be. And the duality within the pronoun filled her breast with a double emptiness, a double negative, she thought, grimly amused.

And she listened to the silence like when a mockingbird ceases in the middle of the night its intricate deception that has kept someone awake listening for the single note of truth. She waited for her son's reassurance to fill the silence, but the song had stopped; the silence rang with the song's cessation. It was the silence she had been listening for since spring—but which one, the one before Fatty's birth or this year's mirror, a long time coming to her hand and quickly broken. And now June was a summer mirror at the halfway mark, reflecting all before and after—aspiration, need, failure. In her conception of a singer by a singer she had doomed the conceived. Starting for the door she thought, No, not by the act; by the misuse of the boy. Because I feared silence, the one thing we're born knowing. Our first yell, our first song, is just an attempt to stave that silence off.

Simultaneously the sister thought about how glad she had been three years ago to leave the school where almost daily she was witness to her brother's humiliation at the hands of the other boys. She had gone on to the new County High School, relieved and, with the appearance of Chigger in her brother's life, somewhat forgetful. Or when she remembered, or was recalled by a question (usually sly; Fatty's name inspired slyness, even in teachers), she tried smearing on honey by referring to Fatty, airily, as "The Genius" ("The genius on our blighted family tree"), hoping the term would catch on and become explanatory of Fatty's difference. The term had caught on, another to be used disparagingly. She went back to her relief at leaving the school that also contained Fatty and his plight, and excused herself for it without apology. Girls had a hard-enough time on their own; a popular brother, even one much younger, was an asset; an unpopular one was another barrier to be overcome. She had, however vicariously, shared his humiliations and tried not to dislike him for it. She believed she had managed, but the distance between the schools had been an additional safeguard. Without his help but in the same school she had won "Most Popular Girl" two years running. The past year, safely away from his subliminal influence upon her total image, among people who did not know of his existence, she had won "Prettiest Girl," though not "Most Popular." Yes, that was what she had been looking for! She thought with a pang about the dubiety of the new honor: the latter without the former to strengthen it had an unfortunate aura of emptiness, of image without content. She pressed bravely on. Without Fatty, the cross she bore so well, whose forbearance was the proof of her character (her sweetness, gallantry, humor), she was out of context; Fatty was her context. Without him she was seen as merely pretty. Empty. The sense of his presence stood beside her in the kitchen like a specter, and then the acute sense of his absence. She had only come home late yesterday; she had not kissed him or petted him nearly enough. She turned to ask her mother to excuse her while she ran to the clump to find Fatty and make up for lost time and saw her mother hurrying across the yard, untying her apron strings clumsily. The sister's legs went leaden. "It's Fatty, something's happened to him," and she crept across the floor with the blood heavy in her legs giving her the gait of a nightmare or—the thought could not be stopped—of the summer stretching before her.

The boys reached the edge of the foul swamp and saw and heard it pulling for sustenance at the barely moist, teatlike clumps of itself. Hody, anxious to go on proving his courage to Chigger, jumped across the moving slime to the first clump of grass. There was an easier way, involving logs, but that was for other days. Hody had felt, since the lane and Fatty's song, that the clump had thrown the day out of balance—that it physically outweighed the land over which he walked with Chigger, making their progress as difficult as if their way were all uphill. He had stepped very hard, trying with his weight to push the earth down again and make it level so that he and Chigger would not fall backward and roll like stones into the clump where Fatty sang. Hody saw the swamp as their salvation: crossing it was unpleasant but once it lay between them and Fatty they would be safe. Hody had never been in the clump and did not know why he was afraid of it, unless he was feeling what Chigger was feeling; if he was, the way he had in the lane with the cutting arrow-words, then he was terrified for Chigger. Chigger was in great danger of being pulled back and dragged into the clump. Hody could feel the lure it had for him, like a terribly strong magnet. This galvanized him into furious movement. He hurtled forward, over the sucking slime, to the next sun-cracked hillock with the sharp dried grass that cut his legs. Yelling in anger and excitement and pain, he turned to impel Chigger forward with his rage and saw that Chigger stood facing (it was the way Hody saw it, even though the swamp was the muck at the bottom of a basin) downhill. As Hody watched, Chigger began to walk away. When he reached the fallen tree without looking back, Hody called out in a flat voice, "Indian." Chigger kept on, mounting the tree as though it were a staircase and descending the other side without slowing his pace. The fallen tree cut him in half; Hody could only see him from the waist up. It was that half-person or child—it looked like both—which Hody tried to reach, not caring if Chigger came back and broke his nose or pushed him into the nasty, green, sucking slime. "Indian giver," he yelled. Chigger kept going.

She found herself stuck in the ionosphere, an unwilling transmitter of thoughts not recognizably her own. It seemed to her that she was receiving alien ideas and transmitting them to herself, and eventually that she was originating and transmitting and receiving, an operation whose sterility outlined her plight exactly. She looked longingly back to earth and saw the long mutilated summer stretching over the farms like a laboratory corpse, one of her own purchase, and wondered for the first time if her father was not right about her, if perhaps there were things she did not know after all. One could not stay wrapped in the cool mantle of science all one's days; one had occasionally to emerge in one's own skin and move about in the world unprotected. The way Fatty did! And take one's knocks, the way Fatty did. Of course, that was the answer, right before her eyes. She and Fatty were really two of a kind; of all those around her this summer he was the one to understand her; to share. She admitted that she was afraid of being called "freak" by those not in her peer group, by inferiors—she thought a moment—and superiors. At home there was a sign on her laboratory door that read THE FREAK, but she had put it there. Fatty would understand! She wondered what she would do if she were forced to live in a place where no one shared her interests, or understood them, or knew about them; a place where she was called "freak" all the time. She knew instantly what she would do. The phonograph had stopped; Fatty had stopped singing. "Oh, no!" she exclaimed, "Fatty, don't!" and climbed off the gate and ran down the road, glad of the chance to get the hell out of that ionosphere, but worried, too.

Bent over the harness in the gloomy tack room, the father thought that it was high time the boy started considering him. That caterwauling in a bunch of trees was something a kid could get away with, but when a boy passed twelve he was on his way to manhood and had to abide by the rules laid down by men for men. Men didn't sing out like that, unless they were on the way home from the fields, or splashing in a tub where just the family could hear. It occurred to him that maybe Fatty didn't know he was an embarrassment to his father. Not that you could outright say it to the boy, but there were ways. And Fatty could be understanding. . . . But what did the boy do in that clump of trees, besides sing? What was he doing in there, the place snake-infested as could be. It was like the behavior of a stranger, somebody not brought up knowing about the snakes in this part of the country. A man could be hit over the head and not have a case in court, just for making the wrong kind of noise behind a man's back, hissing or rattling. Words. Certain words couldn't be whispered in snake country without making a man uneasy. Sissy. Couldn't whisper that word in snake country. It was hard on you in snake country, harder than almost anywhere else, he imagined. Just to survive in these parts proved you were a man. You came to manhood early through survival alone. No other credentials were necessary; just yourself, walking around. Fatty had earned his right to respect and the father was going to see that he got it from now on. The two of them, together, could present a pretty strong front. That would give the bastards something to contend with. He listened for the reassurance of Fatty's voice. Finding the quiet in its stead, he got up, feeling arthritic. The partly mended harness fell to the floor unnoticed. He thought about the way snakes came from holes in the ground, dropped from trees, slid out of logs where you sat, hissed at you from clumps of ivy at eye level, lay sunning on split-rail fences, chilled your hand in hens' nests, coiled there among the sucked eggs. Snakes and laughers, snickerers and snakes, one as inhuman as the other, lying in wait, confusing a man by stealing his money, trying to steal other things; sucking his eggs or taking it out of his pocket on account of a drought, or sneaking around . . . all were thievery. A man couldn't be a leader like he was meant to be if he had to count his pennies all his life, or snatch eggs still hot from the hen, or keep an eye on the back door, listening for snickers and snakes every step he took. He kicked at the harness on the floor, mistaking it for a black racer, tromped on it until it broke in two places. He hoped Fatty was strong enough to do the same until his father got there.

They converged on the clump in the field. Man and wife noticed many small changes in each other—lined faces, stooped shoulders, sympathy. Chigger and the sister glared at each other; their eyes snapped "Deserter!" The erstwhile scientist, amazed at the assemblage that seemed to be weighing each other on internal scales, stepped into the clump, through the green wall, which shivered shut behind her. Nobody made a move to stop her, or to follow. The polymorphous fears separating them from the arena of the clump like a curtain of fluids had ended the long drought so precipitously that they were foot-mired and could not move.

After a time the girl and Fatty emerged, some distance away, she holding onto his arm while he rubbed the sleep from his eyes. Her voice was reasonable but touched with enough passion to carry to those being left behind.

"We simply can't, you know, people like us. Not when we're asleep or anything. We have to keep at it, you see. We can't stop a minute, honestly. Well, that's an expression, but still—" The two children ploughed through the clover heading for the rocket gate. They did not turn around, but the girl's voice floated back. " 'Dedication' and such concepts to one side, the *real reason* we have to keep on is—" The others leaned forward but she whispered, maddeningly, in Fatty's ear, following which she and Fatty laughed in two-part harmony.

She became audible again. "Don't you *know* what we are, Fatty, dear?" The others saw him shake his head. This time they took a step forward in unison, leaning and craning for her answer, but the noise they made with their big feet covered her reply and all they got was the tantalizing signature: the double laugh of the children and one bird call from the clump, a perfect major triad.

WRITINGS ON A
CAVE WALL

I remind me how they divvied up the sticks among us five young ones that day. Our big brother got the short fat stick with most meat on it but it was soon seen that I was best favored for I got the ring. When the ashes and black had been sanded away it shone with a fine goldy sheen and they said twas mine for keeping and the young ones sang finders keepers losers weepers. Our Dam said I should wear the ring outside when amongst kin and inside when abroad in the world. The next oldest of us with a privy mouth said if I went abroad too often with the ring inside me I'd soon wear the gold away from shitting it out when I got back to the cave place. I knew our Dam meant for me to bear the circlet inside my clothes and I had a leathern thong I had been hoping to adorn with some shiny thing ever since our sister fell heir to the wondrous stone as green as moss, and later a fine chain to string it upon.

We young ones did not know what hand our Dam and Sire had in the apportionment of treasure, whether the ring-stick fell to me by chance or by design. If twas by their design then all would understand that it was to compensate me for the loss of my pet, of which I partook like the others, the times being slim to gaunt and sentiment overruled by a more powerful tyrant named hunger. Oftentimes in my dreams following the massacre of my playmate I would hear the screams of her dying and awaken retching at the thought that her life should have gone to sustain my own. But I never shared the dreams nor the regrets, which would have been one of the unforgivables, not the sharing but the practice. Even now I break old commandments by writing so of the past, by recollection and by harboring still these regrets and sense of loss. But, to be hanged for a sheep as for a lamb, I will say here that my piglet—off whose sweet flesh we supped, broke fast, and supped again, the sweet meat divvied among us in morsels, most of the fat going to the hunters—I will say now and in this place of soft stone and silences that I loved in all the world, in all my life, only my book and that pink and playful, wise and sometimes wistful, Little Pretty. When the ring fell to me I yearned at the thought of how it would have glistered in her nose, the placement of which, however painful, knowing the alternative, she would have agreed to with happy oinks and skipping trotters. The four biggest among us ate the trotters, done to a turn.

In an earlier hard time when the ground was froze denser than granite and the roots from which our bread was made were as afar and untouchable as stars, and the hunters came at nightfall with bone weariness and increased weakness their sole bag, we ate my sister's pet talking crow that could converse in long phrases like a man, and even parse a sentence. Although ate is hardly fitting for the feather sucking we children did. The crow had been roasted in its plumage so that the youngest might have whatever crumb of meat should cling to the plucked pinion. In reality twas less a crumb than an aroma. In terror at impending slaughter the learned crow forgot man language so that its last word was the simple speech of its ancestors, caw. I do not know if my sister mourned her pet as I mourn, still, mine, nor if the moss-green stone was a fair exchange for the loss. All I know is, our Dam, who commanded our respect and affection, had inculcated in us the rigid understanding since infancy that sacrifice for The Common Weal was not to be thought of as Sacrifice, worthy of the large effect, and thus perhaps the fine chain upon which she wore the moss-green stone was compensation enough for my sister's second loss of which I find I cannot write presently. If joys are to be multiplied, then mourning must be divided.

I am now only newly one of the hunters and thus my attempt to retreat to past times when knowledge was not a sudden burden. In that past time mystery abode by day as well as by night for twas then, by day, that our Dam suckled us on tales of the pleasanter sort, tales of innocence and the mystery of innocence, and the dream of innocence retained, while the hunters were gone. They returned and brought more mystery, but dark as the sky, clandestine as the word. Then the activity, it seemed to us young, was extreme, a wildness of suppressed sound, muffled cries, slithery and slippery motions heard but never seen, and all was connected to the preparation of food. Thus we learned early in life that living revolved around the central fact of sustenance. We were made to see that the hunters hunting brutishly the livelong day and returning burdened and jubilant or unburdened and despondent—and, betimes, desperate and dangerous; and that the prolonged busyness, involving digging, burning, whetting, flensing, flaying, all out of sight in the deep inner cave—that all of this was so that later on when the first had died down, we might belch and fart, shit and in some cases vomit, due to stomachs filled to various levels of tolerance. The best level was seldom vouchsafed the youngest to know, which was when the belly showed as water shows in a skin bag, by distension and sleekness, how filled it is. In ten years I have perhaps known such repleteness four or five times, and the pain was like bliss and as short-lived except in memory.

We become in our tribe hunters at the age of ten.

Some other facts about us. We are an old people. We are happiest as a mountain people, dwelling near high passes, perilous crossings, in deep caves. In our forebears we have crossed broad continents and vast bodies of water. We have, as they tell it, though I do not know what the words mean, sported at the poles and among cyclades with mammals big as houses. Our Dam, who can riddle with the best a riddle, says we have also swum among comets dodging their sparkly tails.

The sunball has fallen long since and my letters lean upon one another in the near darkness. Would that I could emulate them

and squeeze into myself for warmth and become like the letter *i*
and shiver away up a star beam as one slim line with a seeing eye
and sport among the sparks of the comet tail safer amid fires
than alone in this seeking dark.

In the night I returned again to the day of the ring and the sticks
or stalks of meat. I thought this was partly due to hunger, for in
this rocky high place there is nothing to eat, not even a berry. I
became aware of my body feeding upon itself, which is what
those gnawing cramps imply. I was filled with the horror of what
my book informs me is called poetic justice.

The day of the sticks and my ring. It is as though that last day
of innocence is the hub of a wheel from which radiate the spokes
of my suspicion and learning, or suppressed knowledge and
willfully misread signs, many of these, for it is a thickly spoked
wheel, all leading to the inflexible iron rim that is the circumfer-
ence of my life. This, in the context of Knowing, may stand for
the gods, or a God, for in my book I have encountered Him as
well and as far as I can figure it He represents the massed knowing of a people, yet with mystery intact. My book, the only remaining love in my life, I should say here, is called a Thesaurus
and was my first gift from my parents. Only now do I recall how
the contents of the saddlebag were passed among us, for I was
but five years old. I see now my sister's portion of the booty, a
box of pencils, and my brothers'—various articles that I can view
now as parts of a scholarly life, the which they destroyed as
worthless. I recall their jeers at my portion, but kindly enough,
their contempt amiable.

But from my family I have kept the knowledge that I read
and write and think; that I deduce; believing myself canny until
now. For I think now that they have kept from me their own
deductions and discoveries, my brothers, I mean, for the learning plainly was not for them a final thing as it is for me. I wonder
if they did not always know, if, more intrepid than I, they had
fathomed the depths of the mystery by, using the analogy of my
wheel, putting together the pieces as they fell from the lathe,

constructing the wheel of their lives in an orderly fashion as I believe we were all meant to do so that there would be scarcely any transition upon the day of full initiation. But what I experience is not transition; I know that I cannot complete the journey, not that one; that if I am to live it must be elsewhere, among others. And I know as my family must know that my living must mean their death.

I remind me of the pieces of the wheel fashioned before my eyes, that I let lie where they fell. Things taken squirming and fighting in sacks, taken into the deep inner caves. Sounds that I translated into bleating or baaing or the squeals of Little Pretty, none more horrendous than that. The blue marble fed to my sister's crow, the while I did not inquire if the marble would not kill a bird. The five meaty sticks, meat always sweetest nearest the bone. A lifetime of willful blindness and deafness, absorbed in my book, trusting for a sane reason, I suppose: that our Dam was there humming at her cooking, sleeping by the fire in the dark cold afternoons in all the innocence that she bespoke as our portion.

The inner gnawing now is fierce. It is ten days since I came here, to my sandstone sanctuary. Ten days since I have begun etching in the soft walls of my asylum this account. Ten days since my belly has known ought but the water that I scoop from the declivities. There is reptilian life about me and as there are serpents there are rodents. But they are safe with me, serpents, lizards, rodents. I have eaten worse all my lifetime and will not touch flesh again.

I remind me of the crucial day which was ten days past. Of how the rain slicked the red clay and the clouds lowered from the peak of the mountains hiding us from the road as we lay in wait. Of the wind sounding in the crevices of the rocks like a woman singing. Of the big birds flapping to their eyries, one hawk with a serpent dangling, twisting into shapes like the letters of a word from the hawk's beak. Was it the hawk or the serpent that wrote? When the instrument of words is living is it not the author? Although twas the hawk wielded the living pen. I remind me of my thoughts as they were, broken into by the faraway sound of wagon wheels skidding on the unseen washboard road. Of the sudden alertness of my companions, my Sire and my brothers among them. Of how we scrabbled down the ravines and took sightings and plotted the encounter. Of how the produce, the pumpkins and squashes, the potatoes and turnips, the eggplants, were left upon the wagon. Left upon the wagon poured from their sacks and the sacks filled elsewhere the sacks filled otherwise the sacks reddened where the new contents lay still. The spoiled wheat, the corn, the barley that could have kept us our family alive all winter spilling from the wagon onto the roadbed.

Our Dam made our beds out of balsam branches in the warm weather and of hay-stuffed hides for winter. We slept amid fragrance. There was a tanning cave for the hides. Oftentimes we young ones would go there with her to turn the hides, the pale familiar hides. Pigskin boarskin bearskin deerskin kidskin she said but all the same pale familiar hides.

I have eaten Kentucky oysters my Sire's favorite meat. These are the testicles of pigs.

In my book now I have found stumbled upon Long Pig.

Twas my sister's new babe her second loss of which earlier I could not write.

The blue marble fed the crow was no marble. Marbles are in their nature sightless.

Necessity was never the cause. Else living among them were still possible.

I hear their voices in the night. I recognize a brother's and his Sire's, both mine erstwhile. If the Dam came I would surrender.

I have had no water for three days. I lick the stones. One advantage for them. I could not cry out.

I sleep awhile then awaken. Light falls through my cave roof and then gone. The moonball passes over else I glimpse a star. My writing grows faint for want of strength and for fear they may hear me scratching and come and destroy my tablets. There would be no history of my family and no mark of me.

I imagine I hear my Dam murmur above.

In the night a thing dropped through the hole. By first light I see that it is a chunk of meat. I guess twas knowingly dropped. In secret or as part of a scheme. But think twas dropped to me by my Dam. To fatten me up. It will be fitting. As a babe I fed upon her.

MY FATHER WAS A RIVER

They called me a good child. It made me feel even more set apart, a sort of social leper, for this was the great period of rebellion when youth roamed the streets, rode through the countryside like gathered lightning, and the eternal rule of thumb was that it be affixed permanently to the nose. My parents' indictment had another effect upon me. It caused me to husband my dark energies, out of a sense of loyalty, until I became a walking dynamo. Nothing, through those long formative years, was spent, and there were times when the buoyancy of my reserves made me feel that I might fly straight up into the air and hover above the treetops, looking down and laughing to see their faces. This was the most innocent of my fancies. Another was that I should suddenly, when the family had assembled—aunts, uncles, cousins, grandparents—fly into an orgy of rage and kick tables, legs, faces, until all became splinters. This impulse would disappear when I lay before my tall window washed in the odor of midnight and summer roses. Then I would simply grow and become grass and willow trees, hovering protectively over my mother's grave, watered by my father's dear tears.

My mother was a light woman, quick and evanescent. When she entered a room she had already left it. Her beauty was contained to the point that little of it showed.

When my father entered a room it became too crowded, for there seemed to be too many of him. He extended himself so that he sat in every chair and filled each corner. My father was feral; if he filled a room, he became the forest. My father was a river, a fox, a mountain lion.

In a time when large families were fashionable, my parents were considered odd to have only one child, and perhaps they were pitied. But I knew things that I could have told; things gleaned as I prowled the house listening to conversations and other sounds. I discovered in my parents a sort of desperate passion that would bring my father hurriedly home from his supervision of the fields at all hours of the day, and kept the house murmurous and restless through nights when child and servants were thought to be sleeping. If other eyes had been as watchful as mine, they would have seen glances and touches exchanged in the midst of large gatherings, and departing guests detained past a seemly hour for the same reason that I forced myself to eat slowly through a dish I did not like, but with my eye cocked voluptuously on the dessert that I loved and knew would be the better for the waiting.

It was my mother whom I watched mostly, for her reactions. I came to know her responses to my father's touch and glance until her gestures and movements became my own. When I was alone with her I would stroke her arms and the hands that I had seen tremble for him. When I was small this did not seem unnatural to her; it pleased her and she would laugh and muss my hair, not knowing that it was myself that I caressed. But later, toward the end, she would pull sharply away and her eyes would follow me with their haunted look as I jauntily left the room at her command, turning always in the doorway to salute her in filial obedience.

But when I was younger they called me a good child. Because they trusted me, I was free. Our doors were never locked. I came and went, harboring myself, and for one whole year I did not sleep at night.

The River

I knew many things about my father that no one else knew. An ordinary person with ordinary vision can turn his powers of concentration upon a single object and eventually time will reveal to him each mystery, flaw, and virtue of that object. A stone or a leaf, given the outside force of absolute concentration and the added dimension of time, will unlock itself and lay bare its secret. But my vast reserves of energy, coupled with my singleness of mind, gave me an insight that verged on the supernatural; my imagination was a circle and my father was its nucleus.

I loitered on the edge of my twelfth summer, a dark child filled with heavy secrets, when the first in a chain of revelations presented itself to me. It was my favorite hour, midnight—that perfect hour when struggling day has been completely devoured, its tail disappearing down the throat of night. I lay before my window, listening to the tides of sound. I heard the river and I heard my father, both advancing and retreating, both responding to the syzygial arrangement of sun, moon, and earth, each helpless and triumphant before nature. Suddenly the sounds became one. As with all true revelation the answer was simply there. I had been resting naked; I rose and put on the garment nearest to hand and in that gesture, which was a decision, I pledged myself to the quest.

Through the summer I clung to the riverbanks until each angle knew me by heart. At the beginning, my nocturnal footsteps would send up showers of night birds like sparks from a fire, but eventually they came to sit quietly and let me walk among them. I watched snakes moving from darkness to darkness through the moonlight, their dizzying motion like shored ripples from the river. Gradually the unnatural quiet brought about by my invasion became filled with the normal sounds of a summer night: chirping, chatter of beaver, and other sounds of beasts unnamed by man who inherit the earth when the sun falls. Over, above it all, was the song the river sang. It was a love song that said *come to me* and nature responded. Birds hovered and dipped, swooning; beavers flopped sensuously as they tried to dam up the river's love for themselves alone, chattering indignantly when love slipped through their obstructions and went running lightly the length of the land calling *come to me*. I felt its lure, I felt it, but I played the flirt, running along the shores calling *come to me*, mockingly, *come to me*.

And the night came when I saw the waters advancing to my call. I was not prepared, and showed it, and heard the river laugh. The night was filled with the deriding sounds of laughter. Scratch a challenger, they implied, and you will find a coward; scratch a flirt, and you will find a fool. I took off my clothes and in front of all nature went into the arms of the river. Nature, voyeur, avidly watched as I struggled in the grasp of the river crying, catching at roots and branches, "No, Father, Father, don't."

For a week afterward I kept away, angry and ashamed. But like most lovers' quarrels this one too ended and I was back, cajoling, mocking, wary. I wooed and was wooed, but at a distance, by night. It pleased me, when noon shadows lay on the river, to sit by my father as he fished, dabbling my feet and singing innocent songs, watching him secretly, feeling his knowing that some secret area of himself had been touched. And so I passed the summer.

When frost came the river's ardor chilled. Spurned and spurning, I looked for new diversion.

The Fox

One night when the lateness of the hour and the increasing intensity of my parents' glances told me they would soon go up to bed, a great uproar came from the direction of the tenements where our poultry lived in constant bickering, complaints, and uprisings. My father shouted for the servants but they were long asleep, and if they woke at the sound, merely wrapped themselves more securely in their armor of indolence that my parents had encouraged to grow, layer by layer, through the years. Resigned, my father lit a lantern and together we left the house. As we neared the source of trouble my father stopped. I saw on his face a look of passionate amusement and satisfaction as he gazed at the fox who was emerging from the poultry house, a hen dangling from each corner of his mouth. The fox and my father wore the same expression. They were one. The revelation came as simply as the first. My father, because of the sound I made, gave me a long look, then turned, saying, "Too late," and walked back to the house.

It was that night that I began this record of my days and nights, suspecting mortality.

The following evening I sat shivering on the roof of the summer house, glaring at the moon for its coldness, when I saw the fox moving past me. I turned my head slowly so that its motion might be mistaken for the turning of a star but I was caught out. The fox and I exchanged a look of comprehension. He read my disdain for hens and I his desire, which, considering our position, amounted to the same thing. I longed to become an accomplice, a procurer, a pimp, whose reward would be one bloodstained feather. I felt the same excitement I had known in the river's embrace and recognized the need for control. I let him pass but stayed in suspension of breath and thought until he returned with his victim, leaving a trail of blood on the rimy grass. Again he paused and looked at me and his eyes were filled with mockery and a kind of love.

For many nights I let him pass and the moon waned. He came to accept me there, to look for me. I encouraged his trust and praised him with my silence. Gradually I led him to know that without me he was in danger; that our ritual greeting equaled safety. When the mockery had gone from his eyes and only love remained, when his dependence upon me was entire, I knew the time had come but still I waited, in the manner of my parents and their detained guests: only one lesson in passion is needed by the willing pupil.

The time came when I could bear the burning no longer. An hour earlier than usual I took a lantern and went into the poultry house. In a quiet frenzy I evaluated, chose, discarded, considered, rejected. I was a connoisseur in the slave market as I deliberated over each point of beauty and desirability. I left no feather unturned and when at last I chose I believed I could feel even the victim's approval. I then closed every possible means of access to the buildings, sealing in the hens like Oriental queens. Darkening the lantern I settled down outside the tomb to wait.

I imagined him pausing before the summer house, smiling upward; saw the confidence change to bewilderment, the love to doubt, then fear. I saw him tremble on the brink of turning back, tensing as each gust of wind sent down a leaf rattling in death. I felt his heart flutter and hurt with betrayal, then the tide of his rising anger and arrogance. With him I experienced the desperate decision to brazen it out, then the step backward, the agonizing remembrance of familial duty and the reckless plunge forward on a crest of maleness.

Because we knew these emotions together, when we were finally face to face it was in a kind of love-death. The night eddied around us; we were the center of a whirlpool; the walls were high and sheer and the roar deafening. I watched the pulsing of his heart under the red-gold shield of his chest and my own heart swelled to bursting as I held out to him my gift. I was breathless with his love as the cock crowed and a ring of fire swept the sky.

Farewells are a promise of forever and by arresting love at its peak we remain on that high plateau where the climate is constant and the winds invariable.

The winter like a huge snake wrapped its gray coils about the countryside. Wild youth still roved and marauded or so I was told at family gatherings. They called me a good child and I lowered my eyes to hide the flickerings of my splinter impulse. The hearth crackled with my father's heat and the house toasted in his embrace. Skittish aunts basked under his warmth and dreamed of assault. A slight snow flurry was enough to make them stay over for days; at night they would leave the doors of their bedrooms ajar and scamper about the halls like mice in their unlovely shifts at the sound of his step on the stair.

He looked at me and by smiling in a way I had practiced I caused something dark to appear in his face. It came first to the edges of his mouth; by concentration I forced it into his eyes, so near the brain. I would hide from him and stay away for so long that he would come to look for me, forgetting my mother's hand on his arm. I felt his restlessness grow and the puzzled lines that came to mark his forehead were as sharp as music to me. One night when I had been playing the fool to the accompaniment of my aunts' laughter, I turned to my mother for the approval of her smile and found instead the cold watchful eyes of a stranger.

I was standing on a low stool, for in my game I was Icarus preparing to flee the labyrinth at his father's command. The devil caught hold of me at my mother's cold look and before I flew I improvised a speech to my father, playing upon the words "son" and "sun," giving to the labyrinth a dark meaning as I exhorted my father to free himself from bondage to those passageways and fly with me.

When I flew I deliberately fell and cried with pain. My father rushed to help me up. I gave him, for the smallest moment, the look of the fox—knowing, amused—and returned the pressure of his arms as I said without emphasis, "No need to bother, I am nearly grown." When I turned from him my mother was leaving the room, a spot of color high on each cheek. She looked as if she was overheated by the fire.

Through the rest of the winter nights I crept crunchily around the world and once I saw the mountain lion. It was the same lion, I was certain, that had thrown the countryside into a state of terror a few years back, causing parents to lock their children in houses after nightfall and themselves keeping close to home and light. As all things came to my father's doorstep, so had the lion. Looking at the beast I remembered the way it had come about.

I was a small child in the reign of terror, plump and brown, a juicy morsel to tempt a hungry lion, but in conformity with my parents' enlightened ideas I was as free as ever to come and go. Occasionally in my travels I would be found and carried home, kicking and biting, by some irate community-minded father, and delivered to my parents; I would see the accusing eyes of my deliverer met by the barely polite indifference of my father and mother. As children are easily frightened by adults, I should have been frightened by the fear in my deliverers, but I only resented their intrusion as my parents did, and I grew adept at eluding them. It became a game to show myself at a distance and when the man approached, scolding, to disappear, leaving my spluttering would-be savior to thresh the underbrush while I laughed in my burrow or tree.

One day at dusk I stood with my father in the courtyard of our house, watching the stars appear and dutifully naming them. The mountain lion walked through the gateway and stood considering me. I did, then, feel the quiver of fear and turned to my father, but he did not pick me up or shield me with his body; he did not move from his stance of casual contemplation. I looked at his face, thinking perhaps he had not yet seen the lion.

Now, recalling the face he wore as he returned the lion's gaze, I felt the familiar shiver of recognition. It was enough for the time being. I was tired; I followed my sun-filled tracks home and slept all day in the granary on sacks of summer-holding wheat.

The rest of that winter I confined my night journeys to a small radius. By day I read the classics, for I wanted to be well rounded and worthy. I gave my body more care than ever, polishing my skin with pumice. During this pleasurable exercise I stumbled onto the fact that imperfection can be smoothed away as gentle erosion smoothes away prominences from the land. No part of me escaped rigorous discipline; my hair was brushed until it glittered, each delicate muscle of my body gained and held its proper importance to overall balance, my fingernails were made to reflect objects, my ears glowed. As I transformed myself I told myself the reason: I was preparing for the greatest adventure of all, the adventure of facing Death bare and pure. As a greater gladiator honored with a magnificent adversary would prepare himself with purging and prayer, so I went about my task, with one difference: I observed the ritual purging but omitted the prayer. My task was a secular one.

The change in me did not go unremarked. My maternal grandmother, who romanticized each detail of daily life into little pastel-colored shapes like candied violets, declared that I was the model for all children, a paragon of all known and a few invented virtues. She pronounced me beautiful and her heart fluttered, she said, for the helpless state of the object of my romantic intention. She appealed to my mother for corroboration of her statements.

If I had had any pity in me, I would have felt it then at the changes in my mother. She had always been a tremulous woman, a reflection rather than the light itself, but now the reflection was beset with shadows and the shadows threatened to obscure the thin ray. There was something in her of a firefly in a dark glass, the tiny glow, as air is sucked away, growing fainter and fainter, the dark areas of the glass seeming to loom larger by contrast. I saw her thin fingers tremble as they smoothed the material of her needlework. She had not even the strength of her coldness now, but still her look contained no entreaty. I had thought her weak and slow, but she was neither. She alone had guessed what until then only I myself knew and our shared knowledge drew me to her. I stroked her hair and long pale hands. I kissed her cheek and called her pet names of childhood while she sat helpless under my grandmother's benevolent eye, her skin lumped with revulsion.

The Mountain Lion

When the thaws began green things again fingered up through the soil, and out from their polished caskets of wood buds pushed their lazarus heads. At dinner one night I sang to my zither and had the satisfaction of seeing tears in my father's eyes. Pushing my advantage I made the strings murmur like a river and jump like trout. My father turned a full gaze on me and I felt myself blanch. I pretended that faulty tuning of the instrument was responsible for the sounds and I busied myself with the pegs until he partly withdrew his suspicion. But that night when the house slept I sought out the lair of the mountain lion.

My father had taught me about degrees of beauty, from the planets through Euclid and Pythagoras to Homer to the fox; but here was Beauty.

Tawny would be his color if tawny is also the color of autumn's essence and the heart of fire. If one drop distilled from a vineyard's perfect year should be tawny, then let tawny suffice for him. But to try to describe the eyes, the motion—how does one describe a shape outside geometry's rules? If not recognizable as a shape might it not as well communicate itself as an odor, or Death? I felt his glance and if I say I burned and froze it is because there is no word for their combination. If his breath sated and starved me, what else can I say except sated and starved? I died and was born, dreamed and woke, fell and flew. Dawn came, and empty air.

The pattern became fixed. The trees grew fuller, the grass taller, the dawns earlier. Then one night he did not come. Nor the next. On the third night of futile watch I knew he would not come again and I knew why: I guessed his secret, which was that he had guessed mine.

The following night I slept in my bed for the first time in a year.

That spring procreation covered the land. All things seemed determined that their species should overrun the world. My thirteen cats filled the nights with the caterwauling of love agonies. From the stables whinnyings, lowings, bleatings kept the air in turmoil. The aviaries, the poultry houses, the sties pulsed with reproduction. Under the persuasion of nocturnal torrents and daily deluges of sun the wild vegetation threatened to encompass and engulf all cultivation. Modest and timid vines became boa constrictors, thorny shrubs put forth daggers, and the little yellow lions of grass became full-fledged kings of the jungle. Flowers poured out so much perfume that the garden was a charnel house of stench. In the orchard fruit grew so quickly ripe that each globe dangled a starry bloom from its tip. In the meadows the breeding ponds resembled fountains, so constant was the leaping of silvery bodies into the sunlight.

And my mother's youngest sister, half her age and painfully delicate, sent a message that she was shortly to be brought to childbed and was in terror for the survival of body and soul together. Would my mother come to her?

As my mother went about her preparations she seemed to be imprinting each detail of the house in permanent image on her

brain. When I saw her gazing intently at some object she especially favored I would insinuate myself between them; her efforts to keep from seeing me gave to her eyes a look of permanent unfocus, like a madwoman's.

On the day she left we gathered in the courtyard to say good-
bye. She stood surrounded by servants laden like pack animals.
She turned to my father in the pale sunlight and said something
I could never forget were I given a lifetime in which to try. She
held up her hand at his protesting for the hundredth time her
going and said, "Don't protest too much, my dearest, for I might
stay. And, oh, I don't wish to be spiteful," then she turned without a word or glance at me and a small wind lifted the end of
her long scarf high into the air so that for a beautiful moment
she seemed, with her characteristically tilted head, to be hanging
on a thread of scarlet, suspended from the wind. The procession
moved from the courtyard and each blowing flower of spring
sent one blossom each after them and veiled them in a shower
of petals.

Chaconne

Alone. Silence is a pool and the weight of unspoken things sends
ripples spiraling upward and upward, limpid O's that are both
question and answer, mouths shaped to surprise and assent. Long
spears of sun penetrate the pool but stop short of the final illumination of whatever lurks at the bottom, illusively flickering as
a thought flickers unformed in the brain's wellsprings behind
the eyes. A stair creaks, shifting weight, and the sound is antici-
patory of assault, a bracing sound that stirs the caryatids on the
newels, causing them to shift the entablature that is their cross
and reason for being. The movement extends upward through
the house to the architrave, which, shifting, causes movement in
the figures of the frieze, whose pavane resettles the cornice. The
energy rises like smoke through chamber above chamber and
dissipates on the wind, which enters the regions beneath the house
where the statement originally began.

Everywhere, inside and out, the movement is restated as an

upward sifting of thought. The glass of the day is no longer cloudy; each image is reflected as undistorted. Truth, shedding its dark garments, showing its primeval bones unadorned, walks through the garden. The unsmiling face of Truth is a distant cry from a child's learning. Truth is only part of the equation pointing by parallel lines to a sum of frozenness—a lump of ice without the powerful grace of refraction. The eye, having gazed on Truth, turns forever inward, blind to the world, the shriven pupil staring at the flower of evil that stands to the right of the heart in the precise center of the self.

Is this the soul you spoke of, Mother? Is this the result of the seed you planted in me early, conscientious gardener that you were, abiding by an almanac of Faith that led you, in the proper phase of the moon, to teach me to say, without understanding, like an articulate plant, *"Specs mea Christus"*? Is it my fault alone that the seeds sprouted wild and black branches like a growth from some swamp planet? Weren't you able to see, by the games I played, that the harvest would be alien? But what could you know of the dangerous games of a child in the night when your own elaborate night kept you occupied in a long search for variations on a theme!

But wait, no recriminations, I promise. Only pause, you and your caravan, on whatever plain you find yourself. Never mind the night; you are safe, wrapped securely about with loyal protectors and noble intent. Stop, I ask you, and think of me, for I am left alone in a house with a river, and a fox, and a mountain lion.

See me, Mother, for this moment, and try to understand what I tell you: Here is my room and I am here by the window. There are shadows behind me now. I remember once, in winter, I boasted that I could make spring appear by unleashing my stores of energy. Are these shadows behind me deeper than winter? They must be, for I cannot budge them. Outside the window are roses, black, drained of the sun. Black grass, too, and trees—a world of silhouettes. On your plain, rosy with afterglow, it may be hard for you to look into the gloom of mine, but I ask you to try.

See me as someone you knew, poised on the edge of a world

you suspected; a world, however strange, that was made at least
bearable by your inability to visualize true evil. And this is the
crux: I find myself where I am by the same inability. I will let
you decide whether it is virtue or fault.

I was only playing a game! All children's games are composed
on formulae that are dangerous: pentacles, bits of glass to catch
the eye of Beelzebub, runic rhymes; the games you played as a
girl could have led you as easily to this precipice but you were
probably saved by an unasking innocence. But suppose you had
asked, and looking, found a shape, squat and dark, in the center
of your magic circle? Would you not have called to your mother,
perhaps on her way to visit an ailing relative, "Wait, stop, understand?"

The house trembles with sounds. If only I were not able to
identify them. There is water, stilly and deep, but we are in a
state of truce and its gentle lapping could comfort me. And that
sharp bark, too, is somehow playful and the appetite that it an-
nounces could be assuaged by a hen or a net of birds. We have
had our day, the river, the fox, and I—a day of mutual benefits
on a high plateau.

There is another sound. It is of constant movement, not gentle
as the river nor peevish as the fox. It is purposeful and sharp in
intent as the clacking of claws on the floor. It is the sound of a
Titan hungry after aeons of sleep, all appetites become finally
one.

Wood splinters, something falls, matter gives under force. A
Titan, after so long a sleep, would not understand the function
of walls and doors, would he? He would simply pass through.

And a child. What is a child to an aroused Titan?

What is a child?

HAM'S GIFT

In a region of ancestor worship he was singular for having, to his or anyone else's knowledge, none. He had been an apprentice farmer, a bondsman, from earliest memory, having been found wrapped in an old blanket in a hayloft by one of the children of the family with whom he lived. He had been taken in, the strangely quiet baby, and cared for with Baptist charity, which meant that he was fed, clothed, and housed until he was old enough to work at the age of five.

His first official job was to bring water in a little pail from the distant spring to the house and stable troughs. It was a full-time job, requiring the entire day with time out for a nap after midday dinner. As he grew older and stronger and could manage larger pails, the water carrying was finished sooner, leaving time for other jobs which became officially his. By the age of eight, the entire watering and feeding of the animals was in his care; in addition, he milked three Jersey cows twice daily, gathered eggs, and weeded and hoed the kitchen garden. He did his work well and was appreciated for it, but there was no lowering of social barriers between the boy and the family. He slept apart from the others in a little room in back of the washhouse and joined the family only for meals and the Bible readings which followed supper. There was no pretense that the originless child and youth was other than a stray and a bondsman; he was never asked to call his employers other than Mister, Miss, or Mrs., as the case might be.

He was given a rudimentary, secondhand education by one of the daughters of the house, which meant that she taught him, three evening a week, to read simple books, do simple sums, and to sign his name.

He did not feel deprived; indeed, the word was unknown to him. But when he discovered that he was blessed with a gift he hugged the knowledge to himself with something akin to ecstasy, and gradually the idea of a world in which he would be the aristocrat—an ancestorless world of gifted people who kept themselves apart with amused but kind toleration—began to form in his mind; after a time it ceased to be an idea and became, for him, a reality. At first as shrouded in mist as the distant mountains he wondered about, it drew daily nearer and replaced the world in which he moved and worked, ate and slept.

Without knowing why he knew, he knew: beyond the mountains the others were gathering, they were aware of his existence, and wordlessly he communicated with them at specific times set by his heart. At these moments the stolidity with which he faced the day would become suffused with melancholy and a faint, tugging excitement, and he would know that it was time.

He guarded his secret gift from the others with increasing difficulty. He was growing older and was expected to take part in communal labor, and he felt more than an edge of fear that they might witness him in a state of communication, which would lead to questions and exposure before he was ready. To circumvent this, he became adept at excuses that would allow him to seek privacy at those times. Ordinarily tractable to the point of dumb-animal servility, when he felt the call of his equals beyond the mountains he became almost insolent when objections were raised to his need to seek privacy. His employer, an honest man honestly bewildered, came to accept the boy's sole eccentricity, and because the boy was never absent for very long, soon ceased to question him or to think about it. When he was questioned by others, primarily by his sons, the farmer would say that he guessed it had something to do with body functions, with the boy's shyness about relieving himself in front of others. When they laughed and slapped their legs at such prissiness in a country boy, the farmer would say, gruffly, that it caused no harm; the boy always made the time up.

One son, Ezekiel, who was nearest in age to the bondsman, was resentful and fearful for his birthright because his mind was filled with Biblical stories wherein the rightful heir is deprived of his due by a cunning stranger. He resolved to watch the boy closely and report what he found to his father.

The bondsman, who was eventually called Ham, after the farmer's bent for Old Testament names, set himself a goal toward which he worked: at the age of fourteen, or as nearly as that age could be calculated, he would break his bondage and go to join the others, presenting to them, for the general good, his gift, which he envisioned as having the shape and glister of the prism one of the daughters of the house owned and kept on a piece of velvet. Thinking of the glad reception that would be his on that day, he glowed and trembled and worked as three men to hasten the time and earn his freedom.

The last three months of what he calculated to be his fourteenth year were the hardest. Try as he might, he found the long days almost immovable, like vast stones rooted in the earth. When finally they were budged, and nudged over the precipice into night, he felt drained of more than energy. After supper, after prayers, he would stand outside his small sleeping room and gaze at the mountains, far and gold in the moonlight, and would allow his imaginings of what lay beyond them to fill him drop by drop until he was a vessel containing the purest essence of dreams, like a brimming cup of quicksilver. He would stand so still that he became like a mirror into which he could gaze and see: a great lighted building, blazing with candles; within, happy godlike creatures moved to music, laughed, drank amber liquid from clear glass, and each in turn demonstrated, to loving applause, what it was that gave him the right to inhabit this place of all places on earth. Some performed tricks, but such tricks! Others sang songs that only the nightingale in his heart knows.

Once, in the latter part of the final month, he awoke from a communication and found Ezekiel standing at the edge of darkness watching him with huge eyes of fear. Ham made a move

toward the boy, his hands molding entreaty from the air, but
Ezekiel turned and ran to the house. Ham did not sleep that
night from anxiety and went to breakfast with a face ravaged
and old beyond his years, but no one noticed except Ezekiel,
whose eyes clung to Ham's eyes like sleep, searching there for
some explanation. Ham went through the following days in a
state of apprehension, and fear forced him to confine his com-
munications to his own little room where he might draw the curtains and obtain privacy. When they were working the fields and
he felt the tugging melancholic excitement, he would run without permission toward the harboring woods that bordered the
work area. Once he did not make the woods and fell into a patch
of uncut wheat. He was on the verge of being discovered, and
his heart beat thickly to cloak his anguish, but he knew he could
not deny the call; prayerfully he asked that the message be brief
and miraculously it was. He picked himself up to see Ezekiel
advancing, and pretending that he had stumbled on a root, he
made his way to the woods to preserve the illusion that his mis-
sion had not yet been accomplished. Ezekiel went back at the
farmer's angry call, but something in the look he gave to Ham,
and an added urgency to the communication that was like a clear
call, told Ham that he must not delay any longer.

That evening while the others were washing up for supper,
he sought out the farmer's wife and spoke with her. That was
the first time he had done so, for though she was the only mother
he had ever known, there was no love between them. At times
Ham had dreamed of a look or a word of special kindness from
her, but accepted the fact that he had no right to expect it. And
she, the solid, busy, good woman, felt toward him a kindness
and wished him well but further than that she was not prepared
to go, taken up as she was with the affairs and well-being of her
own brood. Her religion spoke of feeding and clothing the unfortunate but not of loving them. So that when Ham sought her
out for an exchange of words, they were both surprised. The
occasion had about it an air of importance, and they behaved as
strangers at a gathering—formal, and anxious to please by saying the right things.

It was her busiest hour, but something about his eyes caused her to wipe her floury hands on her apron, and, to her surprise, ask him to sit down. To his surprise, he sat. Perching each on the edge of a chair they spoke of the fine weather for harvest, sincerely hoped it might continue until bins, barns, and silos were filled. He told her how much he had always enjoyed her cookery; she complimented him on the excellent work he always gave in exchange. Once or twice during the conversation she shook her head as if to clear it of puzzlement. She was reluctant to break the mood, which seemed oddly significant. Eventually, however, he freed her by leaving. The rest of the supper preparations she performed in a kind of haze, her mind striving to penetrate the meaning of what had gone before. Weighty thoughts tired her after a while, and she gave up. But all through the meal and prayers afterward she rested her gaze on his intense young head as if to bore into its interior and fathom the mystery. She noticed that when he said good night his eyes wandered about the room with a look both happy and sad, coming to rest on her last of all and lingering. Speaking eyes, they were, but she did not know the language.

Ham returned to his room and settled down to wait. Gradually the large house grew quiet, lamps were extinguished, and serenity and sleep flowed from the windows into the warm night. Ham silently put a few belongings into a parcel, rose to leave, and felt the urge to communicate with his friends beyond the mountain. He gave himself up to the painful beauty of the exchange, the most bright, encouraging, love-filled one of his experience. His body trembled and beat as if it were a great organ note vibrating on the late air. He cried out at so much rapture and sat up, arms stretched toward the vision. Ezekiel stood in the doorway, frightened but determined. He came into the room and said, his voice slow and hoarse, "There's something the matter with you. You're possessed of a devil. I'm going to wake Pa."

It seemed to Ham that a shattered vessel lay on the floor of the room, and he saw that the vessel was himself. What it had contained, his gift, seeped in patches like moonlight. He beseeched Ezekiel to wait, promising to explain. The other boy, a shadow in the yard, neither replied nor faltered. In desperation Ham picked up a shovel that stood in a corner of the washhouse and followed Ezekiel, whose shadow looked to him like an eared jug. The shovel caught Ezekiel behind one of the ears. He fell without a sound, and his dark fluid quickly filled the depressions between tufts of grass.

Ham ran blindly, leaving his parcel of goods behind. Past the spring, through the fields of half-harvested grain, to and into the bordering woods and out, straight as a bird he flew toward the mountains. Brambles tore his clothes, and the sharp rocks of stream beds cut his feet, but on he ran. He fell and struck his head on a stump but got to his feet and ran onward through the night, swiping at the curtain of blood that obscured his vision. By dawn he had reached the foothills of the mountains, where he crept into a dark shelter and slept until night fell again.

The pattern of flight and hiding became his way of life. His communicants had not warned him that the mountain was a vast one. Upward and onward he rose toward the moon into the thin chilly air. A few times he was glimpsed by hunting mountaineers and a legend grew of an apparition, mournful and wild, who haunted the mountain passes on nights of the full moon. As Ham advanced, so traveled the legend, and in later years it was a matter of dispute as to which community could lay original claim to the specter.

At last he reached a plateau from which could be seen his objective lying like Canaan below the clouds. Standing at the edge of the old world, gazing with hosannas into the new, his suffering lay upon him like the mantle of a prophet. His hair, matted with leaves and burrs and blood, hung in tatters to his shoulders. His clothing was ripped and torn in a hundred places. His long curving nails gave him the look of a wolf-person, as did his burning eyes. Nowhere was there evidence of his youth. But he was unaware of his awesomeness, for when he drank from streams all that had been reflected therein was his goal, so blazing a vision that it had obscured as well the memory of Ezekiel lying in the litter of his life for having gazed upon the wheel of fate. An incident of Ham's final hour before his descent did not make him suspect the figure of fear he had become.

He lay in a clump of trees waiting for nightfall when some bushes surrounding his retreat parted and a dog sniffed through, followed by a child. The child, intent upon some spoor in imitation of his dog, did not see Ham. When Ham spoke in his unused voice the child raised his eyes and was stricken in the manner of Lot's wife. Tasting recognition, Ham smiled, which broke the thralldom, and the child screamed and ran from the copse followed by the rumbling tail-tucked dog. Ham puzzled out that the reason for the strange behavior was that a snake had hung coiling from one of the trees above his head.

He grew impatient with the slow day, counting the minutes until nightfall and covering darkness. He estimated that he had about an hour's travel before him. The chimneys and steeples of the village could be glimpsed now from rises in the fields. As darkness lowered, lights appeared in the kingdom he sought, and he stepped as lightly as a gazelle, his heart lifting in his thin chest.

An hour past nightfall he stood on the boundaries of Eden. It was a small town, but it seemed to Ham that he stood at the gates of Beulahland. Straight, unerringly, he made his way to the trysting place. He knew it from his visions, and there it was before him, tall windows alight with candles and within figures moving to music, pausing to drink amber liquid from clear glass. When he reached the doorway a small knot of outsiders who were peering at the festivities parted silently and made way for him. It seemed to him that their eyes acknowledged his right, his alone of all of them, to enter the place. They stared at him and with a kindly smile he drank in their recognition.

He entered the hall, in his face radiant with joy. The music stopped and gradually the people turned one by one, silent, waiting for him to speak first. The beat of his heart thundered in the sweet silence; he could not seem to form words that he longed to say to these, his people. To his dismay he felt faint, to his horror he knew that he was falling. But he was *here*. There was no need of silent communication now! He strove to tell them, to tell himself, to speak and be heard above the growing din.

There was great activity about him, above him, and he seemed dimly to hear the word "physician." He looked up through eyes from which vision was fading and into those of a man bending over him. The man's eyes were filled with love and understand-

ing and admiration. Ham felt christened in the light of the eyes.
Through the pounding in his ears he heard the man say words,
simple and dignified, that made the long arduous journey worth
its terrors. They were answer, affirmation, fulfillment: Grand
Mal. Grand! How blessèd the sound of praise, like David at his
Psalms! He had slain, too, young David, and lived to share his
boon, his shining gift, with all the world.

"God moves," said Ham from the depths of his gift, "in mysterious ways—oh ye Saints!"—and drank his brimming tongue
like a cup of thanksgiving.

MRS. HACKETT

Marie Louise would say to inquiries about her mother's age, "Well, if I'm under thirty, Mama *could* be under fifty," and then because her brush was uncertain even when attempting to paint lilies, she would add, "Couldn't she?"

As uncharitable as many of the townspeople longed to be with regard to that "under thirty" clause, no one actually ever said "No" because of their regard for Marie Louise's mother, Mrs. Hackett, who, if she was under fifty, was enjoying the earliest second childhood of anybody around.

She was a tall woman, thin and flat and straight, with fingers that were like weathered bones—"artistic" they used to say, and still did out of habit, though now the hands were all but useless, which may have been exactly what they meant. Her head, too, was like a skull found on a desert: equine, with long teeth the color of old piano keys and skin that bound the bones tightly as though to impede further growth. Her feet, dressed summer and winter in white kid, were narrow and lengthy. She wore leghorn hats with streamers to cover her yellow hair that had come out in patches, exposing the leached-out scalp like a glimpse of the dry earth through clouds. She wore dresses of a bygone cut and material— dimity and pongee which tended to a profusion of sashes and bows and ruching.

Dressed in white organdy with enormously puffed sleeves and

dozens of stiff ruffles edged in red rickrack, wearing a floppy organdy hat and carrying a somewhat thyrsoid shepherdess crook— perhaps a costume from some forgotten gala— she could slow down traffic in midtown on a winter's day.

Her friends had given up trying to make her dress sensibly for cold weather; her feet could not have been squeezed into any of the little, one size fits all, plastic booties which they favored, and they all admitted that a heavy winter coat would look just silly as could be with the organdy hat. Grubbing with her through her trunks in search of a lost doll, they had found an evening cloak of transparent velvet with a wealth of passementerie, and sometimes she could be persuaded to wear it, but more often she eluded even those well-intentioned ones who liked to say that they kept an eye out for her, and in general they left her alone, taking their cue from Marie Louise. "Oh, Mama's all right," she would say, looking wistfully at the snow, thinking for no reason that she could place about death in winter, and sighing.

Mrs. Hackett had gone into second childhood unexpectedly, in the middle of a piano lesson. She was coaching, against the coming event of her yearly recital, her least promising pupil in the nuances of Percy Grainger's "Country Gardens." "No, no," she was saying as the child interpolated a bit of the Beatles into the most delicate section; "No, *no*," and all at once, according to the girl's report, she had gone onto all fours to pick up the pencil she used as a pointer and had stayed that way, crawling under the piano and gurgling. The pupil told those of her own set that Mrs. Hackett had also peed.

If any of the girl's report was true, then Mrs. Hackett grew up at a rate that would have alarmed any parent, because when Marie Louise dropped in on her the next day she was reading *The Wind in the Willows,* and said without being asked that she was nine years old. Marie Louise thought that she said "ninety" and put her foot down hard, pointing out that if *she* was still under thirty then she could not have a ninety-year-old mother without causing talk of a highly nasty nature. Calculating rapidly she said, "My God, Mama, assuming I'm twenty-eight years old, that would have you doing it—subtract two, carry nine months—when you were over sixty-one years of age *and Daddy died when you were forty.*"

She had gone on in this vein, interspersed with her mother's observations about Toad of Toad Hall, until it came to her that she had, as she told her friends, "lost my mama and gained a kid sister."

At first it had amused her to play paper dolls with her mother, but this had soon given way to a cynicism that took the form of teaching the woman who had been famous for her prudery to say bad words. At gatherings in Mrs. Hackett's parlor—a great many gatherings in the first months of her senility, during which time she was courted as a queen by lines of townspeople waiting to gain admittance—Marie Louise would stand by her mother's chair and coax her, "Now, darling, recite a little piece for our friends," and Mrs. Hackett would oblige with the latest pornographic limerick she had learned at her daughter's knee. But she was clever and soon caught on to the quality of the laughter. She would smile sweetly until her guest had gone and then would say, "That verse was naughty, now wasn't it?" And though Marie Louise would never admit that it had been, she grew foxy and consulted the dictionary and certain other books for words more subtly objectionable This too backfired, but it did contribute to an odd kind of general education.

Still, it was not as much immediate fun to have Mrs. Hackett say "fellatio," pronouncing it "fell-lot-e-o" as she had been taught, and get only nervous titters in return. Her audience soon took to writing the words down and looking them up at home and reacting there—surely the "delayed take" nonpareil. And then like schoolchildren they were bringing their books with them. Ranged about her with books, paper, and pencils, writing down the words and looking them up, it was as though they once again attended her opening classes for beginners, in which she had introduced most of them and their children to the preliminary mysteries of music, having them count out and mark with their feet—"But softly, boys and girls, this is an old old carpet on an old old floor"—the different time values of the notes as she drew them on a slate. The hysterical delayed laughter of the adults at the unearthing in their reference books of some meaning was like an echo of the chaos resulting from the teacher's slow counting out of a whole note—"oneeeee Twoooooo Threeeee Foooooour"—which they were supposed to fill in with sixteenth notes, shouting and pounding their feet, "ONEtwothreefour-FIVEsixseveneight NINEteneleventwelve THIRteenfourteen-fifteensixteen."

Mrs. Hackett had brought the audiences to an end by getting sick. At least she said that she was sick and went to bed with a pickaninny doll for comfort, and though the doctor, her husband's best man and her lifelong friend, who examined her with sympathy and loathing for her daughter could find nothing physically wrong with her, she refused to get out of bed. Which meant that Marie Louise had to pay for a full-time nurse to stay in the house and, as she said, "eat like a goddamned horse all day." Marie Louise's husband, being the one who actually paid, accused her of responsibility for her mother's condition and gave her an ultimatum: Get her out of that bed in a week or pack up and move back home.

Marie Louise was frightened at the thought of "practicing a profession for which she was not trained"—namely, nursing—and she approached her mother with a tenderness awful in its supplication.

"Mama . . ." she said, and meeting suspicion mingled with blankness at the address, she for the first time called her mother by her given name, Belle, though she tried for a diminutive and wound up calling her mother "Belly," which was a hard beginning because that was one of the words her mother knew to be naughty. She tried again, so softly as to hide the venom with which a sharper tone would have been tipped, though she was not entirely successful.

"Dear little Belle," she murmured, "tell big Marie Louise what the hell's wrong with you."

Still, she had had a week of grace and in that time her mother had extracted from Marie Louise a promise to keep "the big people" away from her. It seemed that their laughter frightened her ("Of all things!") and made her wonder ("Can you imag-

ine!") whether she had ("The poor old thing whispered it . . .")
soiled her dress in (shrieks of laughter) *"the water closet."*

Following her two weeks in bed Mrs. Hackett had entered a time
of loneliness. When well-meaning friends called on her she would
turn them away at the door, saying that her mother was not at
home, after which she would wander through the house searching, wondering where her parents were, certain that they had
told her exactly when they would return so that she wouldn't
worry, and then she had to go and forget. When she got hungry
she would make messes at the stove but got so she could cook a
passable meal of Quaker Oats and buttered bread toasted in the
oven. Once or twice a week the ugly woman who called her "little
sister" with a smirk when she wasn't being mean and scolding
came to see her and made her eat vegetables and tough meat
and shoved coffee—Mama would just die—at her in big cups.
When she tried to explain about not being allowed stimulants
she was either told to shut up or got stared at in a very rude
manner. "Shut up" was an expression that only very vulgar people used, foreigners who lived in the bad part of town and were
allowed to work for respectable person only in the daytime. Mama
would say, "I wouldn't trust one of them in my house after dark,"
and everyone would nod.

Belle did not honestly know why this was so, for she had been
taught that nighttime is the snuggest, warmest, safest time of all.
When Papa had to go out to attend an accouchement and she
and Mama were left alone in the evening, Mama would tell her
over and over about nighttime being so snug and safe. Over and
over—standing at the window pinching the curtains peeping out.
Over and over—poking up the fire and piling on big lumps of
coal. When Belle got sleepy Mama would hold her on her lap in
a chair with its back to the wall and croon to her about how snug
and safe nighttime was, letting out little screams when a shutter
banged or ice slid off the roof with a funny noise. Once in the
summertime she had made Papa repeat something he had said
to her before they were married, that she said only he would

know, before she would unhook the screen door and let him in. Standing in the hallway while Papa nuzzled Belle's hair and laughed, Mama had said that of course they couldn't use those words as a password ever again because *they* had heard and would use them to gain admittance and have their way. "Who with?" Papa had asked. "You or the String Bean?"—which was what he called Belle because she was so skinny. Mama had said, "Perish the thought!" and she threw her hands up and walled her eyes.

The time came when Belle stopped looking for them to come up the walk, or listening for the jingle of the harness on her father's buggy. She did not forget them, but they became like the doll that she could remember but could not find anywhere, the one that was larger than she was when she got it, whose head had got broken so that the mechanism holding the movable eyes could be seen at work. She knew that she would find it eventually; to look for it each day became something as necessary as keeping herself meticulously clean. And she knew that her parents would come in one day and tell her in fine detail—her father was a famous raconteur—what it was that had detained them. She missed them, but what at first had been a strong pain became a mild ache like the feeling in an old fading bruise when you pressed it; unless you pressed it hard it did not hurt at all. Gradually she began to allow her mother's callers to come in and sit with her and then they were helping her look for the doll and pick out what clothes to wear, and after a while she was returning their visits and sitting in their parlors and eating sweet cakes and drinking lemonade. She had found, though, that she must not ask them, however discreetly, if they knew where her parents were because they would, at best, pull long faces; at worst they would sniffle. It was a peculiar reaction that she did not care to investigate.

Gradually, through such adjustments, the adult world became partly hers once again. She joined more frequently in conversations and was listened to without the unkind laughter that had puzzled her, especially after she revealed a candor that was sometimes uncomfortably on the mark. For example, when she picked a chrysanthemum bud in a friend's garden and gave it to the lady with a curtsy and a compliment, and was asked dryly and yet condescendingly if the gesture were not "premature," Belle replied in a low swift voice, "Compliments are frequently premature, but some manners never show up at all." Another time, when one of the ladies told a bald truth to another of the circle and excused her wounding frankness on the grounds of friendship, Belle observed musingly, as though recalling the words, "Friendship isn't the license to say just anything at all, but the consideration not to say it." In their confusion the ladies explained to each other that "she heard her mother say that." Part of the confusion was because it had not been in her former nature to make such remarks, and though they admitted the pungency of what she said, they felt on more comfortable grounds with their "old little girl."

As they told each other, she had always been a bit otherworldly, for there was no wider chasm known to woman than that separating the old-fashioned girl (Belle) and the modern (themselves). To emphasize the gap, they gave her gifts of dolls and other discarded toys of their children and grandchildren.

She also discovered that they would help her look for lost toys in her own house, but when she visited them she was expected to leave alone whatever toys there were lying about and must not play with the other children. It was, she learned, not the grown-ups who minded; it was the children. As her mother would say, they were a different breed—incomprehensible, selfish, and shockingly common—and they did not want her to touch their things. She had been brought up to share her playthings, but had also been taught not to point out other people's shortcomings, so she left the children to their games and ignored their rude stares as she sat, bored but polite, in a big chair in the circle of grown-up ladies.

Speaking of rude children, there was one house to which she would never return as long as she lived because of a dance one of them did while she was visiting. The girl, who was her own age and the granddaughter of one of the ladies, was said to be a clever dancer and a disc had been put on the gramophone so that she could demonstrate her talent. The machine seemed to be broken, for the noise that came out of it was harsh and bewildering. Belle waited for someone to repair it, which would give

the little girl a chance to fetch her toe shoes. Instead, the child
(Belle later decided that she was a runaway circus midget) had
begun a series of jerky, broken movements that were horridly as
though she were poking fun at old Mr. Symes who had Saint
Vitus's dance and was an object of pity. The girl, or midget, had
gone on to move her midsection in such a way that Belle, without
having an idea why she did so, broke into tears. All she knew
was that something seemed to be pulling at her mind in a way
that was like a nightmare that tries to make you remember something you never knew. The motions—back and forth, side to
side, round and around—filled her with a nameless terror and
brought pain to the most private parts of her body. And the
sound, the terrible screaming sound from the gramophone. Until she cried, the ladies had been smiling and nodding and wink-
ing at each other. Afterward they gathered around her and
murmured and soothed, and the grim little dancing girl had said
rudely, "What's the matter with *her*" and stared at her with eyes
as hard and bold as a boy's.

Needing to confide in someone, she had told the ugly woman
who sometimes fed her unpleasant food about the incident. (Belle
came to accept that she and the woman probably were distant
relatives, but she refused to put a name to the relationship; one
thing she knew for sure was that the woman was no sister of
hers, being considerably older than her own mother. She got
around her predicament by not calling the woman anything and
thinking about her as little as possible.) The woman had screeched
at her story like a parrot and slapped her legs which were encased in some kind of pantaloon and hollered out something
about second childhood being brought on by the beetles, saying
that now it was all clear to her because imogen had told how she
had stuck some of lucy in the sky into percy grainger and mama
had gone down on all fours and peed.

None of it made any sense to Belle, who smiled at the ugly
woman and wished with all her heart that she would go away
and never come back. From that day on she had to listed to others saying the nonsensical words—beetles and lucy in the sky
and all fours and peed. Belle learned how to live with it and how
to smile and how not to listen. Finally, because of her disposition

which was what Mama had said was as amiable as anyone could wish, she came to enjoy her visits with the grown-ups who were really a jolly bunch, the sole exception being the one they called Marie Louise, who was mean-spirited, kinfolk or not, and that was that.

Mrs. Hackett, dressed in her mother's clothes, sat with her dolls on a sofa looking through a photograph album. She nodded over the beloved pictures, studio portraits of her parents and herself taken before heavy drapes in a garden of columns and pedestals holding baskets of roses. She had never grown so sleepy in such pursuit before, as she informed the dolls with mouth pursed in imitation of a fading memory. "My favorite pastime and me heavy-headed as a cabbage rose!" Not only heavy-headed; bored. The word came even as she gazed at Mama's face. She believed she should cry as penance but no sorrow touched her. Instead, the word repeated: bored, bored, bored, bored.

It seemed to her that she gazed down a corridor of growing-up years as static and artificial as the columns and pedestals—imitation stuff, easy to knock over. She did not see how she could bear to move down that inert avenue where the drapes eternally smelled of dust. She saw herself pressed behind glass, rice-powdered, wearing her mother's clothes, gazing from the window frozen in its frame at a world enlivened by the fresh air of change that could never touch her, never get to her and free her. Curiously like a memory she thought that such airlessness could form monsters out of the dust. She did not want to be a monster! Her head snapped forward as though forcibly to blot melancholy like a signature set at the bottom of her thoughts. Mama gazed up at her sadly, seeming to ask, "Am I a monster, Belle?"—for she had been formed out of that dust and a fear of change.

Fighting confusion and disloyalty the easiest way, Belle closed the album and she and the dolls fell asleep.

She woke to the alarms of a stranger who both knocked and pulled the rusty bell handle as though in a terrible rush. When Mrs. Hackett opened the door the woman shoved an envelope at her, gave her a look that made Mrs. Hackett feel as though she were being swept with a straw broom, followed by a strange smile with a shrug in it, and said, "Not very likely material but what the hell," and left. Open-mouthed at the breach of all manners, Belle stared after the stomping woman until she lumbered into an automobile and drove away.

Belle sat with the dolls, holding the envelope, until she felt her courage build up in her, then opened the coarse heavy thing with a thin paper knife and drew out the card, or invitation as it turned out to be: JOIN (it enjoined her) YOUR SISTERS IN BONDAGE TO MALE SUPREMACY AND HYPOCRISY. MEET WITH US! BREAK BREAD WITH US! BREAK WIND WITH US IF YOU MUST! BUT HELP US BREAK THE BONDS THAT BIND US. JOIN M A C H A AND LET US TELL IT LIKE IT IS. EACH LIFE HISTORY SHARED IS A STEP TOWARD OUR TOTAL LIBERATION. HELP US BANISH ALL MEN TO THE MOON!!!

Belle thought and thought. Would all club members be as peculiar as the one who delivered the invitation? Too much like Marie Louise, that one, but she was pleased at the thought of joining her "sisters" in whatever pursuit engaged them. The thing was to get out of that sealed dusty place in which she found herself too frequently alone. Somewhat austerely, thinking as a club member, she apologized to her dolls for the thought, but in her mind she planned her costume for the first meeting: middy blouse, pleated skirt, black stockings—very, she thought, Club.

Mrs. Hackett, used to strange reactions to her person, entered the place of meeting with good grace and control, concealing her dismay to see ugly Marie Louise sitting on a platform with her friend Miss Little, both of them trousered and booted, sitting as only the lowest order of man sat, with legs splayed out. Marie Louise let out a hoot, which Mrs. Hackett took willfully as a version of a kindly meant greeting (if one were a large trousered hoot owl) and waved merrily as though she and her detested relative were intimate enough to have a private greeting (and shuddered at the idea).

As she sat Mrs. Hackett heard a long-drawn-out sound that horrified—it seemed to come from everywhere but primarily from beneath her—and heard raucous laughter grow around her. In her confusion she shifted in her seat and each time she shifted the noise repeated; in her mind it was inextricable from the vision of a *pot de chambre,* sepulchral, shameful, certainly and unmistakably one of life's burdens. And it came from herself though no sensation of incontinence accompanied it. Bright red, the color to her of horror, for it represented the ultimate in breach of manners, she rose to leave the clubhouse only to be confronted by someone she knew, one of her friends to whose house she often went. The woman, also red-faced (Mrs. Hackett thought coldly that there could be no doubt of the red's origin: merriment), drew from Mrs. Hackett's seat a cushion. Compressing it, still unable to speak, the woman managed to indicate that the sound was the peculiar property of the cushion, of air escaping a valve. Weakly, when she could, the woman said, "To break the ice. A whoopee cushion. Marie's Louise's idea."

Marie Louise, as though the mere calling of her name summoned her like a dog, cried out from the platform, "Oh, Mama, relax, what's a little fart between sisters!" and the hall exploded in masculine glee.

The tall old figure turned in a slow circle standing before her assigned seat, her prepared seat, and surveyed the hall. Those who clung to the gallery above could see her long feet in black patent leather slippers, see the black ribbed stockings that met the pleated wool skirt joined to the middy blouse with its militant red silk scarf knotted below the collar, and some of them felt shame. But shame itself is funny, they later agreed, and led them onward to laughter. And what, after all, *is* a little fart between sisters who only a short time before would have been punished for saying the word! But they all admitted, later, that they had a sudden, simultaneous urge—no, stronger than that, a real appetite—to hear the life history of the humiliated woman. *There* was where to start, with the only living example of total ruin in the hall: old, prudish, probably virginal—no, for she had had a daughter, one of their shining lights, in fact; so she *had* been fucked, at least once . . . and as the liberated thoughts and language poured from them some admitted that they wished to see the woman below them, standing in a daze, martyred. *Their* martyr, though, and love flooded each and every breast.

They descended upon her, those clinging to the gallery, and from the auditorium floor they rose up at her. They pulled at her and pushed at her and ultimately, necessity being also the mother of action, some of them took the fainting woman to her home, never knowing that she had retreated—rapidly, like an animal backing into the hole from which it has ventured for food—into the past. The woman or girl who had come to their meeting had been in the vicinity of sixteen years old; what they returned to the empty house was once again a child of nine.

Belle wanted a Christmas tree. Her dolls wanted a Christmas tree. The house had always had a Christmas tree, so tall that the star brushed the ceiling, with real candles that Papa would light for an hour each night of the twelve. The curtains were always pulled wide so that passersby could look in and see the tree, and when Belle and Mama and Papa were themselves passersby, they could look in the houses all up and down Marvel Street and see the other beautiful trees. And carolers sang and sleigh bells tinkled and all the town was a festival to the memory of the Babe. But now they were telling her that she could not have a tree. The candles would be dangerous, they said, and when she agreed with them and said she would not have candles they thought up other excuses, one of which—repeated by strange coarse women—was "So goddamned unmacha," which made no sense at all.

On Christmas Eve not a wreath, not a sprig of holly, showed in the entire city. She made sure of that by dressing in her prettiest frock and walking up and down every street in the good parts of town, hoping against hope to see one glimmer of cheer. Night drew in and still she searched.

Finally, among the shops and press of people, just as the first flakes of snow fell, she found the color she sought. It was a bookstore, cozily lighted, an impression of firelight behind the glass, behind the snow. Shelves and tables of books danced, caught like jewels, so bright-jacketed were they, in the rivulets of condensation on the pane. Mrs. Hackett smiled with glee at the thought of treasures old and new—a splendid-looking new *Wind in the Willows*, or a book of geography with gay maps and descriptions of, as she was learning to say, life-styles of creatures not quite so unlike herself as Beaver et al. Yes, that was it, "armchair travel," as Papa would say; a nice fire and getting to know someone in a country beyond the hills, the sea. Grass huts on stilts beside a teeming river in a country where snow never fell at all. "Where the wind don't blow and the snow don't go," as the old song had it, though the only place without wind that anybody human could testify to was the moon.

Patting her pocketbook where the quarters, dimes, nickels, and some found silver dollars were, she went through the crowd into the deliciously warm store, nodding in case the clerks were friends of her parents. Right away she found just the book, bound in sun colors with the picture of a solemn native on the back cover. *Alabama Black Boy*. The sound was like drums.

She opened it, read: "With my guts, my dick, my bull balls, I hated them, all of them, the white motherfuc . . ." Her gaze wandered to another stack of burnished dust covers as she absently placed the native account back on the table. Here was another, a drawing, this time, of a boy with curls in front of his ears and a foreign-looking hat; he seemed cold, a somber little boy from a mountainous place. She took up the volume and opened it carefully.

"More than the cockroaches, more than hunger, more than the congenital stupidity of—to my private anguishing certainty despite the tenderness of my feelings for (even when I chose to think of her by a more suitable name than((my father having once been pushed, in the old country, into a pile of cowshit by a girl named Betty)) Betty) Betty—Betty; and more than, negating the salty saliva in my mouth when I saw her brought on by proximity to (for spit is spit and my spittle ran for Betty) Betty—Yahweh, my real enemy, our real enemies, my constipated father's real sometimes enema was were was the goyim for more than the unutterable true name of God"—Mrs. Hackett was glad to find the Name, the first word she had so far understood, and it seemed to take her by the hand and lead her on—"was it forbidden to say the name of my shiksa darling (cunt tongue hard as razor sound of her) in the house of my parents, and the houses of their parents, anywhere, anywhere at all except in the precarious privacy (my mother's diaphragm stuffed in my mouth to mask the sound) of the toilet."

She put the book back, not at all carefully. In fact, she slapped it smartly down to demonstrate disapproval in case anyone was watching or listening. Mama had instilled in her that only the most vulgar people said "toilet" for water closet. Sometimes, if one was poor but genteel, one had instead an earth closet; but the word she had just read was not permissible unless one spelled and pronounced it in French, "toilette," where it meant washing your face and putting on cologne.

She wandered, the store practically hers, and sampled wares until she wound up at a book table that proclaimed itself by a sign to contain books suitable for "preteens." She did not know her age but believed herself on comfortable territory.

She selected a book with a little girl wearing trousers on its cover, a hurdle easily gotten over for she was becoming immune to surprises. Still, she opened it somewhat warily. Inside, in a nicely drawn and colored picture, there was the same little girl. Mrs. Hackett found this reassuring. She had been really amazed at the changes that took place, in all the other books, the moment the covers were opened. Over and over she had been reminded of Pandora's box, so prettily painted and carved, hiding so many stinging things. The little native boy hating everyone; the boy with the curls writing "toilet"; the book written by a golden-haired pointy-faced girl that said on the jacket, "A tender, haunting story of love and devotion," and began with the narrator throwing up on a visitor's stomach, the language far worse than the deed: "As soon as he came I lifted my head and puked on his belly." Making an effort, because of the girl's heart-face and lovely hair, Mrs. Hackett had arranged to see the following: a very sick girl lying on a hospital bed; she was recovering from something dreadful—diphtheria, the scourge of its time—and was simply not in control, gallant though she was, so that when her father came in and stood by the bed she raised her bedewed head to smile at him and *unable to help herself* she vomited and some of it got on his waistcoat. "Puked" and "belly" could not be incorporated into the gallant picture and so she glazed them over.

But here at last was a book that had not changed at all. Here was the same little girl reassuringly on the very first page, same costume, same wide-eyed expression, pointing to another bigger girl who wore earrings and some lip rouge; doubtless the little sister would have some roguishly edifying thing, a little moral, to say about the cosmetics. Under the picture were the words, in childish printing, "This is my queer brother. Since Jen and Dave, our sometime parents, got their divorce, he dresses this way and smokes a lot of grass."

Mrs. Hackett sighed over the divorce, giggled at the idea of smoking grass: a queer brother, indeed. Still, it was a story about children who could be her own age and there was some comfort in that, and she paid for the book willingly in spite of the shocking price. She had to tug and tug at a lady clerk to get service, and the woman then tried to detain her, asking her to wait, "at least," she said, "until I can call Marie Louise," not knowing how poor a prospect that was to Mrs. Hackett.

Mrs. Hackett pushed through the crowd and went home, glad to be away from the noise, glad to have a new picture book, but her voile dress was ruined, draggled with mud and snow, and her slippers were worn through to the numbed soles of her feet. She went to bed the way she was, too weary to undress, book and prospect of fireside forgotten.

Periodically throughout the loud night she awoke to see her parents in the room with her. It seemed to her that her room was a chessboard and Papa and Mama the king and queen. Who was moving them (their defenses long captured) she could not tell, but they would have been placed differently on the board each time she looked. It was clear to her that they were trying to get to her bedside, but the players used stratagems, Belle thought, that Papa himself, a most scrupulous player, would not have approved of to prolong the game.

In the moonlight-scattered room the chairs stood angled, one in the middle of the floor, another at the window, abutting it, so that one sitting there could watch the variations of light in the garden and have a clear view of the room. Papa sat in the middle chair, between Mama at the window and Belle on the bed, keeping vigil through the night. He and Mama were staying for longer visits as Belle grew weaker, though if the two facts were connected she had nothing to do with it, for she had not told anyone. She was occasionally tempted to tell, for then someone would go down and bring her up something to eat, but in an odd way the idea of eating, and growing strong again, ran against the grain; it was like an impoliteness, and she did not want either of her parents to go for a moment out of the room. She wanted them, each and every minute of them, for as long as they could stay with her. At the thought, an edge, a narrow edge of light surrounded the picture of Belle wanting them to stay with her forever and she could see it and feel it inside, a warmer comfort than food, smile-producing. And she thought that when the edge of light grew to a certain width, as though prescribed by law, then it would become solidified, would be a permanent frame, so that the picture could be lifted up and hung on the wall as an unchanging fact, like a painting or a daguerreotype: Papa and Belle and Mama Together Forever.

By nine o'clock on the evening of the gala there was only one empty seat in the amphitheatre, the one to have been occupied by Mrs. Hackett. Marie Louise had tried to dress the old lady with the intention of taking her to the celebration in the back of the station wagon and somehow propping her up in her seat, believing that nobody would notice anything strange, but she had to admit defeat; rigor mortis made Mrs. Hackett's limbs unmanageable. Marie Louise would have taken her anyhow, except her mother had died trying to get to the bathroom and her bedgown was spattered with night soil, as she would have called it. She could have been cloaked—her old velvet cloak with the passementerie lay across the foot of her bed as though she had meant to dress herself and attend the great liberation ceremony. But there was no way to disguise the odor, which Marie Louise found out the expensive way by pouring over Mrs. Hackett an entire bottle of perfume, which made Marie Louise, understandably, she felt, angry. Finally, unable to restrain a last impulsive comment, Marie Louise kicked Mrs. Hackett. Kicked and kicked her.

Looking at her lying with huge blue empty eyes walled up, all at once it came to her just what it was her mother most resembled: that old broken doll that she had cared for more than she cared for her daughter, that she was always searching for but could not find because Marie Louise had put it in the furnace the first chance she got, after her mother had gone off her rocker. Kick, kick, the way one whacks a stopped clock, but the old woman was a lump of yellow dirt with never a tick left in her.

However, all things have their good side. Marie Louise, being the last to arrive, received the undivided attention of the svelte audience as she walked slowly up and down the aisles. She managed the long intricate parade so well that her sisters broke into sustained applause. She was final proof that liberation has at last come to womankind and that it was not only "macha" but wondrously *womanly* (at last they could say it!) as well. For her long good moment she was the bride of her world and in a last nod at tradition, among her apparel of new, borrowed, and blue, she wore, on the tip of her odd-grained stomping boot, little identical patches of something old.

THE MOON, THE OWL, MY SISTER

We are an agrarian family, living by the field. We have been taught that those who live by the field will die by the field, and we accept this. We are necessarily nomadic. Our belief in the equal division of landed property is not shared by the owners of the property we till and work, and thus we must move on from field to field, gleaning as much of the harvest as we can, using the residue of its materials to build our seasonal homes. Sometimes we fall onto good seasons, a double-edged remark, for by it I mean those times when land is allowed to lie fallow, and we must then go far afield for our food; but, the good edge, in such seasons we put down roots and foolishly, according to our mother, build dwellings that have about them the look and feel of permanence.

For the past two hunter's moons we have lived in one of these "permanent" dwellings. We add on rooms as the fancy strikes, and fill storehouses as though we at last had come into property of our very own, which no one could take from us by revolution or otherwise. "Otherwise" must remain undefined, for it is the stuff of instinct; but "revolution" as we define it would grant us the right to our piece of earth, which would be no larger nor smaller than those of our fellows, and so covetousness could not have a part to play.

We are a small family though we have in the past been large. Indeed, the lady of the house whom I gratefully call mother is in fact my stepmother, and in this sense "our family" is a comparatively recent term. My own mother, the product of whose loins by my father I am the remaining specimen, was taken from us when I was very small, though I remember her well. My father formed the new alliance as much for my sake as for his own, and the excellent creature he took to spouse has provided him with another brood, diminished now. Altogether we are only six; two of us were taken in hunting accidents, one by drowning, and another is simply gone, we know not where.

My favorite sister—though the word looks unfair, as I have only one other now, a baby still—is beautiful, poetic, and moody, and was born to my stepmother in her first alliance, before I was conceived.

Our father is stalwart and revered, and though sometimes we laugh at him, it is my belief that he deliberately fosters it to relieve rebellious instincts. We seldom quarrel among ourselves, due to the peaceable example of our parents, and we are allowed a large degree of independence meant to develop our individuality. That some of us have died is thankfully not seen as the result of such latitude, and we are not made to suffer in addition to our sense of loss.

In our current situation—may it continue unbroken and unresolved, which supplication I will try to make clear in the course of this narrative—we each have our own room, which reflects our independence nicely. My youngest brother and sister, whom we refer to as "the twins" though they are the survivors of sextuplets, have made their connecting quarters into one labyrinth, diabolically intricate; to visit them one must be prepared to stay awhile.

My room, because of my "thoughtful" bent, is plainest, and though I do not have any books entire, I have sections of books which I have arranged as I have seen them in houses (the houses from which I took the leaves, patiently unlawful, a leaf at a time); among these are almost all of the *f*'s and *m*'s from the dictionary (Microtus pennsylvanicus rather proudly underlined); there is also a shattering poem by Robert Burns and, a dark and perhaps sinful secret, parts of many adventures from a curious book called *Master Tyll Owlglass.*

My favorite sister's room is the one we are most eager to be invited to visit, for it is both strange and cozy. She has allowed— proof of the benevolence of that good housekeeper, our mother!—cobwebs to accumulate, entire with occupants and sometimes their would-be dinners. In most cases both occupant and prey are preserved in the mere likeness of life, but there is always at least one active web and one can sit before it and watch the tragicomedy of life and death and meditate upon it, as my sister frequently does. My mother, somewhat testily, is accustomed to say that this spectacle accounts for a certain streak of morbidity in my beloved sister. But as to my view of it, I will only say, not wishing to dispute our mother more than necessary, that the word—morbidity—seems at odds with my sister. As I have said, she is poetical, which means, I believe, that she is more prone to meditations upon fate than others among us, but within herself I believe the word would not find a congenial atmosphere. Unless morbid and philosophical are synonyms bound together, like halves of a peach pit, by a seamlike thread that we can acknowledge to be poetical foresight.

And yet. The owl in winter flying low and calling draws her, draws her like a thread from the upper world. Draws her out of her room and toward the door. The look on her face at such times is one a brother would like to erase or to forget. And yet it is not morbid, or has not seemed so since my dreams began. For the moment I will characterize the look thusly: it is intent, as though she hears a music in the cry that we cannot; it is curious, as though words were being used that she does not, but would, understand; and it is something other. My mother and I, the watchers, would have that "something" changed for another look, one that remembered us, for at such times we are forgotten. She will walk among us as we are gathered together for warmth and pleasure, and will not see us, the multiple expression upon her rapt countenance creating the face of a stranger. Even now, with the insight I have obtained through dreams, I find it disquieting to dwell at length upon that look, that unfamiliar face.

Curiously, my father does not seem to share the apprehension that my mother and I feel. When my sister sleepwalks through our little group, father will loudly say something about the quality of the corn we are eating, and perhaps even toss a grain at my sister's head, but if he does it to bring her out of her trance, one has the feeling that it is done without awareness or planning. His protectiveness toward us extends the length of him, like a backbone.

We all hear the owl. Some of us tremble to hear it cry its shivery cry so close to our lock, but this lack of control is confined to the dead of winter when the frost has pushed the entranceway to our house moonward. And though the tremblers may be soothed by our mother's quiet caress, the reason is never spoken of. We learned the name of the author of such a fearsome song in the fields, among our playmates. Because of the secrecy surrounding the name we have come to know that to speak it before our parents would be to mouth an obscenity, worse than to say "cheese" in polite society. We spare our parents our knowledge of the name as they spare us; it is for this reason that I keep *Master Tyll Owlglass* hidden, for I think it would profoundly shock my mother. Nor do we children compare notes among ourselves, such as "Did you hear the wings brush the roof last night?" I think we all imagine something dire would follow such confidence, and when we hear it each of our embarrassed ruses to cover the sound could be considered comical.

My sister does not always make these spectral appearances among us when the owl hunts. Many is the time she has sat with us, and heard the swoop and the enticing cries, and only trembled. Lately, since my revelation, once again she sits among us, but without trembling, for it is as though she has divined that she has an ally now, and need not— But I am unable to finish the thought. A lot is clear to me that once was cloudy, but there are many things that I would conclude, or draw conclusions about, that are still veiled, and so I, like my sister, wait.

I would not give the impression that we live perpetually under that shadow. If death, personified by that owl, inhabits the sky, so does life in the presence of the sun. It is the sun that makes the grain grow; it is the plenitude or lack of grain that most informs our lives. As we are shortsighted.

Even the lesson of the cheese is taken as a laughing matter by the twins, and during those exercises I confess that my mind wanders. There is something ludicrous about that piece of rockhard cheese upon which we are instructed to concentrate our loathing. It would scarcely seem to be the stuff that wistful dreams are made on. My sister sits embarrassed during the lesson, for it was she who was glancingly wounded; she wears her slight limp as penance and to my mind, it is reminder enough. But twice a week the bait is hauled out and we must howl our derision, hold our noses as though it smelled to heaven.

The twins love the exercise for at those times they are allowed to chant and howl out the word that at other times can only be whispered behind the backs of our elders. Once I asked our mother if she did not think my sister took this somehow personally, as though she were the object of our concerted hatred, but mother assured me that it was standard procedure in the best households, even those that could not boast a survivor of the trap.

We are a happy family. Believe me, we are. The twins scamper outrageously, our parents teach us old games and invent new ones, my bookishness is the cause of both pride and amusement, for I have lied about how the library was acquired, and my sister, an artist, gives our household stature. Throughout the field we are known because of her. It is my belief that because of her, when last we had to move our dwelling, others chose to cluster around us, so that we are—a rarity among our breed—a community with a center and activities outside the home. Through the end of the season of goldenrod we played at our communal games; into the first frost we foraged as a community, sharing the spoils, as befits agrarians. Thus every storehouse is equally provisioned, except in the cases of overwhelmingly large families, who are given more. Nobody grumbles about this.

Now that winter approaches, we seldom visit back and forth, and in our house my sister's room is the scene—though by invitation only!—of memorable evenings.

More of my sister's room: branches of berries against the cobwebs, pods of milkweed like hoary heads, a carpet of silvery husks.
It is a fantasy room in which one, rustling, becomes part of the
fantasy, as though one moved in an autumn field, dodging the
moon, instead of in the safety and glamour of my sister's ambi-
ance—a rare combination expressing my sister exactly where
others are concerned. If there is no safety for her within that
radiance beyond which we cannot reach, there is also little if any
sense of personal glamour. In my sister's room there is no evidence of vanity, hardly anything of personal adornment. To
amuse us, she may wear a wig of corn silk, or playing a great
lady, a necklace of strung bittersweet, but she is at her best when
she parodies the ways of the world without props or costumes,
stretching our imaginations through her pantomime.

Her purest success is chrysalis-into-butterfly. She always stops
in her dance with the maiden flight of the enchanged insect, at
the peak of its intoxicated freedom, and the tragedy of its brief
hour is tacit. For the youngest among us it is unimaginable, for
the twins are blessed with immortality, conviction being the soul
of philosophy. That the flight of the butterfly is in the direction
of one of the webs, that a "wing" brushes a web, is the dark
implication kerneled within all art, and may, as is frequently so
among artists, be without conscious knowledge. But I have noticed that when she performs this pantomime for our parents,
the flight is confined to the middle of the room, is circular and
lyrical and nowhere approaches a web. I believe, therefore, that
the other version has contained all along a message, a plea, if
you will, for me. But this belief began with my dreams and is
retroactive. Our mother says that this act, performed without
hurry and embellished each time with subtle and new inspira-
tion, is as constantly surprising as a sunrise. Our father beams
and tugs at his whiskers, saying, "Well, well!"

On evenings of the butterfly we part thoughtfully with whispered good-nights. But other evenings, when she has outraged,
or so they pretend, the sensibilities of our parents with something ultramodern—even at times scatological—the partings are
raucous and the twins have to be looked in on time and again
and warned to be quiet. If it is a silent night of no wind and a

cold moon, our mother says that our high spirits can be heard by the neighbors. Watching my sister's face, I see that "the neighbors" is a euphemism for the owl.

Anyone but my sister would find it strange that it is those evenings of high times that I have come to dread, when she, having been reckless in her invention, is dangerously wound up. Alone with her in her room when the others have finally gone to sleep, I am sole witness to where recklessness could lead her, for she does not act for my benefit. It is as though her sense of achievement wants not to be contained, wants to be carried afield. I have seen her—not oblivious to me, but trusting, which is a kind of oblivion—rake her nails against her low ceiling, at times savagely, as though to claw through to the world, but at other times with a rhythmic and terrible softness as though she were sending messages in code to a listener above, a lover with his breast and ear laid to her roof.

Scrabble scrabble—pause—scrabble scrabble scrabble. It is almost unnerving, I can feel my nerves jumping along their length as though to tear through my skin, their roof. But I am no longer young enough to plead, to cry her name, squeaking like a baby. And what would I say? "Don't leave me, dearest sister"? It would be a violation of our basic and necessary fatalism, and I can imagine a scornful reply or sore disillusionment which would be worse.

She trusts me as an equal and this, I believe, led to my dreams and fostered my revelation. Does this make them artificial, the products of a deep wish to accommodate myself to her needs, her superior philosophy? I am a fledgling in the shadowy field of dreams and hunt there half-blinded like the owl by daylight.

The last time my sister performed the butterfly, when the frost crackled about us and the earth creaked in the silences of her artistry, when she emerged from the chrysalis, unaware of her beauty, wondering at the sights and sounds of the world, it happened that the owl cried and it was as though he sat upon us, separated from us by no more than a membrane. For the first time in a dance my sister spoke. "How innocent you are! Look at you, how innocent!" My parents took this as improvisation, as a cry addressed to herself, the butterfly. But I saw that she spoke to change her face with words, to erase the expression that had lived there as though indelibly etched with acid. To hide herself from us, from me, she violated her art.

What I had seen on her face when the owl cried, in the moment before she became a talking butterfly, was passion. It was profane. I had finally isolated and defined the "something" that our mother and I regretted and that I feared immeasurably, having seen it. Did Mother see, too? I could not ask.

That was the night I dreamed my sister, dreamed the owl, saw my sister drawn irrevocably to the door, saw the door open, the moon beyond. I woke with a shout, an outcry to frighten all but the owl. When the others had gone back to bed, our father grumbling to reassure us, I again saw the dream while it was fresh and horrid, wiped out all extraneous detail and concentrated upon the look on my sister's face. Yes, it was profane, it was carnal, it was sexual. But at the door it changed. Standing under the open door with the hunter's moon behind her, she turned as though to say good-bye and the look said, clearer than words, "Be glad for me!" It said, "I know what I am, now."

To speak of revelations is difficult and dangerous, for there are would-be disciples waiting to misinterpret and misuse the dreams of others. Therefore I will be as plain as I can be and interpret my own dreams. Within the dream I was informed of this: dreams are given to us as projections of light from the parts of our brain to which no passage exists in the daytime, the corridors swollen with everyday thoughts and frets and wishes. In sleep these corridors contract, and philosophy and art emerge as themselves, for they would not be recognizable to the everyday brain of an average creature. Thus: in all dreams we are all philosophers and artists. In sleep, I saw with my sister, the artist: I saw what she sees in her waking hours, and I understood.

I did not wish to, do not wish to, and I do not accept it yet, but I have seen within the radiance.

I ask myself: do I understand to the extent of not stopping her when the time comes that she is drawn to the door and upward, and I—we all are—wide awake and able to coax, to divert, if necessary to restrain? My instincts are of no use. Our mother would not even understand the question, I feel. My father? Again, I do not know.

My conclusion: it would be best if it happened when we are all late at our hunting and my sister, who is forbidden to hunt at night in winter, is alone. I pray that it happens that way. We could not forget her, but if she were gone when we returned we would not *know*, and thus could keep here memory alive, however somberly, through speculation. We could avoid somberness by inventing travels for her, and successes in the wide world; we could tell each other that any day now, any night, she might reappear with gifts for the twins and tales to keep us up until all hours, and new pantomimes! Our mother could weave for us the colors and textures of the costume my sister would be wearing, and the jewels in her ears. I pray that she may, like another of us, simply not be there when we return.

And my dreams tell me further: there is something maiming about bearing witness to another's epiphany. Assuredly there is an owl in every life, but the terror, my dreams inform me, is that it will prove in most lives to be just that: an owl. I was advised that of all the humors, yellow bile, or envy, is the most destructive. This is one dream that I cannot fathom at all.

In my latest dream my sister turns at the door, the moon behind her but I see them as one. Then the owl is silhouetted against the moon, my sister, and they are a trinity. In any combination of pairs the sum is the third. This, I think, is a wistful dream, for if she were the owl I would not miss her, could bear to look at a future without her, would kill her if I could. . . . Perhaps in an effort to join her, inseparably, I tell myself that the last cause above makes me, too, the owl.

In the meantime we are a happy family. I say this determinedly. Our home is snug. The remains of a nearby harvest are still plentiful. We do not have to go very far to gather grain and can best the low-flying owl by twilight, teasing his dazzled sight and ducking into our doorway and laughing; at least the twins laugh, for until the ground is hard frozen and the moon sits implacably pointing at our entranceway frost-buckled above the ground, foraging and life itself are games to them.

The dreamers among us are learning to keep our dreams to ourselves. Lately my sister has sat with us in the evenings and when the owl gives its shivery cry she does not tremble but seems to grow drowsy with indifference. Our mother smiles and nods, her eyes confiding in me her relief. I nod back, and smile. Our father cracks corn for us all, masticating it for the twins, for winter is upon us, moon and owl, and the corn is half frozen.

THE GREAT
GODALMIGHTY BIRD

The boy and his grandmother were best friends. They smoked Bull Durham hand-rolled cigarettes together and she did not mind his cursing if he kept it moderate, as he generally did. At his request she told him what it was that happened between men and women that was so mysterious to the young and pronounced judgment upon it: "It don't amount to much except babies," although she said he might find it otherwise because "a lot of folks do."

She was a tiny woman. By the time he was a tallish eight years old, one of them growing up and the other down, as she put it, they were comfortably face to face.

He called her Mammy and his grandfather Pappy, as his mother and aunts and uncles did. Sometimes lying awake in his grandparents' house on summer nights, hearing the creaking of the well rope as the bucket was drawn up to satisfy his grandmother's frequent nocturnal need for cold well-bottom water, he wondered what it was that had brought together two people who were so unlike each other, because his parents were as like as the halves of an apple. His grandfather wore a high collar and waistcoat, which he called a weskit and his grandmother called a vest, even when he milked the cows. Over the years the grandson came to see that the waistcoat, tightly buttoned from early morning until bedtime, was a perfect indicator and not a cover-up of his grandfather's inner self, just as his grandmother's long hair escaping the constantly poked-at coil at her nape was a good indicator of her inner rebelliousness. She wound the coil each morning, whipping it around her hand with great energy and an expression of grim dislike, pulling the hair so tight at the temples that her eyes slanted, twisting it and jabbing in a large number of long mottled pins, but by midmorning it would be slippings its bonds.

If there was something to annoy her, such as an obviously brooding hen giving the two of them the slip when they tried to sneak behind her and find the nest, his grandmother's tendency to anarchy would take the form, inevitably, of ire directed at her undisciplined hair. "I'm aiming to take a scissors and cut the dad-blamed thing off at the roots as soon as we get home!" If she was greatly annoyed—her flowers broken in the night by some trampling thing—"dad-blamed" could become "damned." On one occasion, just the once, therefore branding the already memorable day upon his mind, her long switch of hair became "this Goddamned thing." Remembering it years later he acknowledged that it was the despair in her intonation that defined for him the awesomeness within the word "blasphemy." On only one other occasion did he feel so distant from her, bereft within the insignificance of his small age which offered neither shelter nor comfort.

That day when they got back to the house she took the scissors from her sewing box, her gestures angular and jerky, and went to her dresser mirror as though slipping up behind somebody. He was no more to her then than the armadillo shell, weighted inside with a brick, that held the door to her bedroom open onto the wide cool hall. Standing before her dresser she let down the offending rope of hair. It came to the backs of her knees and fanned out at once on the light wind, stirring as if it might escape the sharp blades. In response, he thought, watching the silent dialogue in stillness, his grandmother gathered the hair at the scalp and tightened it and lifted the scissors, aiming, as she had promised, to whack the glossy tail off at the very roots. But something arrested her. By reversing the direction of her eyes in the low mirror he found that the image staying her hand was the reflection of his grandfather's likeness in a round frame which hung over the bedside just opposite the dresser mirror. He watched his grandmother's expressions shift and change, as fascinating to him as the waves of color that washed a salamander when it would crawl from her hand to his and then onto a leaf.

The friendship between him and his grandmother was so true a thing that he felt he would have something real to offer someone he might meet and like a lot in the years to come, as she said he would, his great gift to that person being an introduction to her. He kept her in his mind as a treasure through the winters when the occasions of their meeting were family days, beginning with Thanksgiving and ending with the cold spring Easter. At those times they could hardly do more than make private faces at each other across the crowd, for the family with all its branchings was a big one and everybody wanted as much of her time as they could get.

It was in the summer that he visited her most often, and stayed as long as he could, both of them aware that as he got older and his muscles hardened he would be required to spend more and more time at work on his father's farm. While he remained a child his labors were light enough to allow him to visit her on weekends, leaving home, if he was lucky just about noon on Saturday, or close to nightfall when his luck was low. Whatever the hour, he was always given permission to set off alone on the five-mile hike to her house, to arrive sometimes after she and his grandfather had gone to bed. The screen doors were never hooked so he could go in and go to bed whenever he felt like it.

If he had a mind to, though, he could wait by the well, sitting on the curb, leaning against the cool resounding weathered boards of the well house, hearing the constant light fall of water as it condensed on the stones inside and fell; sniffing with such enthusiasm as to make him grow light-headed the perfumes of tobacco plant and four o'clocks and roses, and especially the breath of a red-leaved bush that grew close by the well, a scent unlike any other in the world, definitive and yet secret. He called it the Summer Bush. And through the arches of the trees he would watch the moon and stars and clouds, and stroke with fingers and bare toes the emerald moss that ringed the well, sensing the movements of the country night around him; for sooner or later she would come out, her arrival heralded by the low singing of the spring on the screen door. Then like a haunt in her billowy white nightgown, long-sleeved and high-necked in summer as in winter, she would appear to float onto the porch and from the shadows spy him where he waited so that her step coming down and to him across the dewy grass would be visibly lightened with her pleasure. In the dark of the moon, hearing the door spring, he would whistle like a night bird and hurry to meet her.

The drinking was leisurely and voluptuous, each taking his turn at the deep gourd dipper that imparted its own quality to the water, like a memory of sun-dried seed and fiber. Then, inwardly cooled and faces dampened to invite the night breezes, they would often go for a walk, both of them barefoot, she holding up the long skirt of her gown and looping and knotting it at the side so that it would not draggle in the dew of the grass and dust of the road and give her a muddy hem.

It was on such walks that he would ask for verification of tales he had heard at home, of his mother's growing-up years and the phenomena that seemed so plentiful in that long-ago time, a good deal of it frightening. Was it true that clumps of fire had rolled out of the darkness as the family sat on the lawn, and darted around their chairs and between their feet like fiery croquet balls? What about the night when something let the horses out of the barn and chased them, the horses thundering around the house neighing in fright, knocking down fences? And what about the footprints found next morning in the mud, as big as dinosaurs', and was it true that Pappy mixed some plaster and made a cast of one footprint, and where was it now? Could she shed any light on the rapping under the floorboards that had followed Cousin Eva wherever she went and drove her nearly crazy so that she bit Pappy and the other men who tried to hold her, and did they really have to be treated for snakebite with hartshorn and bleeding?

It was not that he doubted, or wanted to, his mother's dramatic stories. What he wanted was his grandmother's versions, at the same time more matter-of-fact and more hair-raising, for she was surely the world's greatest storyteller, giving a story its head like a horse, instead of leading it, as his mother did. Also, he could not help feeling that when his mother told the tales she was leaning down to him and his younger sisters, scaring and patting them at the same time. His grandmother did not lean but lost herself in the recountals, her reedy voice attesting to the truth of what she said and yet standing back, waiting as he waited for the climaxes, which always surprised her. She told him about a bird, a great bird with odd mating habits and strange native habitat, with visage so striking that when it was rarely seen by a human being all that person could say, as she had said, was "Great Godalmighty, look at that bird!" When he asked her what the bird was called she thought a long moment and then said it was called The Great Godalmighty Bird, and he, charmed and surprised by the appropriateness and logic, saw that she was charmed and no less surprised. Had she forgotten until he asked, or did she put it away each time in pieces to be unwrapped, each section a surprise, the way chapters in books were always surprising?

If a story was scary, when the climax arrived she was not the less scared of the two. The night they saw a great *M* made out of flaming stars take shape in the sky over the Negro church steeple, the comfort they gave each other in their fear was equal because their fear was equal.

She was impatient, he discovered, with teaching as teaching, with a certain tone of voice that indicated she was instructing him, or was herself being instructed, usually by one of her children; when that happened she would cut off the lesson at once and as soon as not purify herself with an irreverence, so that if he wanted to know a thing he had to be roundabout in his method of seeking it, had to cover for her in a manner of speaking. When he was grown and thinking about it he concluded that she had had enough of teaching her twelve children and that none of them, including his mother, had turned out the way she wanted. But what she had hoped for any of them she kept inside with her disappointment, if that was what it was.

On their nocturnal walks it was the pupil who primed the lore within the teacher by drawing from her such things as the names of stars and constellations, yet seeking always in vain to know how and where and from whom she herself had learned. Her parents, he knew from his mother, had stayed "on the other side," which was in the Highlands of Scotland, but beyond that Mammy had not talked and never would talk about herself as a girl. His mother expressed resentment and said if she could ever afford it she would hire somebody to trace her family for her, so she could know what kind of stock she sprang from on that side. She was glad to say that on Pappy's side the line was a long straight one going clean back to the century before last, Scotch-Irish and one Cherokee Indian great-great to put spice in the potpourri.

The surest way to anger his grandmother was to shake or wag a finger at her, or, using that same finger, tap a table to empha-size what was being told her. He had watched her temper flame when his grandfather did that, or any of her children, their never having learned in a lifetime that you did not use that gesture, the schoolteacher's tool of admonishment, when you spoke to her. "Why, Moetta," his mild grandfather would always say; and, "Why, Mammy!" the others would exclaim, offended. He con-cluded that there was something bad enough about those early years of her life to make him learn to protect her from himself and his curiosity, and even in the intimacy of their summer night walks he taught himself not to ask her about her own schooling though she might be inquiring about his. Or rather, she might be testing his ambition, for she wanted him to become a musi-cian, or, as she called it, a musicker. He never mentioned at home that she wanted something for him besides farming, knowing the stir it would cause, but sought to gratify her by delving deep inside himself in hope, looking for the hidden music there that would be like stacks of victrola records.

Her last son was still living at home, and uncle and nephew shared
room and bed for a few years, but by the time the boy was near-
ing the age of ten the bed was often his alone for his uncle was
staying out until nearly morning milking time. "A-courting" was
what his grandfather called it, and he would sing a few bars of
"Froggie Went A-Courting" ("and he did ride, ring tom bonny
mitch a cambo"). In his grandmother's book what was going on
was Tom Catting. In her satisfied-sounding opinion her son was
playing the field and no one girl had her hooks in him. She would
mention an old girl who lived over at Locust Grove whose hopes
she had been told were high; and another one who, according
to the peddler—this one "over to Providence"—was filling up
her Hope Chest at a good rate, buying trinket and dishpan, garter
and washrag alike from the peddler's truck. To no avail, she
said, because her son Jim was a bachelor born.

This belief was responsible for the elopement coming as a shock
that the boy thought was like an earthquake, during which you
could feel your trust in the solid earth under your feet separating into territories like the islands in clabber. He would never
get used to the tremors underfoot, enticed, his grandmother said,
to Kentucky by all the caves that undermined the state. And he
believed that she would never reconcile herself to the way her
son had gone, perhaps because it seemed dishonest.

The boy was always awakened by his uncle as he changed from
his suit into overalls and boots, and the omission of the ritual
woke him anyway that morning, to the several clocks tolling and
chiming and cuckooing the hour of four. It was just past four-
thirty when his grandmother came into the room and searched
it like someone with premonitions. He knew she was looking for
a clue as to why Jim had not come home to do the morning
chores, knowing that his father's growing arthritis made milking
especially difficult for him. Finding the letter on the bureau
weighted down by a hairbrush she asked her grandson's complicity with her eyes and put it inside the bosom of her nightgown.

When Pappy, buttoned into his vest, had done the chores and with his grandson's help milked the ten cows, his wife contrived, for it was a Sunday, to send him off somewhere for the day. The talk at breakfast had touched only lightly upon the missing son, the two adults sharing what seemed to their grandson like an off-color explanation having to do with dogs in heat, which made Pappy blush; but when he had gone the boy could see that there was no joking in his grandmother that day, that she had been acting a part. She took herself and her grandson and the letter off to a grove of trees where there was the grave of a young kinsman of Pappy's who had died of smallpox during the Civil War. There she opened the envelope and read the news. It was then she blasphemed and rushed back to the house and nearly cut off her hair. When she was thwarted in that by Pappy's painted eyes she did something even more curious: she draped the mirror over her dresser with a shawl.

The boy was amazed and jealous at her prolonged reaction and believed that she was still putting on a show. She and her son Jim had gotten along well together, an amiable and jokey relationship, but the boy had always felt that Jim had gotten too old for his mother to care much about. As time passed he came to believe it was only the method, the elopement, that she minded so much.

But that Sunday afternoon, which turned thundery and rainy with thick air that smelled of sulphur, the two of them wrote a song, laboring at the pump organ, to allay or incite his grandmother's peculiar grief.

> Left out on a limb
> What'll I do with him gone,
> Got those my son Jim gone blues.

She said she knew Al Jolson would sing it if she could just figure out a way to get the song to him. They called it "My Son Jim Gone Blues."

In the course of repetition they fell in love with their blues song and sang it each time with more feeling until he, going on eleven, felt in his soul that he had lost a son named Jim. For the only time in their life together they cried. When Pappy came home he found his wife blazing with angry tears and his grandson sniffling along more in sorrow. Later through the walls the boy heard his grandmother's condemnation of the bitch who had led a man to run away from his home in the middle of the night. She said it was the contempt that froze her marrow. And, she cried out with passion that distorted her voice, Jim had not even in his note said "whichever one of the bitches it was!"

But that afternoon Pappy's astoundment at their carrying on, so great that it slacked open his mouth, had changed their tears to laughter and that also got out of hand for a while.

When the house was quiet the boy lay wondering about the old girl who had hooked Jim, hoping it was the hard worker who had so patiently filled her Hope Chest with things from the peddler, Bunie Huffines.

Bunie's identifying call was "I Jod," the way he pronounced "By God," which made people laugh. He peddled gossip over the countryside along with merchandise, hawking and spitting brown juice, playing the clown for the customers. The boy went around with him on the truck one day and for eight hours received inculcation in the art of rooking. Bunie's rook, or ace, was to turn people's amusement at his speech impediment and hijinks to his own advantage. Long before the day was over the boy caught onto the fact that he was being used as a kind of shill. His first value to Bunie, he knew, was his strangeness, for in what Bunie called the "hills and hollers" of deep country the people seldom saw a stranger; seeing one, small enough not to be threatening but still exotic, they could not resist questioning him and while they did, Bunie, counting their change aloud, made alterations to his own profit. They were so successful as a team that Bunie, confessing what had taken place, offered the boy what he called "a nice piece of money" to go with him often. The boy had made up his mind not to do it before he consulted his grandmother, obliquely, not wanting to snitch even to her. Her advice was mild—"Stay clean of peddlers."

Lying awake thinking about the girl filling her Hope Chest, paying a higher price than she knew, he thought that he would tell his grandmother that the girl had, in a manner of speaking, actually earned Jim, and if she saw it that way she might not mind so much.

Soon afterwards Jim turned up with his bride and the mystery was cleared up. It had been his notion to run off, not hers. She was neither one of the girls mentioned but was a schoolteacher of whose courting not even Bunie had got wind. She was pretty and precise and chilly, the opposite of her mother-in-law, or so the prejudiced grandson thought: pretty where his grandmother was thrilling, precise where his grandmother was flexible, and chilly to the other woman's great warmth that was like a summer night. The boy was puzzled and disgusted by and with Jim. According to the song, a man was supposed to marry a girl *just* like the girl that married dear old dad. And even if he didn't how could he go so far wrong!

Still, the boy was prepared to make the best of it for his grandmother's sake as well as Jim's. He shyly asked of the new aunt what he should call her. She gave the matter her full attention, then said kindly that Miss Martha would do. Miss Martha, the schoolteacher. He saw his grandmother's nostrils open and close, saw that the tip of her nose was white, but Miss Martha could not know what that implied. The boy felt the distancing of himself from Jim's wife, saw himself being pushed out into the hallways. Time was bided and passed. When his grandmother had to address the woman her son had married in secrecy, she, too, named her Miss Martha, with a prissiness of pronunciation that was as like Miss Martha's as could be this side of pure libel, or so his scandalized mother later said, for she and all the family were present to greet the bride.

He made one more bid for Miss Martha's sympathy, not sympathy for himself but for his grandmother, thinking that if he could swing it disaster might be averted, for his grandmother had mocked her not once but several times until it was an embarrassment even to him. When he found his uncle and Miss Martha alone in the parlor he told them about the song and began to play it, the "My Son Jim Gone Blues." He vaguely imagined that the playing would effect some change, perhaps remorse on Jim's part as well as forgiveness on hers. Midway, hearing a sound, he turned, expecting to see tears but instead he found a blushing Jim and a sniggering Miss Martha. He saw then what he had done, how he had betrayed his grandmother. He felt frozen to the organ seat, wondering if the sound of the song had got to the kitchen where all the women but Miss Martha worked at preparing a feast. His mind supplied a picture of his grandmother in the middle of the kitchen floor, frozen as he was, aware of the knife her grandson, her supposed friend, had plunged into her high back.

Maybe it was in retaliation for the mockery, but Miss Martha took Jim away to her home state of Indiana and their trips back were infrequent and never occurred at important times, such as Christmas. To some this was a relief because there was an ugliness in Miss Martha's highly personal behavior that made the boy, for one, feel strange and helpless; but he had overheard his mother deploring the schoolteacher's behavior to his father and others, and had seen her shake her head and look disgusted. His own unfamiliar impulse was the desire to slap Miss Martha's face with its thick-looking skin like the surface on a pan of cream. He was shocked to want to hit anybody, especially a woman, but he could not think of her, no matter how he tried, as a relation. How could she be, and act as she acted, refusing to look at his grandmother, sitting at the table with head down in such a way that it seemed a slight only to her mother-in-law! He tried, verging on puberty, to instruct himself that her maddening behavior was based on shame at taking Jim away, not just from home but to another state. But he came to believe that his grandmother's original assessment, sight unseen, had been foresight, an actual look into the actual future. He knew that the evaluation of Miss Martha as a bitch was not changed by any subsequent knowledge but was reinforced; and he felt that both word and condition, in case they differed slightly, were tied in with those experiences of his grandmother's that she would not talk about, that would remain for her grandson a mystical and mysterious circle like the thought of predestination.

Eventually he had to admit that what he felt for Miss Martha was probably hatred, and detested her further as the schoolteacher whose hard lesson he had had to learn.

Then all such circular considerations, wearying over a length of time, were made unimportant. Soon after the New Year his grandmother was taken to her bed from where she was found lying in the hen yard in the scattered feed.

In the inordinately rainy months that followed, warm and rainy with a clamminess that was said to be especially bad for her, he was not allowed to see her but would overhear those who had been there talking about the coughing that drained her. When blood was spoken of the voices descended into whispers that made it all the more terrible. He wrote to her and her replies were delivered verbally for it was feared, he overheard, that even the paper on which she wrote might be contagious; and those returning from the bedside with her replies to his letters in their mouths would make him wait until they performed rituals of cleansing. The clothes they wore would be fumigated before they wore them again; they would come to him scrubbed and antiseptic, smelling of medicine, of liniment. There was nothing of his grandmother anywhere, none of her special scent that usually clung to people who had been near her, a distinct odor of dried roses; and for his nose alone to identify there was the faint smell of tobacco, of their private sessions with the sack of Bull Durham and an occasional corncob pipe. When at last the messages from her were given over they sounded, in the voices of the deliverers, a little playful and a little foolish, like his mother's "leaning" tone of voice; so that even in the exact words she had said there was nothing of her self.

He wondered incessantly if he was going to lose her, the only friend he had ever had and ever would have or want, for without her to offer someone as a bribe he would never make a friend or even an acquaintance in his life; and he felt despair at the thought in which he saw how his wonderful grandmother was a commodity, an object of barter like something on Bunie Huffines's truck, for the repossession of which he would willingly shortchange the whole world.

He grew acquainted with death, in preparation. But she recovered. A dry spring came and settled into dust the soggy land. Reports from the bedside turned favorable. Then the reports were coming from the chairside where she sat by the window, and then from the side of the chair on the porch, and one satisfyingly dusty day he walked barefoot toward her, squirting the dust like water between his toes, and they were reunited. People had warned him that she had changed, but he could find only one big difference, which was that she seemed much tinier. But of course he had grown in the long months and now stood above her, protectively.

Soon after the boy became thirteen he came back from his grandmother's house one Sunday to find that the old Roark place down the road, that had been vacant all his life but had been kept up by terms of a will, had been reclaimed. There was a son, Luther, who was almost exactly his age. His own birthday had swung him into the grown-up domain at 10:15 P.M. on the twenty-fourth of August, 1937, and Luther had made it at 4:25 on the twenty-fifth. They were just six hours and ten minutes apart and could have been twins, Luther said, because it often took that long for a twin to get dropped. He said, "While your mammy was just easing up mine was just starting to bear down." This was taken as a sign by both of them, and a further secret sign to the boy was that Luther had said "your mammy" though he did not call his own mother that; he called her by her first name, a matter for criticism in the countryside until the Roarks settled in and it was forgotten.

Theirs was just the age for friendship to catch hold violently, to be as near passion as it could be and stay chaste. Perhaps the only thing that kept the final barrier in place was their ignorance, and at the same time the satiety that comes from constant touching, poking, tripping-up; and on summer nights when they slept high on the moonlit tops of haystacks, the arm one threw across the shoulder of the other as a part of "good night" was left there by mutual consent and was enough of flesh for them, added onto the day's harvest.

They discussed and explored the very crannies of each other's souls, and by the time Christmas was approaching both families took it for granted that they would have to share their festivities or one family would have to go without a son.

The boy of this story, grandson of Mammy, had kept back from his friend only the extent of his passion for his grandmother. References to her had been kept light because the revelation of her—her ease with boys, the comradeship she offered, the lack of demands, the many gifts of spirit and the constant surprise— were to be offered in the way, perhaps, that a ring is given, or the chalice or the sacred sword. It is difficult for someone my age to recall except as words the symbols of boyhood; actually it is, I find, impossible for me. There were and still are holes in my memory like the holes in a Swiss cheese I once had: the holes had been filled with a stuffing and the cheese wrapped in pastry and baked. I never knew what the stuffing was made of for it and the cheese had melted together. And so the symbols and meanings, both passionate and casual, of my boyhood have become like that stuffing a part of the cheese, and, further, wrapped in a complex pastry of which the cheese has become a part: the *feuilletage* of my life.

There the fragment would have ended, an unsuccessful attempt like many before it to prod memory like a rock with a magic rod and bring forth a gush, and if not a gush a trickle—some sort of release. Would have ended and did. And then I went on a rare visit to one of my sisters, propelled by a death, not in the family we shared but in the one I had made for myself, thousands of miles from those of whose blood I am part. My sister and I were talking, quite naturally, about death, but both of us now at an age when the morbidity of fascination has given way to practical interest. My bereavement was in check; I would no more have discussed my loss with her than I would have discussed with her the soul and its possible fate. We leave those matters to people whose upbringing was more churchly than ours, or to those who have compensated for what they may feel was a spiritually deprived childhood by embracing some heavily organized belief. Still, my sister tends toward the East, I know that much, but she lets me in on only the most superficial aspects, and I conceal, if that is really the word, from her my midnight suspicion that reincarnation is as inevitable as that a plant will grow from a seed, *if* the seed is given the most rudimentary care, such as not being wantonly destroyed by pulverization or blown to smithereens by some patented device or other. A very big *if* in today's world.

In the course of the discussion of practical matters, disposal and so forth, I told her of my chagrin at not having gone to Mammy's funeral and especially at not being able to recall why I had not gone. What, I asked her, could possibly have kept me away?

The look she gave me was probably one of the faces of Zen. It was a long scrutiny, kindly I suppose but detached as well. Then she got up and left the room. An eccentric, my sister, growing in her secret conviction to look more and more like an Asiatic. If she had returned in a turban with some esoteric tool of divination in her hand I would not have been too surprised.

When she came back, unturbaned, she handed me a little booklet. I saw that it was one of those funerary programs of scriptural quotes, names and page numbers of hymns, presiding minister's name, and names of pallbearers. Mammy's funeral program. I had not seen one and felt as I might have expected to feel if I had sat there anticipating it—a bit in awe, a bit afraid of holding this forty-year-old relic, reliquary really because of the treasures of old names associated with a past that seemed much longer ago than forty years.

I was going to ask my sister if there might be another one, or if it would be an irreverence to make a Xerox copy if this was the only one. I had been distracted from my question of why I had not gone to the funeral though this would seem to have been her reply and I still did not know. And just then in a list of pallbearers I found my name. I had helped to carry the coffin which I instantly visualized as being as small as a child's, a little white virginal box. Was this a memory? How could I have forgotten!

When I could I asked my sister these questions. She did not know how I had forgotten but surely it was important to me that I did; didn't the depth of mourning answer the question, she asked; I had loved Mammy more than anything; had I forgotten that too?

I pressed her on the matter of the tiny coffin. Wasn't this in fact a true memory returned all in one piece? I said I felt more complete, just a little bit satisfied, as though a gap had been filled. Lamely but in character I said times like these always made one think of Proust, and saw that I was trying to set distance between us at the same time I asked for the great intimacy of her true memory to fill in the holes of my faulty or missing past.

No, she said carefully, it was not a memory at all. The coffin, in fact, had been somewhat ungainly, a plain pine box but wider and deeper than most. Feeling congested I asked her, Why? Because, she said, giving me her quiet Zen look, because of Mammy's hunchback, which, by the time I had helped to carry her body away, had grown, oh, a foot above her head. They said she had been suffocating for years, her lungs pressed and squeezed as though between two boards. She had been tubercular, which affected her spine in that awful and painful way, making it as bendable as rubber until it set as hard as stone. The tuberculosis flared up again—did I recall that long illness when we could not see her? I said I certainly did; it lasted from New Year's until spring. But no, my sister said, it lasted over a year; from New Year's to spring of the following year. You, she said, lost more than a bit of memory. You lost a year.

She was compassionate, I could tell, and wondered if she could feel how my lungs, my heart, were being squeezed, not just by the revelation at hand but by a more terrible one, for me, that followed on its heels, this time a true memory, a jagged chunk of the past like a lethal stone in a rockfall: Luther's betrayal of me and my grandmother, of my love, of our life.

Here, as simply as I can tell it, is what unearthed the day of the funeral program in my sister's living room in Tennessee.

I had begun with Luther to build up to the revelation of my grandmother, to whose house I was going to be allowed to take my friend, the friend she had predicted for me. We were going for a part of Christmas. I don't know if Luther was an actor, I suppose all kids are to some extent, but his excitement seemed to match mine, our anticipation like two horses trying to outrace each other.

I see the day arrive, I see us packed and waiting. To accommodate the packages we are going in a buggy, one of several in my father's barns, the buggy to be drawn over the snowy roads by a roan called Big Red. I see the journey, feel the crisp air and the warmth of legs under the horse blanket that somebody, over our manly protests, has tucked around us. Luther has had a cold, that was it, and it was his mother who insisted on the blanket. I hear the show-off whip crack—Big Red knows I would not touch his glossy back with a whip. We pass farmhouses and people we know, we are passed by cars that slow down for an exchange of greetings and information; there are no strangers in our world that I can see stretching on forever: me, Mammy, Luther; friends and family, Big Red, dogs and cats I love, summer nights by Mammy's well and snowy days with Luther. The sky is cloudy but in the distance there is a blue sky pond that will be just over Mammy's house. My heart is rather full.

Luther gets sick almost as soon as we arrive. Luther has to lie down. He does not want my grandmother to attend him. Luther has to be taken home but not before he makes me want to kill him, to take a pitchfork and impale him and throw him high and far like a bale of spoiled hay. His behavior to my grandmother is exactly the same as Miss Martha's. He will not look at her, will not take the hot chocolate offered by her hand, sits and acts like somebody paralyzed by the sight of a snake. How can I know why? How can I condemn now, as I did then—then, not knowing; now, knowing? His, and Miss Martha's, inability to look at my grandmother's twisted spine looming above her head—do I call this cowardice? Is there perhaps some superstition shared by the world about hunchbacks that I do not know about? If I try Luther and Miss Martha I wonder how many others should share in the trial, those people who kept my grandmother from going about normally, to church and socials, because, I imagine, she put consideration of their plight above her own. Do I condemn all these people for not sharing my standards of beauty? Maybe someone in the family should have told me, Look, Mammy is a hunchback and a kind of freak to some because of that, and you just have to be careful who you expose her to. Then I could have said to Luther as breezy as March, Look, Mammy's a hunchback so let's get going, she'll be watching out the window for us to come over the hill. The chocolate will be hot and you straightback you what do you mean you're not going? At least that would have spared my grandmother. The Great Godalmighty Bird of her own imagination.

Well, the memory must end somewhere. I'll let it end with our Christmas that year, the best of my life for I put Luther out like a snake that had got in the house and my grandmother and I were even more Christmas-y than usual, and Pappy in his weskit watched us like we were actors in a tent show and we wrote new Christmas songs and rewrote old ones we didn't much like. The nights were high and heavy with light, a billion galaxies swirling around; and we stood in the brilliance of snowy grounds reflecting the blazing heavens and watched as curtains of Northern Lights billowed across the sky as though trying to close down that act of the heavenly show.

I actually saw the Northern Lights with Mammy once. But that was not in December.

THE
CONSEQUENCES
OF BREATH

I ENVY YOU YOUR GREAT ADVENTURE

"Cheryl is the only gentleman in the American Theatre," Omerie said firmly. "You should let *her* produce your play."

Augustine was thoughtful. "Naturally, I'd thought of her *first*, but one musn't ignore completely those others." It was an entire statement and having fashioned it he turned as though to open the window and let it fly like a bird too lovely to be kept imprisoned. He stood looking down onto the formal gardens and the lemon groves beyond. In the same musing tone he said, "There goes the Duke. It really is too bad that he looks like a gardener."

"Well, the head gardener looks like a duke, so I suppose that balances the ledger." Omerie made an Aubrey Beardsley gesture with his left hand, but the gesture was not successful because he had no left hand. He looked intensely for a moment at the space that should have been occupied by the hand. "Augustine, wasn't it extraordinary that there was no blood when my hand fell off last night?"

Augustine smiled at him, very nicely. "Not in the least. You always were fastidious." He yawned and said, "I suppose we should do something or other about dressing if we're to go to the casino tonight."

"We would attract more attention if we didn't dress."

"Oh, who cares what they think in Estoril? The nicest thing about Portugal is that one can be oneself here, and wear dinner clothes any time."

"Do you think," said Omerie, "that we will ever go back to New York?"

"Who knows—or cares, for that matter? Perhaps we'll slip back some summer and peer in on the carnage? If we stay at the Waldorf, dine at Sardi's, and refrain from smoked glasses, nobody will know we're there."

They dressed at a leisurely pace, occasionally ringing for this or that, and after an omelet and strawberries in the garden and coffee with the Duke, they got into their automobile and drove the short distance from Setais to Estoril, where they won money until Omerie's right hand dropped bloodlessly from his wrist, which meant that he could not handle the chips and so had to stop playing. Augustine stopped playing out of sympathy and boredom and cashed in their chips.

Humorously, he told Omerie, "Now I shall have to feed you like a little bird. Will that amuse you?"

"How can I tell? It might be more amusing to sip things through a straw and simply not bother with the rest. However, we shall, of course, see."

When they returned to the palace they walked for an hour in the gardens and groves, talking of this and that. A touch of mist muted the night which without it would have been like a golden trumpet. Occasionally a cock crew and the two young men agreed that the harsh note was as destructive to the night as a political discussion to a dinner party. Since they feared the false propaganda would penetrate to their rooms they sought out the offending creature in the stables and Augustine wrung its neck with finesse so that his white gloves should not be soiled. They then returned to their suite and were ready for bed in a scant two hours. This was the moment to which they both looked forward—when, in brocade and silk, they settled comfortably into bed each night and Augustine read aloud his play. Tonight would be the four hundredth reading and the number appeared significant enough to lend an air of extra festivity to the occasion. When the tiny mother-of-pearl marijuana pipes were lit—or, tonight, only one, which Augustine from time to time held to Omerie's lips—Augustine began to read. He was in excellent voice and his rendering of the part of the Amethyst Tongue Scraper, for whom he would ask that Fontanne be engaged, was especially effective. They had heard recently that Alfred was sick, so the role of The Tongue, which had been tailored to his talents, Augustine read sadly, hauntingly, with a touch of doom that was, according to Omerie, the only way it should be read. The locale of the play was A Mouth, and the characters represented objects introduced into it over a span of twenty-four hours. It was allegorical and poignant, almost excessively the latter, so that both young men were reduced to tears when The Mouth finally closed for the last time on the horde of brightly colored Sleeping Pills. However, Augustine did not for long allow emotion to color his fanatic objectivity concerning his magnum opus. Indeed, it seemed to Omerie, who did not hesitate to say so, that the release of tears led Augustine to a harshness of judgment that verged perilously upon the *professional*. Tonight was hardly an exception. The loveliest speech in the play began "*The* fullform'd phalluscy . . ." which was so exact, so immediate, that Omerie's eyes produced more tears at Augustine's insistence upon changing "the" to "a."

"It *spoils* it," Omerie moaned between sips at the held marijuana pipe. " 'A' is so terribly *general*. The edge, the beautiful *hurting* edge of the specific—" He choked and motioned with his streaming eyes for Augustine to take the pipe away. Augustine was pitiless, adamant. At last Omerie, knowing the battle to be lost, told him with a touch of well-justified malice, albeit mixed with sorrow, "Very well. But you will get no star to play an 'a.' You might as well forget Marlon." This did make Augustine thoughtful, at least, which he hated, so that his "Good night" was circled with coolness like drops of dew. Lying in the dark, Omerie reflected that this was far from the first time they had fought over matters aesthetic, and that he had always, heretofore, been the one to concede. *Heretofore,* tonight he would not do so, nor tomorrow, nor the day after that. He would carry his convictions like unfurled banners in his eyes, to the very edge of the abyss which is the only surviving child of battle. He fell militantly asleep and dreamt of Jeanne d'Arc.

The following morning, or noon, when they had arisen and were performing their toilettes—rather, when Augustine was uncomplainingly tending them both—Omerie's decision of the night before to carry his banners silently in his eyes took on an unavoidable air of the prophetic, because when Augustine was scraping Omerie's tongue—their tongue scrapers were made of palest jade—the tongue came away with the scraper. Omerie marveled—of necessity, silently—and wondered if he could be just a touch clairvoyant. At first the thought was pleasing, but then images of fat clairvoyants—Madame Blavatsky, Eileen Garrett (though her eyes were splendid), and Marie Powers—took his pleasure from him and he determined that he would not be clairvoyant; not in the least.

When Augustine had scraped his own tongue he said to Omerie, his face wearing an expression of slight displeasure, "We will really have to go straight to Italy now. I do dislike missing the Spaniards this time around, but as Portuguese and Spanish are *your* languages, we will not get far with bargaining, I fear." He made a little *moue* of distaste. "Sign language is too barbaric to consider." He sat on the bidet and turned Omerie over his lap, applying their own soft tissue gently, as to a child. "I do regret the fishers at Nazaré—so fiendishly reluctant, in their leathery way, you will recall—" He stood Omerie up and smiled warmly into his eyes. "But there. You mustn't think that I blame you, my dear. Perhaps you won't find Italy too soiled this time around."

He led the way to the dressing room where he dressed them both in the softest of summer flannels, pale yellow for himself and for Omerie the beautifully elegiac lilac. This was a special concession given, Omerie knew, as compensation for his coolness of the night before. Augustine usually insisted on the more dramatic expression for himself.

When the Duke's valet had packed for them, they managed to escape without having to bid the Duke farewell, a thing they loathed doing for the Duke was old and sometimes grew slobbery and embarrassing on the subject of Perhaps Last Meetings and so on. As Augustine had said to Omerie the last time it happened that they were caught in a Farewell Scene with the Duke,

"Last Time, Pastime." And Omerie had murmured admiringly.

They drove to Lisbon where they abandoned their automobile in favor of a chartered jet plane to carry them to Rome. Augustine spent some time forward with the pilot but now and again he would come back to where Omerie lay among their special cushions and feed him bits of peaches soaked in an infusion of Chablis and hashish. It was typical of him, they both felt, that he could interrupt his own pleasure to perform thoughtful acts. He told Omerie that the pilot possessed in equal measure the qualities of anger and avarice, and that there might be an Incident when the plane landed, although Augustine could not promise this. The unfurled banners in Omerie's eyes seemed to snap in a sudden brisk wind. Augustine appeared to be, for a fraction of a second, disconcerted and then his face resumed its customary lack of expression. After a while he went forward again.

In Rome they found a plethora of tourists and not much else. Even the fountains displayed nothing for which a bribe might conceivably be offered.

The nightly reading of the play became alarmingly burdensome. Augustine changed more and more words until it seemed that he was bent upon total destruction. In three nights he recklessly changed five words and abandoned two. Carnage stretched behind him bloodily. Omerie's flags signaled with increasing frenzy, to no purpose: Augustine avoided his eyes. In desperation, Omerie stamped his foot, something he would never have done ordinarily. It was, he knew, an extreme measure, but he was rewarded. Augustine could not with good grace avoid his eyes when he had picked up the leg that separated itself at the knee and slid from the silken pajamas with a reproachful little sigh. Augustine stood holding the leg and his eyes filled with genuine sorrow as he told Omerie, "I know I'm being beastly, my dear, but surely you will agree that it is at least partially warranted? Something quite frightfully unexpected is happening to the climate of the world when *Rome* should appear to be sterile. *Soiled* is one thing, but *this* . . . Though it is a cliché, I would welcome even a common cold as evidence that *something* of an adverse nature could still occur."

Omerie felt his misery and considered attempting a sneeze,

but he knew that Augustine would see through the ruse. Also, he knew that Augustine considered sympathy to be condescending and therefore he was careful that his expression remain noncommittal. The play was the important thing, and though Augustine was kindness itself, he could, on occasion, if goaded to it (as he had been on the past three nights), take his pound of flesh even when it hurt him to do so. Omerie felt that one more excised word would be beyond his own endurance.

Fortunately, when Augustine returned to Omerie the following night, he was able to report that circumstances had taken a turn for the better. He had struck several good bargains and there had even been a slight Incident following the execution of one in the Colosseum. Nothing spectacular, but a skirmish. He read beautifully again and, to Omerie's breathless relief, returned with teasing casualness one of the abandoned words to its rightful place. Omerie was not religious, but he approached the edge of prayer that night with his fervent wish for a really *big* Incident for Augustine; something big enough—though he hardly dared wish for so much—to cause Augustine to change the devastating "a" back to the eloquent "the."

Omerie had never felt himself to have much willpower, which was a drawback; he hadn't, he felt, individuality enough for that. His function had always been to guard the treasure of Augustine's genius and to help feed its source. It was to this end that he had learnt the barbaric Portuguese tongue, because for Augustine to know it would have been a blight on his purity of expression, like a birthmark on clear skin. Omerie crossed his handless arms upon his body in the darkness and sighed as he felt the arms loosen at the shoulders and roll down to lie along his sides, slightly bent at the elbows, enclosing him in a set of parentheses. As he fell asleep it amused him to think that perhaps this was what was meant by the expression "self-contained." He told himself that it was a thought of absurd levity under these circumstances when so much was at stake, but he did not honestly feel that his little self-amusement could affect in any important way his large wish for Augustine.

He continued to wish and, though there was no way of knowing whether it was in response to his wishes, Rome improved.

There was, true enough, no really big Incident, but Augustine was able to report several medium-sized ones, and, on their last night together, to exhibit the evidence of an *almost* satisfying one to Omerie: the thin line that a knife blade had traced around the base of his throat. This had given Augustine justification to shoot, with his exquisite little eighteenth-century pistol, the man— not, alas, fatally; the skirmish warranted only a shot through the shoulder. But it gave one reason to hope for the near future. That last night Omerie lay with eyes closed in thanksgiving as Augustine read and in the process returned the other abandoned word to its place and reinstated four of the five changed ones in their pristine offices.

Omerie lay awake in the Roman night, unable, perhaps due to hunger-induced weakness, to put off any longer the revelation that what he had told himself were wishes were in actuality prayers: real prayers to a real, existing, undoubtedly exacting God. Nor could he feel humiliated by such proof of his insignificance. His smallness of mind matched perfectly the smallness of his body, which was no more by this time than a torso without limbs or genitals on which his tongueless head with its flagless eyes perched with a look of impermanence. It was not quite correct to say that the eyes were flagless, but the banners had furled as wish became prayer and prayer became answer. There was little actually left to wish (or to pray) for; Omerie had every reason to believe that Augustine would, of his own unflawed taste, change back the offensive "a" to the sublime "the." If wishes could be called disguised regrets, then he did regret his inability to communicate one last request to Augustine, much too complicated for his asking eyes to accomplish. It was possibly just as well, for it was a selfish request. . . . Even as he thought it, through the open window there flew a bird of bright plumage which came to rest on Omerie's bosom. The oddity of the occurrence was that Omerie and the bird could observe each other despite the darkness of the room. The bird looked into Omerie's eyes and repeated what it saw there in an accent very like Omerie's had been. When Omerie ceased to think, for fear that the voice might wake Augustine, the bird was silent.

The following noon, as Augustine dressed, the bird spoke to

him in Omerie's voice, a bit hesitantly phrasing the request, as Omerie would have done. Augustine was the soul of kindness, agreeing to the letter without quibble, merely remarking, because it was a fact and should be known, that he would have to postpone and possibly miss altogether an arranged meeting with a promising prospect. But this would not for a moment keep him from obliging Omerie, and let no more be said. When no more was said, surprise winged across his face, or perhaps it was the shadow of the bird's wing as it fluttered to the door and sat waiting there.

Augustine carried Omerie to the Via Sistina and placed him there in the sunlight on a little canvas chair, quite near the other torso with the monkey and the tin cup that Omerie had remembered from other times and envied. The bird perched on Omerie's head, stretching its wings once as though saying good-bye to flight before it settled down. Augustine looked at Omerie for signs of tears at the parting—surely there should be tears? Omerie felt it too, but none came. He wondered if the bird was crying, but he could not, of course, see. And still Augustine delayed his departure. Surely some last plea to save his great work? Omerie felt it too, but none came; the bird was silent. Augustine frowned and Omerie's heart beat thickly, telling him that there *was* something further he could do to feed Augustine's genius: he could lie. The bird fluttered and craned its neck and spoke clearly into the crystal air: "I envy you your great adventure." The words, new-minted, rang like bright coins dropped into the tin cup of the blind torso with the monkey.

"Grazie—grazie," said the torso, smiling sightlessly about, nodding his head in all directions. *"Grazie, signore."*

Augustine smiled a smile plural and dazzling enough for a host of seraphim. He lifted his hand as though bestowing a benediction upon all present.

"Prego," he said, and walked away to keep his appointment.

IF BEGGARS WERE
HORSES

Ordinarily we are like painters, mixing out of all the various colors of sensations within us the exact hue to suit our mood, or to cover mistakes made at the time of happenings. Was the day really bleak? Swipe a touch of sun from another day and dab it there: what a difference! But the sick, those voyagers in the land of no-color, cannot perform such tricks; euphemisms are too bright for their eyes.

Marriott watches himself carrying Lisa through the hedges from one parent to the other, both mothers crying, standing on their stoops, facing each other like mirror images: it was their day, for each had pressed her bereavement like a funereal flower between the day's clear amber leaves. Marriott watches himself staggering under bride-weight, then thinks that he does not actually stagger but is only aware of how much heavier she is than she looks. She is not fat, nor will she be so for years, nor is her solidity antiromantic since he has not believed himself to be marrying a piece of thistledown. It is only that her reality grows for him with each step, therefore excluding even momentary thoughts of wonderment about her actually belonging to him now: obviously, someone as increasingly heavy as she could hardly be a figment of his longing imagination. A few people have gathered on the broken sidewalk beyond the hedges and applaud either politely or ironically and Lisa presses her face into his neck. Can she tell by the heat of his neck that he is blushing?

The scent of his mother's lilacs drips heavily onto his head as though shaken from a large bottle of hair oil. The tallest lilac tree brushes the windows of the bridal chamber and, he thinks with frustrated resignation, one foot on his mother's step, it will tap there throughout the night in the wind that has begun to rise, a sound his mother cannot muffle through precautionary measures such as she has taken with the bridal bed, swathing even the wooden frame in heavy quilting. Finding the swathed bed, fighting anger, he had thought it was as if she said that what you can't hear doesn't exist. Love is sounds too, Mama, he says across the years from his sickbed. But the effort to stay in the present for a moment longer is too great for him and the great rubber band of the past, stretched beyond endurance, snaps him back into the then-present.

One foot on the stoop, then two feet, then the door, which his mother lets him struggle to open as though saying she cannot help him anymore now that he has a wife, although she stands as nearly in his path as she can so that he has to maneuver Lisa to keep her from kicking his mother in the stomach. It is as if she has said silently that he will have to manage all openings by himself now; and there is no bawdry in the thought, only the cold spade-calling of the loveless rivalry between old mothers and new wives that excludes men as other than objects like bones to be pulled at, merely tangible reasons for the surfacing of the duel as old as Eve's with God. He thinks: Women relentlessly hunt down and bag wives for their sons for the same reason that God created Eve—to have someone to fight with on their own level.

In the hallway he sets Lisa down, relieved to have it over with, feeling her own relief. His mother's eyes daub at the screen separating them like two acid-soaked wads of discolored cotton. Surely, she says, you are not deserting your bride at the foot of the mountain!

The stairs are narrow, steep, dark; his mother has bound the one railing like a wounded limb with a white-flowered vine, bound it tightly to preclude the possibility of one graceful and airy swag lending to the processional route a touch of triumph by its suggestion of even a reflected arch. Such tight binding was an act of extravagance on her part, requiring the sacrifice of twice as much of her treasured vine, but in her extravagance there is yet more reproach.

Turning away she says, Well!, trying to sound amused with Lisa and him at his inability to carry his bride up the eighteen steps (though none of them are amused), for it is inability: his back would have broken under the burden of his bride and his bride and his mother know it.

Can that, then, be her reason for deriding him? With a broken back the groom could not warm his virgin spouse into womanly flowering, and the mother would remain the only mature bloom in the dark hothouse redolent of other night-openings as joyless as the cold-odored dew of night-sweats. But perhaps it was protectiveness that made his mother wish him broken-backed, the fellow feeling of the cleft against the pronged.

He sees that his mother has no such fellow feeling. The clarity of his sight is microscopic: he sees her flesh ripple with loathing at the thought and under the flesh, stretched tight on gaunt bones, he sees both intent and desire as though the thin veins were decipherable stencils. If she could have managed it, his mother would have been like a piece of ivy that grows on air, an air parasite practically weightless that thrives pinned to a window curtain. It is not him she mocks, but Lisa, for having human weight, earth-mired wants and expectations.

He stands, the product of his mother's secret propaganda, in the hallway with his bride, afraid to mount the stairs where he will come to a place in which he will have to mount his bride. Is it the mounting that frightens him? There is an irrevocability to that particular athletic stance; once assumed in earnest it is as though a dial were set. It is like hypnosis with posthypnotic suggestion: at such and such a time you will. . . . A lifetime of *you wills*, making puppets of us all. This his mother tells him from beyond the screen, as she has told him, screening her words slyly, since adolescence: Please take a handkerchief to bed instead of blowing your nose on the pillowcases; or another time, Is it catarrh, son?—the complaint that eventually choked his father to death in the night. He sees that she has known all along what it was and he longs to shout out its names to her: *come, jism, jazz;* and imagines her falling to the floor, compacted with shock, made square in shape as if molded in a loaf pan by all her meager juices and organs rushing to peripheral positions in an effort either to escape shock's implosion or, like the brave boy and the dike, rushing there to stop up the holes his words would have made in her hide.

Mother, forgive me; and he turns to the stair with its peeling stained wall as brown as used toilet paper, carpet runner frayed down to its sinews like a piece of cheap-cut veal. Along this trail he is to lead like a calf a young girl with tightness between her legs and is to break her to the condition of comfortable saddle animal, and is periodically to ride her through nightscapes which rest on a base of directives, a pamphlet not of *How-Tos* but of *Why-Tos,* of *Becauses* and *Ergos,* a set of equations the distillate product of all being: a man who does not enjoy gutting a woman is no man. A noman. A woman and a noman twisting in swathed distaste on the mother-made bed. How many couples, his mother asks him from beyond the screen, of women and nomen on all the earth can there be struggling bi-tri-weekly to render lubricious nocturnes as dry as powder? Through her he hears the rasping loins devoid of the oil of humankind-ness not from overweaning fastidiousness but from cold fear of violence by and to. Such women and nomen are bred to the terror of delicate bones collapsing within them, around them.

He sees womb-hung creatures clinging as precariously to the mothercave as young bats, receiving the first inbleeding of claustrophobia to their veins on slow tides of fluids. The mother's fear of internal injury; her equation of fetus with injury accomplished and permanent; her identification with trapped child, bellows of her lungs pumping mightily to dispel illusions of suffocation, crowding the sightless evolutionary into a permanent corner of fear which he will bring with him, folded like a blanket, his first and permanent plaything (little portable prefab shelter), when at last he flounders from the flume onto the dry shores of earth and is greeted, without surprise, with violence.

His first scream is a seeding, a planting of fear. His life from that moment is a progress toward the flowering of the fear-tree on that first night (lilacs tapping the pane) when he mounts to gather blossom-hung fruit (cherries, the heman's Grail) and his mount is revealed as nightmare prescribed as therapy by the family internist.

Marriott lay like a microscopic link of chain within himself reduced to the pair of genes which carried the burden of instinct. Marriott, ill on the edge of extinction. Then, somehow, through galaxies of deoxyribose he journeyed out and outward, avoiding by instinct meteorlike scarrings of nucleic acids and all the other hazards of inner space, and rejoined the convalescent Godhead lying on the soaked pillow.

Because of curious markings on the inner throat that seemed unconnected with Marriott's inability to speak or to swallow food, one of the young nurses in whom Marriott's frailty and infant-like passivity had engendered maternal concern remarked that it was as if Marriott had been calling out for years. Calling out what? she was asked. And she replied, *Help*, I think; that word distends the throat terribly.

The story was repeated and one day Marriott—by then well on his way to recovery, so they told him—heard it and it set him off on a quest to prove or disprove the young woman's remark, for that was his way with things. He was not a man to categorize, at the outset, by tending to place remarks or observations or people under general headings, such as "fanciful." His practice was to start with a remark or a person as they stood, taking on faith their right to occupy such and such a space, and then accumulate unbiased evidence until there was a stack of it big enough on which to pass what he trusted was disinterested judgment.

He began with himself and his marriage to Lisa twenty-five years ago, for if he had been crying out *help*, he felt that it would have been to her, and that what was meant would have been *help, don't leave me.*

He had carried Lisa fifty yards across the lilac-strewn lawn that separated his house from hers, or rather to the house that he had thought of, until his mother's death, as exclusively her house. He and Lisa had lived with his mother in her house for two years and then it became their house; but having been bred to the subtleties of matriarchy (all the fine points down to and including examples of anthropopathy such as the house, which was a female, being capable of anger if he muddied its carpets) he mentally switched the ownership from his dead mother to his wife. In this way he placated the house, which might have been angry at its owner's desertion, and put off what could have been a troublesome reaction to his mother's death.

Lying first in his hospital room and then in a bedroom at home attended by a male nurse, he saw that he had unwittingly made Lisa carry the double burden of wife and mother, as far as his deep emotions were concerned, and he wondered if she had known this, or sensed it, or if she had been as unwitting as he. That he might have been continually, silently calling out to her did not necessarily reveal himself as the four-year-old who had lost one parent and feared abandonment by the other. He did not rule out the possibility for that was not his way. But he could remember of his father only what his mother had told him, and as far as living in fear that she might leave him too, he sincerely believed that the thought had never occurred to him that she could leave, even if she had wanted to. Part of the apparently bottomless security of the female house in which he grew and flourished, and from which he occasionally ventured forth to modest scholastic achievement and to fetch a bride, was his mother's ignorance of her own mortality.

Therefore it seemed to follow, if he had strained at words in the night until his throat bled and scarred, that it was to Lisa he yearned to cry out and somehow never could. He felt, after a try or two, that speculations were pointless as to whether, if he had managed to do so, she would have stayed on rather than leaving and divorcing him after twenty-five years. He thought that if someone had cried out to him not to leave, and had gone on doing so until the throat bled, he would not have waited twenty-five years to go. He doubted he would have been able to stand it for more than a few months. Was that why, he had never done so, had never even said the words, had never even consciously thought them?

Yet there was a persistent feeling of accuracy about what the nurse had said; and he wondered when it had first occurred to his deep-seated sense of bereavement, locked in its little secret room waiting, that in Lisa it had found its reason for being there in the first place.

He had always known Lisa. They were two months apart in age. They had played together as small children, ignored each other for a year or so around the time of puberty, studied together in early teens, graduated from high school together, married in their final year at the college to which they commuted from the Island, a sixteen-mile round trip. He had always felt that he knew her as well as he knew himself—in fact, that there was not much difference between them other than biological, a difference never so pronounced that it could have led, as it did in others, to jealousy and philandering. From the beginning she had had her garden and her clubs and other daytime gatherings with women. He had had his good job and her.

Ah, he said, his first sound in many months, which so pleased the male nurse that he trotted off to the telephone to make a report and missed the next two words from Marriott's abused throat: *I see.*

For a moment he thought that he did see. In his enumeration of their separate blessings, his and Lisa's, he had omitted himself from hers. It had been an automatic omission, which probably meant that it had never been one of his beliefs that he was important to her in the way that her garden and clubs and other women were. He thought sententiously: Unimportant equals dispensable. But he could not proceed with it. Her belief or disbelief in his importance was what was required, and it could only come from her. His belief, suddenly too firm to dispute, was that she had stayed with him because he was important to her, and when he ceased to be she had left him. So that through all the years of his silently crying out to her not to leave him, she had probably had no idea of doing so.

Like his mother's ignorance of her own mortality, Lisa's ignorance of her potential as one who leaves her husband seemed a basic condition to the pleasantness of their twenty-five years. He placed it on the stack of evidence against the nurse and noticed a simultaneous lift in his spirits and a sudden hunger for the sight, sound, and smell of the outside world. He considered calling out for his attendant but feared the man had had a surfeit of joy for one day and a further pang might injure him. He rang instead.

Using sign-language, in which Marriott was by now as facile as a deaf and dumb person, he requested the curtains open, the blind up, and himself placed as near April as could be managed.

The first thing he saw, and it hurt his chest with an inward blow as though sight activated an actual hammer, was a moving van in front of Lisa's old homestead, which had stood as Lisa's mother had left it, kept in perfect repair by the terms of the will, for fifteen years. Furniture, pieces he recognized from childhood, stood about on the lawn and sidewalk, and other pieces, new, some of them swathed in plastic, stood on the veranda, plainly on their way in.

He could not imagine what had happened, who could have broken the will of Lisa's violently opinionated mother, whom, he felt sure, death had but temporarily bested. The will had stated that only if Lisa had need of the house—*its refuge,* was the way it was worded—

No, he said aloud, reasonably, his hand pushing at the curtain to close it. He lay back on the pillows and shut his eyes. For all the shock of her leaving, his illness a direct result, he still believed that he knew her well enough to know that she would not go so far as that. She was in the South, an island off Georgia where they had gone on their belated honeymoon; she was on that island where they honeymooned, living in the cottage which had afforded them their first freedom.

He rang for the attendant and asked for a sedative. Complying, the man murmured pleasantly of not overdoing.

Marriott lay thinking that he did not know Lisa well enough to know anything that she might or might not do. Up until a moment ago something had shielded him from what had to be callousness on her part, that would allow her to leave him, divorce him, and settle down to make her life in a house that still surely contained him. He remained here, or had decided to when convalescence let him make the decision, primarily because of her indelible presence, the impress of her on every item in every room. He was not a proud man and would take what comfort he could find. Nor did he think it was morbid to be willing to live among his memories when they were what he had; fatalistic, perhaps, but not morbid. But she, who had not wanted any part of him—no alimony, no division of property, not even his name, for she had reverted to her maiden name—suddenly he could not think how she could have gone and lived for nearly a year in that house on the Georgian Island.

Or, rather, he could imagine how; and that was what chilled the sleep into which he fell as though it were a bath filled with particles of ice. He did not so much dream as enter a state of alien indifference where he and things that were connected with him had no more stature than a traveler surrounded by luggage has to a stranger in an airport. The stranger's eyes see the sticker on a bag—FRAGILE—but if he accidentally kicks it in his haste and there is a crack he will pass on unless apprehended. It is not wantonness but an indifference beyond carelessness; a condition of almost perfect vacuity.

And yet, Marriott thought, ringing for breakfast, sleep refreshes you whether you want it to or not. He asked for the curtains to be opened and recalled that he had come from that peculiar refreshment with the words *a new lease* struggling on his tongue. After pondering it, he decided that it had been wishful thinking, and that what he had meant was probably *a new Lisa*. Tasting his excruciatingly sweet coffee, he told the attendant, If beggars were horses, wishes might all be sugar lumps, and the attendant, who approved of jollity, said, They would be fattening, anyway, so come on: eat like a beggar for a change.

Marriott settled down to house watching, keeping his mind as clear of negative thoughts about Lisa and himself as he was able to manage. After days of no activity beyond the hedges, and nights of no discernible light there, he came to wonder how much of what he saw had been his own invention, necessary because it had led him to what he believed was a plainer, if more painful, idea of what Lisa might really be like now. If she had become callous, though it hurt him to think it, he felt that knowing it might help him to a more balanced view of what was to matter to him and what was not, especially as regarded his future treatment of her. He still could not see a future unrolling without her and envisioned himself countering her selfishness with generosity, somehow without her quite knowing it. He had dreamlike glimpses of himself indulging her, but the glimpses were so true to dreaming that they eluded head-on scrutiny.

In about a week the couple arrived. They were past middle age and appallingly industrious. Mounds of carpets, more than memory could account for, were beaten in the yard; woodwork was scrubbed down beyond bare windows which were themselves scoured with what looked like viciousness in Marriott's increasingly amused view. Once he noticed a neglected pane, and it became as though he were directing the spring cleaning from his own window because the woman instantly returned and corrected the oversight. Marriott began to play a game. Do this, he would think, and one or the other would oblige. Uh oh, he would think, watching the man clip the hedge, you've fouled up there; and the man would go back and smooth the minute raggedness away as though with a plane.

In this hubris? asked Marriott on the fourth day of the game as a loose brick in the path of peony bushes was resettled at his command. He was eating his first solid food, a little beef filet and rissole potatoes after so much porridge, so many boiled eggs and pieces of milk toast. Since the arrival of the couple and the game he had made huge bounds toward health and, to hear it told on the telephone, he talked the attendant's ear off. Of course the underlying cause of so much rejoicing was that he was finally putting on flesh; this morning he had tipped the old scale at a hundred and ten pounds, just sixty-five pounds under what he had been when Lisa left him. So that it was with the arrogance imparted by returning health and a full stomach that he lay back and smugly asked if this was hubris.

If so, he said, his heart beginning to knock in an excitement that was peculiarly like remembered lust, if so then let me warrant the fullest penalty by going whole god. He sat up and glared at the house beyond the hedge as though it were both a tribunal of Olympians and a woman of such Medusa-like beauty that one shuddered to imagine her.

It begins today, he said.

He arranged a pillow on the windowsill and lay with the back of his head resting on it and held his shaving mirror up at such an angle that it became a metamorphical shield through which to watch the house and its events. It was in the mirror that he saw Lisa arrive, stepping out of the taxi and pausing and looking around as if she had never seen the place before. If his shield caught the sun and winked at her she did not appear to notice.

She looked young. Her face was smooth, without lines; her hair was soft and bright without artifice; and she was slim. As though attesting to his observation she ran her hands down her hips in the slender skirt and then patted her tummy. It's lunchtime, his thought went out to her; you're hungry. She ran up the walk and the steps with the eagerness of real youth and went inside.

Carefully, in fine detail, he thought about Lisa's slimness through all the years when others were going to pot in their complacency. He saw it as indicative of an inner restlessness, and, further, of foresight: the huntress staying lithe for the day when her provider was gone and the quarry had thinned out and her fellows would have grown too clumsy and out of practice to offer much competition. That she had counted on him dying first was probably realistic; statistics were on her side. But it was he who cried out, *Help, don't leave me*, and it was she who had gone.

She had grown impatient, that was all. A lifetime of preparation against his going and then one day it must have come to her that he would hang on until they were both sixty or over and what good would her sacrifices be to her then? She must have thought of all the parfaits waved aside, and the sugar-encrusted cakes and creamed dishes and buttery croissants and third martinis forfeited to a necessary ideal, which was a really good second marriage.

She must have seen herself, in a sudden bleak light, sitting with the other old widows on some seedy boardwalk, competing—unequally, for her flesh would be more pendulous from a

skinny frame—for the attentions of the aged widowers and sus-
picious old bachelors. What he had sensed all those years was
the ceaseless activity of her plotting, manifest in part in her refusal of potatoes and second helpings of starch, her refusal to
join him in the serene acquisition of middle-aged bulk, one of
whose compounds is trust.

It was not, he told himself, vindictiveness at which he arrived
through his mental peroration, but rather a conviction that both
he and Lisa were entitled to be vindicated for holding onto opposite beliefs. Or if that was not possible, then compensation of
some sort was forthcoming. He so instructed the tribunal of gods,
following which he slept the natural sleep of the right-minded.

Freed of the toil of turning the stones of the past and examining their undersides, he grew to fit the shape of the present
and found strength to draw the outlines of a more robust future
and to look forward to growing to fit that shape, too. Lisa's near-
ness was not something that he ever forgot for very long, but she
settled comfortably into a secondary position in his consciousness, snug as a plump cat under a light blanket who occasionally
came forth at his call and was fed. As though acquiescing in his
desire not to see her again for the time being, she kept out of
sight.

At the beginning of June he was able to let the male nurse go
and do for himself. He was not a bad cook and he enjoyed his
meals, which leaned a bit heavily on cream gravies and starch
and desserts. He ate his dinner at twilight, in the kitchen from
which he could see the lights and movements in Lisa's kitchen as
her dinner was being prepared.

He knew her financial situation, which was about the same as
his, thanks to her mother's estate, and he did not feel that he
could have afforded a couple to look after him. In a day or so—
as though letting them go were harder than other compliances
and took longer—the couple left, with their luggage, and he and
Lisa were, so to speak, alone together.

Preparing his meals he would mentally admonish Lisa, telling
her not to stint on the good things, telling her to follow his example with the butter and the cream because they made you

sleep and contented and filled out sag. Eat up, he would say, lifting a fork laden with buttery potatoes in a toast to her shadow beyond the windows. He took to sherry in the daytime, recalling her fondness for it and her self-denial; he kept a decanter of it in his study and at intervals would drink her health in the creamy rich wine and advise her to do the same. He began to wake in the night so that he could see the lights go on in her kitchen as she raided the refrigerator. Good girl, he would tell her, and would summon a clear picture of a quart of ice cream mounded in a bowl and would watch as it disappeared by the tablespoon.

One hot August night he awoke thinking with some panic that he had slept through Lisa's feeding time. He hurried to the window and was glad to see that her light, for once, was already on, glad to know that she could manage for herself now. At first he thought that she was entertaining a guest, because there seemed to be several shadows in her kitchen. But when she passed the window he saw that it was only Lisa who cast so much shadow. Despite the double chin and the large bust thrusting in profile, he could not mistake his wife for anyone else in the world. He nearly leaned out and called to that comfortable middle-aged shape that he loved her, but it was late and there were other people who could have heard him.

He drank a glass of cold water and went back to bed, thankful that he could begin a spartan regime tomorrow, for the unrelentingly rich food of the past several months, while bringing him back to his former weight exactly, had begun to pall, and worse, to give him gas.

Lying in the dark, he drew, as carefully and lovingly as a child filling a coloring book on a rainy afternoon, a detailed mental picture of the house next door. It was a picture of a day in the future, perhaps a near-future day; a winter day in the hour before a snowfall, the first one of the year. There was both sadness and excitement in the air because one season had died and another was moving in, like ladies in succession in an old house.

A truck, which could have been a furniture delivery truck but was not, pulled up before the house. Several men got out, two of them carrying tool boxes and the others lugging what looked like a rolled-up hammock. They went up the walk and onto the veranda and the men with the tools began to work on the front door.

Has the lady of the house locked herself in? The men remove the door, and then the doorframe, and then the wide glass panels on either side, and then, after consultation and some measuring, they remove a section of the wall. The men with the canvas—which seems, as they unroll it behind them, to be a sort of harness, a bit like the rigs used for lifting beeves onto cattle boats—go inside and the others arrange themselves in the tableau of waiting.

Marriott froze them there, in that tableau, for as the author of the picture he knew what was to come next. He asked himself if he had perhaps gone too far, but the drowsy boy within him, to whom it was unthinkable that there could ever be too much billowy femininity, entered sleep smiling.

CANCER

He sat watching the TV Marathon Benefit for the Cancer Fund, a glass of ginger ale in his hand to induce belches and help relieve his heartburn. Occasionally, when one of the comics would say something especially telling or ridiculous, he would call out his own shorthand version of it to his wife who was writing Christmas cards in the next room. He chuckled automatically when the colored man was introduced, an anachronistic reflex that he was still unable to control despite daily headlines, daily occurrences, that devoured as voraciously as cancer his healthy happy memories of The Kingfish and Stepin Fetchit. But it was the man's costume—a suit of Far Eastern influence, a heavy necklace—which in Bill's own thought "put the quietus" on his anticipation, for it recalled that other black comic who a couple of weeks back had enraged and frightened him with a string of blatant insults directed at The White House, The President, and The President's family. He watched uneasily, crouched forward in a position that gripped his stomach like a hand, while the comic warmed up.

He relaxed when it was clear that the man was neither anarchistic nor especially funny; his mild folksiness caused Bill Williams to type him as a black Herb Shriner. He was about to call to his wife and tell her this—"Hey, Bess, this fella's a kind of a dark Herb Shriner"—but she called out first, saying, "That man has the most beautiful speaking voice," and Bill heard the scrape

of her chair as she got up to come to the door and see the man
with the beautiful voice. He barely had time to twist the horizon-
tal hold, creating herringbone, and settle back, before her voice
revealed by its tone her disappointment.

"Well, what on earth . . . How long have you been watching
that?"

"Happened this minute. You know the way she is: sometimes
just walk across the room and she goes out."

"Yes." And then, "Well, what *did* he look like?" her self-exas-
peration and amusement inviting Bill to share. Instead, he jig-
gled the vertical hold, turned the sound down unobtrusively.

"Oh," he teased her, "tall, dark—" She laughed, retreating,
saying, "I bet he wasn't good-looking. I never saw a good-looking comedian."

Bill listened until simultaneously he heard her settling at her
desk and the faint applause signaling the end of the black man's
act.

"Herb Shriner," he said.

"What?"

"I said, you used to think Herb Shriner was good-looking."

"He sure was," she said, engrossed once more in her efforts to
be at least cordial in seeming spontaneity, in writing to people
she and Bill did not see from year to year end, whose individual
faces she could barely summon to mind. It seemed to her that
her husband's family were like apparitions formed of ashes violently stirred once a year, but there never was time to wait until
the ashes settled into some semblance of features. Her own family she had not even communicated with in any fashion for years,
too many years to bother trying to count; enough, certainly, to
have formed a sheath for what once was a cutting edge to wound
her, especially at Christmastime. She shook her head, nibbled
her pen, wrote, "We are both well."

Bill turned the set slowly to brightness, using as a key the blond
hair of the girl perched on a stool singing. He favored blondes
of platinum stripe, out of loyalty to Jean Harlow's luster, and he
felt a bit like Frankenstein at work in his laboratory as he used
the tools of *bright* and *contrast* to create a blonde to his particular
liking. But no matter how far he turned the knobs he could not

bleach the complexion of the man who, with exaggerated stealth—
plainly a "surprise appearance" by the way the audience inter-
rupted the song with applause—crept up beside the girl and
straddled the stool beside her, responding to her welcoming grin
with weavings of his torso that brushed her shoulder with his.
Swiveling toward him, then away, then back, both of them exposed pulses beating with gathering force, the girl slanted her
eyes as he walked along the beach " 'he just doesn't see.' " " 'How,' "
she said (Bill no longer heard music nor recognized, through
the theatricality of his inner turbulence, the girl's rueful and
pointed artistry), " 'can she tell him she loves him?' " The man
beside her, the black man, answered the question unambigu-
ously by gazing at her breasts; to swelling laughter from the audience Bill got up, saw the television set in perspective, switched
it off with trembling hand and took his empty glass into the
kitchen. He rinsed it and put it in the dishwasher, loaded and
waiting for it, and started the machine. He stood by in a position
of listening, waiting for the electric hum, the machine's brain, to
call forth the cleansing jets which he imagined as being the coun-
terparts of emotional release in a man.

Bess came to the kitchen door and surprised her husband in
the attitude of apparent mourning. Although his back was turned
to the room she saw his reflected face in the windowpane, saw
the closed eyes and rigid suffering lines of his brow. She was
worried by what she saw, for it was not the first time that she
had found him thus. She had come to the door deliberately quiet
and apprehensive because of his long silence in the kitchen, afraid
that she would find him as she found him. *Pain* flashed across
her mind, followed, this time, by *cancer*—the thought due partly
to the TV show and partly to a story she had read today in one
of her magazines about a woman who had kept her hideous can-
cerous torture secret from her family until it was to late for treatment.

Bill heard a small sound and opened his eyes to his wife's image in the pane. Because of the way the light struck her skin and
projected its colors onto the viewing screen of the window, she
seemed darker than she was; nearly black. His eyes in the window—remote, divorced from his conscience by a collaborative

act of science and natural law—almost gave the truth to her watchful image. The threshing suds in the machine cut across the film of hate in his eyes and washed it down the drain like a layer of grease. His lids lowered briefly, gratefully, as he turned, and rose again on a peaceful hard-won shining in which comfortable love was discernible to his wife's anxious seeking glance.

"Nearly went to sleep," he told her, "standing right there."

"Bill—" she said, then, "Well, good gracious, go on to bed. I won't be too much longer—"turning and leading the way—"I hope and trust."

He caught up with her, took her arm. "Come on now," he said, trusting her to hear his urgency, but surprisingly she did not, or chose to ignore it.

"I can't. This is the last peaceful minute I'll have, probably, and I'm nearly done. Just about a dozen more . . ." She tapered off into vagueness as she stopped at her desk. "It's what to *say* that seems to get more and more troublesome. Sometimes I wonder—"she paused—"why we try to keep up . . ." In spite of her inflection he heard it as a statement, not a question. His hand still grasped her arm. Both he and she noticed that this was so with detached interest, when Bess had pulled the chair out and started to sit and found herself fettered.

What Bess saw was a wanting hand that she knew as well as if it belonged to her body. A tide of vigorous reddish hair rushed toward it from the cuff of his shirt sleeve, but an inch below the cuff its course was deflected and channeled to the right where it flooded in such density, against the roughly ovate shoreline of the hand's bare back, that it seemed as if it would cascade over the edge onto her smooth flesh, but there the aggressive rush was stemmed, as though drawn back by the moon, and became thinner and paler as if washing over an upgrading not discernible to the eye, a built-in safety device to prevent floods. . . . Drawing back mentally, she saw that the nails were slightly whitened by pressure, each showing a thin line of tension below the thread of dirt.

To Bill, his fingers looked like dead-end paths cut into a jungle. Perhaps they once had led somewhere, but the jungle had overgrown them, pushing them back with feverish growth. Soon the paths would be wholly obscured; in years to come legends would arise of inroads once made but evidence would not be found. . . . The hand was tanned but her dark tones made it appear to be a pinkish-gray, the color of ashes. He separated his flesh from hers and watched, intensely subjective, for the darkening of his hand as he returned it to himself. Was it darker for having clung for so long to her? Was her arm lighter for his hand's having rested, interminably, there?

They thought to touch lips, smile; she sat and began to ponder, gnawing the pen. He stood a moment longer gazing down at her hair that was only a little bit kinky.

"You hurry up," he told her, ordering rather than asking, believing that her talent for total absorption would continue to filter for a while yet the harshness from his increasing commands. He turned from her, hearing in his head her usual docile reply. When he had almost reached the door and still she had not answered, he turned to find her contemplating him with a smile that did not touch her eyes. Only then did she say, "Yes, Bill," and her eyes told him that she was answering a deeper question—a question no longer as submerged as it once was and yet still too hidden in the various strains of their blood to be isolated into the shapes of words. But because of the impendence of that time when blood would become word, because of the look that had penetrated the first, toughest membrane which guarded the source of all vitality, he knew that she would come to him sooner than she had said; was even now laying the pen aside.

IN THE MOOD

The two women who sit facing each other across the oilcloth-covered kitchen table have not seen each other for twelve years. Both are middle-aged, though one might not guess it of the newly arrived Californian, softly smart in cloud-gray. The women are sisters but this, too, might be difficult to guess, because of the opposite ways in which they have been tempered by life. However, it would still be possible for an expert to place their origins in the same Northern Ireland town, which they, glad deserters, left to come to America while still in their teens. Both girls were pretty and lively, and both married young. It was their wish that they could live near each other—Upper New York State, where they met and married their husbands, seemed ideal—but when Martha's second son, Johnny, was two years old, Mary and her husband left for California where work was said to be plentiful. That it was not, that money was indeed scarce, was evidenced by the fact that Mary had made only one trip back, in 1936. It seemed fitting that she should somehow afford the trip rather than Martha, because—as Martha put it in her letter, grace-noted with a little *ha*—Mary was not saddled with kids. Since 1936 there have been weekly letters, but letters, as Martha has said many times, are poor substitutes for the voice of an only sister. It is Martha who is doing most of the talking and how she has longed for the outpouring shows in her flushed face and taut body which may be able, when the dark words are finally said, to relax and know deep sleep again. It was this hope of sleep, as much as unfamiliar helplessness, that let her find the courage to ask her sister to come such a distance, knowing the great cost of the trip.

The visitor has removed her beige shoes and hat but not her gloves. The fact to which she now and again carries a coffee cup or cigarette reflects little, but this is not from lack of interest or sympathy; it is due, rather, to the fact that two face-liftings have taken from her the ability to show any but the most extreme emotions. When, from the taxi, she first glimpsed her sister waiting for her on the porch, her features had writhed upward in the aspiring curves of happiness, but when there was no longer that distance between them to falsify the records of twelve years, when she saw her sister as she now was rather than as she had been, her face protected both of them with kindly blandness. She had once had what were known as "speaking eyes," but the face-liftings revealed that the eye, unassisted by the subtle registering of the flesh around it, is merely a two-way mirror, incapable of any language of its own. Fortunately for both women, Martha chooses, still, to see reflected in Mary's eyes those minute and sympathetic changes of expression that were once the property of the twice-discarded flesh. In the future she will recall, and speak of, her sister's mobile, sorrowing face which, she will say, told her so much more than words and, because of her own blindness, so much less.

In response to a soft question, Martha says, "July," then slowly, with real surprise, "1947—only last year! It's hard to believe, sister. It seems like I waited forever to write you—waited, I guess you'd say, for the skies to clear. Sean dying, and then Johnny going out of his head—I just couldn't burden you with so much all at once. But there—I've done it anyway. Ah, well. July, yes. That's what made it so queer, you see. Of course, it would've been queer enough, just *buying* two winter overcoats and us poor as church mice—but coming home in the heat of July, all but wearing 'em! What I mean is, he was carrying them over his arms, one on each arm, and them flapping together in front of him—it was almost the same as having them on, you see. He came in the front room and sat on the daybed, still holding the coats. I can see him, the coats hiked around his face when he lit up a cigarette. I said to him, 'Be careful, son, you'll burn—' But then I stopped because of the look he gave me, so lost and—well, *hungry*, it looked like. Oh, I wanted to tell him it was wicked to buy two winter overcoats when we'd be needing the money for bills—still paying off his dad's funeral expenses, so much a month—paid off now, thank the Lord—but all at once I recalled the Christmas just past. He'd got cold on Christmas Day and hadn't got warm again for two weeks. I didn't have the gall to use words like *wicked,* not when he was maybe recalling how cold he'd been in the foxholes and trenches. So I piped down. I can see him now, smoking, sad, and the vacant way he nodded now and again, like he was agreeing with somebody I couldn't hear myself. I didn't know then—he didn't tell me, you see, till later, just before he was admitted to the hospital, and out of the blue he started telling me about the time he slept all night with a dead Jap—Yes, darling, I know—"

She reaches across the table and takes her sister's gloved hands.

"It gets worse, sister. That's why I couldn't write about it—I guess I didn't believe it." She pats the beige gloves commiseratingly before she plunges on.

"It was then, during the night with the dead Jap, that he heard somebody calling to him. 'What did they say to you, son?' I asked him. 'They told me,' he said, 'not to get mad—to keep my temper.'"

She gets up and goes to the stove, not wanting to see her sister's face when she voices a thought more dreadful to her than having to sleep with a dead enemy through a long night of searching, articulate shells.

"I couldn't ask him what losing his temper would have made him do to the dead man. I was afraid he'd tell me. Oh, and that's the worst part to me! I was afraid of something in him . . . some . . . *thing.* . . ."

It is not until she shudders with all her body that her sister rises and goes to her in stockinged feet, laying expressive hands on her shoulders.

"Now Martha, listen, dear. I've read that when people go—when people lose their way for a time, as Johnny has done—that they don't do anything they wouldn't do *before*. I mean, they wouldn't do anything that wasn't in their mind, somewhere, all along. Now, can you picture Johnny—that dear, sweet child— doing anything brutal to a dead body, enemy or not?" She turns her sister around to face her, her lips intending a small reassuring smile. "Can you, dear?"

Martha looks at Mary, an unprotected look, before she says, "I've no idea what was in his mind, ever. With Tom, yes. Never with Johnny. If I had—" She takes the coffeepot to the table, fills the cups erratically enough to cause the china to rattle complainingly. The harshness in her voice is due not entirely to fatigue. "And whose fault is it that he was a secretive boy? Mine? His dad's? Tom's?"

"Secretive?" The well-modulated voice gives to the word a peculiarly disproportionate freight of interest, strives immediately to counterbalance it with volume. "But you never wrote me—if it worried you, you should have confided in me—"

"No, I never wrote such a thing because I didn't know it at the time. I was too busy seeing to their food and clothes, seeing they went to confession and to school—then, before I could turn around, there was a war and two grown men were leaving the house to join up. Two grown men—I guess that was the first time I noticed—"

"That Johnny was secretive?" Mary's voice clings to the word.

"That the *children* were gone, I mean. I know that sounds like I didn't see the children while they *were* children—" She looks puzzled, faltering in her speech. "I've thought about it since— about how I can see them as children plain as daylight, now that they're grown men—" She is about to give up when Mary says "Ah," and Martha continues, thankful that she is understood. "That's how I know that Johnny was secretive, you see, and Tom wasn't—through looking back. It's what they call hindsight, I imagine. Sit down, Mary, and have your coffee."

It is that time of day when, in California, Mary is accustomed to having a drink, sometimes more, but she sips her coffee dutifully, remembering her sister's active aversion to the idea of women drinking. When last the sisters met, Mary was in the grip of a terrible marriage, though hypocritically pious on the surface. At that time, coffee was the strongest drink to pass her lips, too, and her appearance then was a warning of what her sister's now is. That she has long since divorced her husband, gotten an education at night school, and made a modestly successful career in managing the line of beauty parlors known as Miss Edythe's are secrets to be kept, always if possible, from Martha. This means that Mary cannot offer her sister financial aid, which she would like to do, but she believes that Martha would not accept money from a divorced woman, even an only sister. She also believes that Martha would find her secrets more intolerable than Johnny's, if she could know them—the secrets, that is, of her divorce and the *reason* for divorce. They would carry an equal weight of horror to Martha's already overburdened mind. Because of this, the happy facts of her education and career must share the same veiled fate, and this hurts her. She knows the pleasure Martha would find in learning that America had, however tardily, lived up to the promise it had seemed to hold out, so long ago, to the two deprived daughters of Portballintrae; it would be Martha's victory, too.

Thoughts of her own secretiveness circle back to Johnny's and her heart put forth, in the vague direction of the hospital where he walks about in response to the bidding of strangers, a tentative yet strong filament of understanding, its strength the result of years of existence, because he had been her favorite as a baby and as a sweet-faced, quiet boy of ten. On the train from California she had asked herself repeatedly if she would have made the trip, knowing the risk of having her secrets found out by Martha, if it had been Tom instead of Johnny who was sick. For she had not questioned, from the time Martha's strangely formal letter came telling her that Johnny was "out of his head" and that her presence was needed, that it was Johnny who needed her. Despite the apparent illogic of the thoughts, she told herself that if it had been Tom, he would have had Martha; Johnny had her. Even if she had never told him in words that he was the kind of son she had yearned for (her mind sharpened and veered, stabbing like a dagger at the all-too-solid, perfidious memory-image of her divorced husband), still, he must have felt it, and in his confusion, reached for its reassurance as a half-asleep, frightened child reaches for a warm object—a teddy bear or a bunched-up blanket. She gives her sister her attention again, belatedly; she has missed something so that the words now spoken float unattached in the air like drops of spume above a wave.

"—won't say *who* it is he is, not even to the doctors, or I should say *the* doctor, because Johnny only talks to one of them, a young fella not much older than him, quiet-spoken, not impatient and hurrying like most of them—not that you can outright blame them, I didn't mean that. The Lord knows they've got enough to do and Johnny one of the quieter ones, counting his voices and all." Mary is still lost in the choppy tide of words but what Martha says next clangs like buoy in her mind. "Or maybe it's not true anymore that he hears voices; maybe once they told him who he was—thinks he is—maybe the voices went away."

"Thinks he is—?"

"Somebody else, darling. That's it, you see. Him thinking such a thing. Oh, I just can't tell it straight. There's too much!" She grows a bit excited, her hands coming up to hover over the cream pitcher and sugar bowl as though bestowing hurried benediction upon the familiar objects. Helplessly she says again, "Johnny thinks he's somebody else now. And he won't say who."

Mary thinks how odd it is that a heart can lift at such a time, but she thinks further that it is, perhaps, because she feels no strangeness at Martha's words; it is as though she had known all along, and thus being proved right proves also her right to feel so close to Johnny. Beneath the cloudy thought, beneath her silence, in some region barely touched by recognizable emotion, a struggle takes place in her. What is struggling she does not know, but the skirmish ends with the further strengthening of the bond that runs from her breast to Johnny. Martha is aware only of her sister's control in the face of this final, terrible revelation, and is grateful for it, knowing how difficult it must be and for whose comfort. She shows her gratitude by wrapping her next words in amusement, though it has always been hard for her not to feel an embarrassed amusement at a thing so ludicrous: "The young doctor told me that Johnny did say once that he'd had a long conversation with the Pope, during the night—" Her eyes invite her sister to join her in the relief of levity but when Mary does not do so, Martha—merry eyes, solemn mouth—explains further, "Johnny said they spoke to each other in Gaelic—"

"I'm sure," Mary says, smoothing a crease in her glove, "that the Pope can speak in any language," and she waits.

"Ah now, Mary—ah now, *Johnny* can't" and Martha plops softly into laughter like a big soap bubble bursting. Mary joins her after a moment as though recalled to politeness by her hostess. The laughter does not last long but it has its good effect; Martha's rigidly held shoulders begin to point downward and inward in the curve that can lead to sleep, if nothing happens—as it has before—to set them on guard again.

Mary sees the therapeutic effect of so slight a thing upon her sister and is moved by love for her, and a many-sided regret, and an anger; the anger makes her wonder what language the Pope has used to address Martha most of the years of her life, knowing the speculation to be strictly unfair because her good, tired sister has always spoken directly to the Virgin, and to God on special occasions. Only Johnny, in his lostness—that place without ego—would think that going above the Pope's head was presumptuous.

Once begun, the thoughts of religion lead Mary to a timeworn path: loss of self, she thinks, is loss of God, and her bitterness at the inextricability of Self and God this side of madness makes her resent her sister, whose complacent belief evidently remains entire and Job-like. Her resentment, following its ancient rut, goes back to include, once again, their dead parents and grandparents, ever-religious stoics in the fact of outrageous fortune, and so on back into the mists where only God stands, massive as the sky turned stone, waiting for her to come butting through and hurt her head against Him as she has been doing most of her life. Knowing that she has lost the possibility of His comfort through the willful act of divorce, she is infuriated and frightened that He is still able, in spite of the identity she has forfeited along with her faces, to recognize and hurt her with His denial. And there is was again: His denial. The words continually broke into her mind like masked thieves, and what they stole she did not know; she knew only that what they left behind them was circled with a question, like a changeling on a doorstep: Where did the child come from? *Denial of what?* She fervently wishes it were tomorrow and visiting time at the hospital.

Martha thinks fondly how well Mary is looking. It occurs to her that she has not asked after Bill, Mary's husband. She will do so soon, but at the moment she is enjoying the lovely silence following laughter. She cannot recall when last she laughed out loud—the time the boys put paper boots on the cat? Ah, no, she thinks with the bafflement; they were twelve and fourteen at the time. Wasn't there something pleasant in the last years she could remember, and mention to Mary?

She begins aimlessly: "Tom's marriage last May—of course I wrote you. Such a sweet girl, Annie. You'll be meeting her to-morrow—we're going there for supper. I wanted you to myself tonight. They've got a nice big house—seven rooms, if you count the kitchen and bath, on a nice street. Tom is foreman at the plant, did I write you? Making good money for his age, the Lord be praised—" Finding her point: "He got married in May and Johnny took sick in July. Mary, do you think it was jealousy made him do it?"

"No," Mary says promptly, feeling her certainty to be curious but trusting it nonetheless.

Martha is doubtful: "His own girl married while he was over-seas. Maybe Tom's getting married brought back thoughts of—"

"No," Mary says again. "No, Martha. You're forgetting the dead Japanese."

The sisters stare at each other. In a moment Martha says help-lessly, out of her depth, "Me? Forgetting such a thing?"

Mary plunges glibly into an explanation, any explanation to end the awkwardness and free their locked eyes.

"I meant that you sounded as if you were going to say Johnny was all right when he came home, and he couldn't have been—not after the dead Japanese, and the voice. Don't you see—" and suddenly she does see, so that her words have conviction—"Johnny *pretended* to be all right, for your sake, as long as he could. But when it got to be too much—" Martha's face stops her.

"What did, Mary? Being home with me? Why would being home with me—"

"Oh, Martha," Mary, impatient with herself, aware now of her splitting head, makes an abrupt movement, justifies it by bending down and slipping on her pumps and rising, purse in hand, from the table. "I'd like to wash up, if I may."

Martha rises less gracefully.

"If she *may*. Hear the girl talk, will you!" She comes around the table and slips her arm about her sister's thin waist, propelling her toward the doorway. Slyly, hoping to raise another liberating laugh, she asks, "Do you wash up with your gloves on?"

Mary does not look at her sister but the set of her head would be expressive, to any but Martha's eyes, of indignation edging up to outrage—an old indignation, Mary's associates could have told Martha, born of recurrent questions similar to hers. Mary's voice is crisp and final but Martha hears the crispness without the finality and thinks of it as her sister's "California brogue." The words spoken are merely eccentric and Mary has always had her share of that.

"I don't like my hands. I don't like to look at them. I always wear gloves, even in bed."

"Goodness," Martha says mildly, restraining a laugh which, though suppressed, has the effect of clearing the air, allowing her to get back to the point. "What got to be too much for Johnny, Mary? If you know, girl, come on and tell me."

Mary's relief at the idleness of the question about her gloved hands lets her make a real effort on her sister's behalf. What she had meant, of course, was simply that being *Johnny* had got to be too much, and yet the simplicity was complicated by the relationship: the mother would not be able to see the son and his actions as apart from herself; was not Martha looking into herself for the answer to Johnny's condition? Son and mother, self and God— there was the same inextricability this side of madness, and even mad, Mary felt absolutely certain, a mother would still recognize her son. Then was it the son alone who, through madness—? But no. Martha had not said that Johnny denied her; he protected her still, by not telling her or the doctors who he had become. As it stood, his identity unrevealed, Martha could continue to call him "son," but if he ever said "I am—" and gave the name of a stranger, whose son would he then be?

The thought causes a second unexplained lifting of Mary's heart, and the pleasurable lightness makes her determined to protect Martha from any possible idea—and it *was* possible—that Johnny had chosen madness as the one means of escape from her. Therefore she dredges up a phrase so overused since the war to condone or condemn the newly reinstated citizens that it has lost all meaning and this she gives to her sister with only the slightest twinge of guilt.

"Adjusting to civilian life," says Mary, and pats Martha's shoulder, glad of the ease she feels there.

Dead words, she thinks, climbing the narrow stairs behind Martha, are the greatest comforters; and imagines for a moment that she hears an echo of Latin from behind the dusty curtain of time; though, as usual, the cadence and accent prove to be false beneath the dust, for the first time Mary is able to think flippantly about the deception. She frames a whimsical sentence concerning it, which she mouths to the unemotional woman in the bathroom mirror: It is thus in vain that we try to re-create in our minds the speech of a dead lover. But the act of removing her gloves and being forced to look at the puffed veins and spots of her old woman's brittle hands deprives her of the illusions of youth and dispassion. Averting her head, she turns on the tap and laves her hands with that mixture of care and repugnance reserved for very old invalids.

After supper the sisters sit in the front room of the little house surrounded by the paraphernalia of Martha's livelihood—Singer sewing machine, neatly folded dress patterns, catalogues, piles of garments in various stages of completion—and Mary's questions encourage Martha to continue filling in the unwritten pages of twelve years. Despite the fact that there is no photographic record of Johnny's growing up, Mary feels, by the end of the evening, that she has seen many of her nephew's faces as a camera might have caught them: happy, defiant, sad, arrogant, hurt—a lump the size of a duck's egg on his head where the baseball struck him; his rueful smile at twisting his shoulder in an overly vigorous (according to Martha, show-off) dive; she has seen him, through what Martha continues to refer to as her "hindsight," wearing bogus mustachios in a school play and his first real moustache at the age of sixteen and a half. She has seen his face closed and secretive on many an occasion, in contrast to Tom's ever-open countenance. (Tom, good and modestly accomplished in the All-American Boy tradition, is actually the sung hero of the evening, but as he seems to lack surprise he arouses in Mary only the feeling of distant indulgence that she once gave to Andy Hardy.) She sees all these faces of Johnny and more, but never, through her sister's memory, does Mary see him frightened. As they are getting ready for bed Mary inquires about this, casually. Martha tells her, as though dipping into a foreign language, that as far as she, or his dad, or Tom ever knew, Johnny had no fear.

The sisters say good night and soon Martha's gentle snores can be heard through the open door across the hall, but Mary lies awake thinking that a person without fear would have no cause to be secretive. She rejects as unrealistic the idea that a fearless person would be safer than one haunted by fear; it seems to her that his position would be more precarious because of being so unguarded and unsuspicious and therefore open to all the very real horrors that lie in wait for the unwary. She thinks that fear and, for example, arsenic have this in common: small daily doses help build up a tolerance so that one who tastes it each day is more likely to survive a massive dose than one who does not. She wonders if Johnny, by becoming someone else, had escaped *from* sudden fear or—her throat catches at the thought—*into* it. As she has done.

She falls asleep with the picture of Johnny's face before her, grown-up and angular beneath the cocky overseas cap. His eyes stare straight into hers, level and fearless—it may be because he looks into the eyes of the mirror-woman and takes her eyes to be his, as Mary believes them to be hers when she needs to. Perhaps the woman in the mirror can help them both by allowing them to meet within her, on that neutral ground.

The next day at the hospital Mary hurries into the visiting room ahead of Martha and recognizes Johnny instantly. The attendant, as she brushes past him, seems for an uncertain moment about to stop her until he sees Martha trailing behind. Mary registers his mistrust and files it away for future examination.

"Hello, Johnny."

"Hello." He looks at her with the photograph's levelness plus the intentness of a man meeting an interesting stranger, but his voice is merely polite.

Martha says, with a touch of disappointment, "Johnny, don't you know your own—" but Mary stops her with a gesture. Johnny's expression grows more alert as he sees Mary's gesture as a signal for the beginning of some new kind of test. He and Mary take each other's measure, both sets of eyes seeming to be intent upon something other than the guessing game of identity, but still Mary says, startling herself, "Johnny, who am I?"

Martha and the attendant stand on either side of the silent boy and the waiting woman, as though they were the judges of a contest. When Johnny finally speaks, it is in a slow, kindly voice.

"I don't know, but I think I can help you. I'll try."

Martha is terribly embarrassed. She steps up and takes her son's arm, shaking her head in chagrin at the attendant. She speaks in an overly loud voice, even a bit gruffly.

"Johnny, this is your Aunt Mary, my sister Mary. You were ten years old the last time you saw her but—well, for heaven's sake! It's your *Aunt Mary,* boy. From *Anaheim, California.*"

"Hello, Ma," he says, smiling at her, before he offers Mary his hand. She takes it and he says, "Hello, Mary. What happened to your face?"

All the way home on the bus Martha apologized. Johnny had never, she told Mary, done anything like that before—never. Getting no response from her sister, who sat looking out of the bus window in a state of bemusement, she tried to explore, with many sidelong glances, the mystery of what made Johnny say such a thing. Even then, searching for evidence, she could see nothing unusual in Mary's face. Repeatedly she told herself that Mary hadn't aged a day in twelve years, and *how* could Johnny think she had! Finally, coming to the conclusion that Mary must have considered the source of the remark—as you had to do with the dear boy and no unkindness meant, the Lord knew— she put it out of her mind. That night at supper when Tom asked Mary if Johnny had known her, it was Martha who said, with conviction, that he had, with no trouble whatever. She and Tom and Annie agreed that it was a good sign. Mary said nothing, which strengthened Annie's opinion of her as standoffish and stuck-up: *gloves* at the supper table.

Mary finally became aware, through several of Annie's cleverly veiled remarks, that she had aroused the girl's antagonism. She made one or two efforts to be more the kind of woman her new niece might take to but she soon found that she really didn't care what Annie thought of her, or what Tom thought, or, to her surprise, what Martha thought either. Having decided it, holding up her corner of the conversation became easier for her and by the time she and Martha bid Tom and Annie good night she had corrected, through indifference, the original bad impression. Somewhat cynically she thought that now that she had their approval, their indifference would meet hers equally and make possible a bland, uncritical relationship, since their kind of approval, won by default, was nothing more than a defense against further seeing.

When Martha had gone to sleep, Mary lay on Johnny's bed smoking, in the room he and Tom had shared and left nothing of themselves in. It was as though, she thought, the boys, like Martha, had not seen themselves during the string-and-brass-doorknob acquisitive days of boyhood and so accumulated none of its prizes. The room reminded her of her apartment in Anaheim, which was also barren—no, *clean* of any testimonial to the past. She had taken the apartment after her graduation from night school; its mirrors knew only the second Mary, who had a face scraped clean of the past, a new job, and—surely it had been indicated?—the chance to mold a different, better past from the material of the future. She had managed too, up to a point, by refusing to speak of anything that dated before her educational and cosmetic transformation; but perhaps now she would have to change that and acknowledge the older past with something tangible, such as a wedding photograph on her dressing table. She meant the thought to be sarcastic but it failed because tonight she had actually taken the first, or final, step toward such acknowledgment with her glib answers to Tom's questions about her husband.

She faced it squarely: she was at last committed to the outright lie she had dreaded for years, in contrast to her former comparatively harmless lie-by-omission to Martha, who had made it easy for her by never doing more than sending PS regards to Bill. It was Mary's belief that Martha had always distrusted Bill without knowing why, but distrust, however vague on the part of sister-in-law or deep on the part of wife, would never justify divorce to Martha. The lie had had to be told, and now that it was, Mary found that it committed her more thoroughly to Bill than marriage to him had done after the first few hopeful years. By extension the commitment included that other Mary who had been his wife: when she had exhausted, through telling, what she knew of those two people that was fit to tell, she would have to invent; invention is creation and the responsibility of the creator to the created is at least as long as life. They were, in a sense, her children now, and her maternity would see to it that they were treated well.

She thought that her experience must parallel her nephew's experience with the two Johnnys: the one who still called Martha "Mother" to spare her feelings, and the person he had become— the unknown, clear-eyed person he had become. She felt no surprise at Johnny's immediate recognition of her as someone who needed his help. It seemed to her to be positive proof of his love, much more so than knowing *who* she was would have been. Let Martha believe his madness had prompted the remark. Such belief would make it possible for Mary to see Johnny often without divulging her real reason.

She told herself that she was tired, and that that was why she had such a thought. She fell asleep pretending day was near, as a sick person does.

It was Martha's habit to visit the hospital twice weekly. Mary suggested that while she was there, Martha should take the opportunity to catch up on her sewing rather than doing it at night, which was bad for her eyes. It was the kind of sensible suggestion Martha would have made had their positions been reversed and she accepted the offer gladly. She would still visit him on Sundays, and would be better company for not having work on her mind.

Mary waited until the next visiting day according to Martha's schedule—she did not want to appear to take over at the beginning. She got to the hospital early and waited for Johnny in the shabby room with the coverless magazines and the family groups who seemed, like the magazines, to have been badly used and left with their contents exposed. She felt with some amusement like a patient waiting for his first interview with a highly recommended doctor upon whose reputation many hopes were depended, like fragile ornaments on a tree. She asked herself what she expected from him—whether it was help for herself as pertained to her directly—and if so, how? and again, what?—or indirectly through his acceptance of her help in trying to decide who it was he had become. She turned the word "decide" around in her mind and found that it was accurate according to her feelings; she did not feel that Johnny knew who the other person was.

Lassitude descended; her body grew heavy and her thoughts pleasantly fuzzy. When Johnny stood in the doorway with the attendant, Mary made no move to get up but let him find her and come to her. He did not inquire after his mother and though he seemed gravely pleased to see Mary, he showed no surprise at her being alone. He sat beside her, with the attendant a short distance away so that if they spoke quietly he would not be able to hear them.

"Mary," said Johnny, "I've been thinking about your case."

"I've been thinking about you, too."

"About my case?" She wondered if it was a test question but did not wait to answer. There must be only honesty between them.

"I don't think of it as a 'case' because I'm not a doctor." He could, if he chose, take her answer as implied criticism of his referring to her as a case, but he did not seem to nor did he follow up his opening remark. It was enough for both of them to know they had been in the thoughts of the other. Settling down with Johnny into the silence that, it seemed to Mary, had a quality of the timelessness before emergence from sleep, it occurred to her that their relationship, at this stage and rightfully, was not dependent upon words. Words used as mere fillers could grow into obstructions to their future understanding of each other. It seemed to her that an ideal balance existed between them, mysterious and marvelous—the balance of a mystery in which each of them had been given one clue concerning the other, the clue itself a mystery: I am not what I seem. Theirs differed from the usual encounters between strangers because they really *cared* to fathom the mystery, and that fact made wild guesses and irrelevant remarks out of the question. Not, however, that rules should be established; when Johnny noticed what Mary was wearing and named the items and colors at some length, she listened, indulgent but serious in case he should express the disapproval, which would be her cue to avoid making the same mistakes in the future. Looking at his artless face she thought that he was like a little child in the newness of his other self—this self, rather, who was a little over a year old as far as anyone knew.

When the attendant, who had slouched on his spine, motionless and somnolent through the visit, stood up and indicated wordlessly that it was time for her to go, Mary looked about her and saw with a sense of shock that the others had left without her noticing. For a split second she had the disoriented feeling that it was she who was to go with the attendant. How deeply, then, she had been in touch with Johnny! The realization allowed her to take the chance of a rebuff. Holding Johnny's hand, she said, "Would you like for me to come often?"

"Oh yes," he told her. "Maybe you could come back tonight." It was the simple trusting request of a child and she was certain that she would burst into tears if she had to deny it, his first request of her. The attendant, whom she had thought a dull beast, incapable of more than fetching, carrying, and disapproval of her, put his hand on Johnny's shoulder and said jocularly, "Hey, old fella, you know girls ain't allowed in the dorms after dark!" He did not look to see how Mary reacted to his little joke; he seemed to care only about Johnny's response and, Mary saw, getting her second unpleasant surprise from him, the quality of his waiting was that of a trusted friend rather than of a jailer. He relaxed visibly when Johnny laughed and took a poke at his arm. There was implicit in their behavior an ease that gave Mary a twinge of jealousy. On the way to the bus she told herself that she couldn't be too careful where the attendant was concerned. And again she told herself that her tiredness was responsible for the thought. It was the last time she stood at a point distant enough to think an excuse was necessary.

When she went to the hospital again it was in the company of Martha, Tom, and Annie. She thought that it did not count as a visit with Johnny, because she and the others rendered each other anonymous except as parts of a mass called "the family." But the fact that she had not been anonymous was made clear to her when she went by herself the following day. On Sunday, Martha had introduced her to the young doctor who was Johnny's *friend*—she had used the word in the introduction—and Mary had found him pleasant and unforceful; when he came in, however, with Johnny and the attendant on Monday and asked to speak with her, she sensed a very definite force of purpose behind his easy manner. She armed herself mentally.

The attendant took Johnny aside but made no further attempt to disguise the doctor's wish to speak to Mary without Johnny hearing. With her eyes on Johnny, Mary said, "This seems awkward to me. He must know that we're talking about him."

"Yes. I told him I wanted to talk to you about him but I want him to wonder what we're saying."

"Why?"

"I need his curiosity. He's curious about you, did you know?"

"He told me so."

"He told me, too—several times. You're the first person he has shown any interest in since he came here. Did you know that?" She shook her head, wondering if the doctor could hear her heart pounding.

"I wish there was a way to tell you how rare such interest is for someone with Johnny's delusion, or what it could mean if it could be sustained." He paused until she looked at him, then said quietly, "I'm afraid I can only tell you the odds against its meaning anything at all." At her gesture he shook his head, indicating that he, too, was at a loss. "We live with such contradictions here. Everything looks possible until you consider the odds."

In his eyes, as he spoke further of the odds, Mary imagined that she saw the figure one, representing Johnny's "chance," solitarily facing an astronomical number which apparently stood for his delusion. Something about the image was distorted: if Johnny's—was the word *delusional?*—if his delusional personality had that much potential strength—if he could become firmly established as another person going by another *name*—then wouldn't he have earned the right of recognition? How many ordinary people had the guarantee of such odds against going insane as Johnny had potentially against what the doctors chose to call "sanity"? Surely, under those circumstances, a cure for him would be tantamount to murder! Mary could not, of course, pursue such reasoning with the doctor because—because? Yes. Because she knew very well that if she did, she would not be allowed to see Johnny again. She managed a thoughtful voice as she told the doctor that she understood and asked him what she should do. She saw that he was staring at her hands and only then did she become aware of clutching her handbag too tightly. Something perverse and arrogant in her caused her to tighten her fingers until the pressure hurt. At that moment Johnny called across the room, "Hey, Mary, I've been thinking about your case." There was a hint of laughter in his voice but it had the sound of goodwill. Mary freed one of her clutching hands and waved to him. When she again looked at the doctor she saw that his eyes were bright with speculation and humor.

"That doesn't embarrass you," he said.

"Why should it?" she decided to see what he would do with the whole truth. "I'm as much of a case as he is." The doctor's smile was dazzling and his voice caught its spark and ignited into warmth.

"Lady, we could sure use you around here!" Mary felt triumphantly that she had gotten over the hurdle, with Johnny's help, and when the doctor told her that he was leaving the hospital soon and would be away for three or four days, possibly longer, she pressed her advantage and asked him how often she would be allowed to see Johnny. He told her as often as she liked; he would leave instructions to that effect. He shook her hand and turned to beckon to the attendant; when he did so, she realized that a most important matter needed to be settled. Breathlessly she asked him if the attendant was necessary—if she could not take Johnny from the ward herself, or meet him outside the visiting room and bring him here alone. In the young man's puzzlement and faint air of disquiet she saw the possibility of losing some of the ground gained with Johnny's fortuitous help. Therefore she spoke with straightforward gravity when she told him that the attendant meant well, she was sure, but he kept interrupting Johnny and her. The doctor's answering look told her plainly that he considered her responsibility doubled, but when he left the visiting room the attendant went with him.

For the first time, Mary had Johnny to herself. She wondered if he shared her feelings of excited complicity. His young face was serious and "professional"; the fingers of his two hands lightly touched, making a "steeple" at midriff height.

He said, "Mary, tell me about yourself. Start anywhere. I can correlate the facts later." He nodded encouragement. "Just relax. That's the most important thing. We probably won't get far this first session, so relax. Now—" he said, leaning forward. "What is it you do for a living?" The light, streaming through his silky fine hair, made a halo around his head and she thought, This is like an interview in heaven. She fought her body's weariness, telling herself that she could not afford to lie there in the chair like a lump of clay when he so clearly expected something more of her. She regretted his words and especially the final question; she had tried so hard to avoid concrete facts. But he was expectant. She answered him obliquely, half apologetically.

"I try to make people happy."

"I do too. I try to make people happy." He beamed at her.

"My work could be called 'vulgar'—" She was tentative lest the word be misunderstood.

"Mine too! Longhairs—" He stopped and laughed. How strange that he should mention hair, she thought. It was as if he had read her mind. She wondered briefly and unpleasantly if the new Johnny was a hairdresser, then she smiled inwardly at her foolishness; he was nothing of the sort because he was nothing at all, except in embryo. Without her help he would remain so. She gave him a fanciful clue to her thought: "I take people into a—*place,* and more or less transform them." She laughed, thinking that the words applied to the beauty parlor as well as to her fancy. Envisioning the hard-faced beauty operators, she added, "With the help of a band of angels."

"Why," he slowly, looking at her with uneasy speculation, "so do I." His expression snapped her out of her self-indulgent game. She considered the words she had just used and saw that they were also descriptive of his imagined role as doctor. If he thought that she, too, was posing as a doctor, he would close the door on her. Nervously she told him, "I manage three beauty parlors in Anaheim. It's a good job and I like it." He said "Oh," and his apparent relief proved the accuracy of her conclusion. Though she did so without interest, she launched into a description of her job and how she had won it by first peddling cosmetics door-to-door. However much she realized the necessity for such "safe" conversation—he asked many questions and was attentive to the answers—it seemed to her to be a comedown from their previous level of communication with few words. She left the hospital dissatisfied and somehow dispirited; undoubtedly she had expected too much of their first time alone together.

She began to go to the hospital every day and when Martha protested that she saw practically nothing of Mary, that Mary came home exhausted and went to bed with the chickens, Mary had to restrain herself from being short with her sister. She was sleeping less and less well and what sleep she did get was invaded by a growing sense of urgency. Awake, away from Johnny, she felt imperiled; it seemed to her that she occupied the air the way a needle placed on its point would do: her sharpness, her potential to penetrate, to impale, could be rendered impotent by the slightest push. But when she was with Johnny she was able to be both serene and gay, and to conceal from him that each day held an unavoidably bad moment for her. When she checked Johnny out of Ward D the person who gave him over into her care was the attendant whom she had, in a manner of speaking, dismissed. The man always looked at her as if he had some intelligence of her that was denied the others around him, and his daily reluctance to give Johnny over to her got so apparent that she had to invent little ruses to keep Johnny from noticing.

Not that she didn't understand how the man felt; if *she* had lost Johnny she would not have accepted it so silently. The worst part of the moment came when she had to admit that she could not prove his silent acceptance. How could she know what he said to the boy in their long hours together? Walking with Johnny to the visiting room she made herself think positive thoughts—calm, lovely thoughts that were a conscious effort to influence their time together which did not seem to begin for her until they emerged into the room which she thought of as their place. Each day she allowed herself hope that some revelation during their visit would make Johnny's return to the ward unnecessary—much better, impossible. She began, in a shadowy way, to imagine herself and the boy together in her apartment in Anaheim.

On the fifth or sixth day of the young doctor's absence, following a night during which Mary became fixed on the idea that her breasts were producing milk, she told the boy, in detail, about life in Anaheim. She spoke generally at first: the town itself, its social possibilities (accent on youth), its athletic facilities, some of which she had to invent. After a while she got down to the specifics of her more desirable—to a young man—possessions: her late-model car, hardly used by its original owner, and her apartment—its central but quiet location, its generous size which allowed for privacy, its solid, unfrilly furnishings. She watched him closely during the recital. His expression was dreamy and wistful and she believed that her words had caught at his imagination. She saw clearly the contrast her word picture presented alongside the inevitable image of Martha's cluttered little house. In her mind she and Johnny stepped out of the apartment house in California, into the streets, and saw the palm trees, felt the warmth. She told him about the warmth which, she said, choosing her words like fruit in a market, made Christmas a semitropical fiesta.

"Think of the novelty of that," she said. "Think of a really *warm* Christmas!"

He cocked his head, considering it. Casually he remarked, "You wouldn't need overcoats."

"No," she said eagerly. "Just sports clothes—nothing heavy, or formal."

He spoke abruptly; there was a note in his voice which she heard, with disbelief, as boredom.

"When are you going back there? You've been here a long time." She found that she had reserves of will and energy unknown to her, and she drew from these so surely that even she forgot, from time to time, that she was engaged in a fight for life.

That night she put off going to her room as long as she could, afraid of what waited for her there. Martha was touchingly glad of her company and the sisters, as if by design, talked about Portballintrae and the old days which seemed suddenly to have been happy ones. It was Martha, finally, who remarked the lateness of the hour. Mary considered asking her sister if she could share her room but she did not. She went to the stuffy bedroom and lay down on the bed with the awareness of a person who, in a primitive place, suffering a gangrenous limb, lies down to submit without anesthetic to the knife. She began by trying to think as Johnny would think so that she might understand the reason for his withdrawal from her—his abruptness and boredom, his terrible, unfeeling question. The effort resulted in such a confusion of personalities that inside her head there sprang up a tower of Babel with a horde of people, begotten by Johnny and herself, trying to speak all at once: there were the other Marys— two or three, she could not recall which; there was the new Mary, who was Johnny; there was the Johnny who was himself and someone else, and the Johnny who was Mary, if she were he. All of them spoke in their own voices with voices beneath those which spoke words with other, so-far-hidden meanings. One of the voices told Mary that it was as if she were trying to take Johnny into herself, into that part of her that was undefiled and healthy, and worthy of him; as though, if she could somehow pass him through her body and out, when he emerged she would then be able to name him. She quivered on the brink of a discovery for which she was not ready. She sought refuge in the only thing that seemed powerful enough to afford it: her hatred of her divorced husband. She thought, more fully than she had done in years, of Bill's deception, of how he had let her believe that she was barren, counting so cynically on her naïveté to provide the blindness to what he was doing when he protected himself against her and the possibility of fathering a son. If she had not innocently told the doctor—describing Bill's actions and the object itself— if. If. She would still be Mrs. William Lonergan, too old now to have a son, locked with Bill in the bitterness of deception and old age. But now—yes. *Thank God. Now.*

There followed a lull during which Mary thought about Martha: old envy was tempered with regret for some imminent loss Martha was to suffer; regret was tempered with envy of some loss Martha had already suffered. And yet, with the discovery more than half-wedged into her brain, flashing on and off like a white light, with the ONs growing more and more prolonged, a shocklike sleep took consciousness from her.

In sleep Mary is Johnny. As Johnny, she lies at the bottom of a shallow gravelike hole with the body of Bill, whom she has just killed. Lights flash around them and she knows that the lights are held by people who are searching for her, to find and punish her for Bill's murder (his face yellowish in death).

"He was my enemy," Mary-Johnny says over and over, rehearsing the defensive phrase for a higher court.

Enemies are as strong as God. We give them their strength because we cannot see them; the strength of the unknown, the unseen, the suspected. When we pray—when we pray in battle, we pray to our enemies as well as to God—"Miss us this time, spare us this time." Because we pray to them, they become God to us. When we kill them, when we find ourselves at the bottom of a hole with their dead body, we know it is God we have killed.

Such guilt cannot be supported. We become—we become— Yes. We become little unborn babies with our lives, with our emergence into life, before us. While we wait they call us crazy.

Mary awakens calling Johnny's name. Martha hurries into the

room, alarming the air through which she flounders. She turns on the lights and sits by Mary, soothing her.

"I thought you were dead to the world. I was at the window watching the flames when I heard you call out. It's that warehouse down the block—every fire engine in town must be down there. . . . You called out Johnny's name in your sleep."

When Mary does not answer, Martha finds in the room the vaguely general sense of guilt which has puzzled her by its elusiveness in the past several days, like the sun hidden by clouds, and focuses it upon herself.

"I was wrong to ask you to share my burden. I've been sleeping like a baby while you've had nightmares about the crazy people—the way I did before you came." She draws her shoulders up to their accustomed rigidity. "Well, girl, now I know. You'll not have to go back there again." She rises and straightens the sheet which her weight has creased, pulling it as tight as the line of her mouth. Mary's eyes blaze at her sister in triumph. Martha's obvious jealousy has taken from her the need to feel guilt. Martha reads Mary's silence as agreement and her sister's accusing eyes force her to a martyr's decision.

"I know you and your sense of duty. And I know you'll say it's not so to spare me." She goes to the doorway and turns, speaking with finality. "Mary, I'm going to call the hospital and tell them you're not to be allowed to see Johnny anymore. The least I can do is try to protect you, the way you've done me."

Martha leaves and Mary lies motionless, feeling in her own body the flames eating the warehouse. After a while she turns off the lamp and gets out of bed, groping her way toward the window. She stumbles over a chair and falls, striking her hands brutally, at a twisted angle, against the floor. She crouches there for a long time, listening for Martha, and the pain reaches from her hands up her arms to her breasts. When she is able, she gets up and sits in the chair. When dawn comes she dresses with difficulty, fumbling at buttons with the hands that swell the seams of her gloves. She goes into the hallway and sees that Martha has, for the first time, closed her door—overt proof of her sister's alienation through jealousy, suspicion, and resentment.

She waits in the cool outdoors as long as she can, walking the countrified streets that bound the hospital, and still it is only nine o'clock when she presents herself to the attendant behind the visitor's desk. Over the woman's demurral Mary says that yesterday Johnny had come close to a *major* divulgence; time, she says, feeling it to the tips of her swollen fingers, is of the utmost importance. The young doctor would never forgive her, would never forgive *anyone* who stood in the way. The emphasized word does the trick. Nor is there difficulty at the ward; the attendant who is Mary's enemy has not yet arrived.

Mary and Johnny have the visiting room to themselves.

"Your gloves are too tight," he says. "You've cut off circulation. Your arms are all red. Take your gloves off, Mary."

"No, Johnny. I can't."

"Do they hurt? Here, let me do it."

"No. Please."

"Aw," he says, reaching for her hands.

"No." She speaks sharply because the time for authority has come.

Mutely he holds out his hands, palms up, for her to put hers in. His expression makes it difficult for her to refuse. To safeguard herself she puts her hands behind her back, feeling a resultant throb in her heavy breasts. Her gesture—of hiding, of exaggerated reluctant refusal—stirs in Johnny a memory of flirtatious girls beside the town swimming pool, in parked cars, and he reacts now as he did then, with teasing, subdued excitement: grinning, eyes mischievous, he reaches around Mary and there is a little struggle before he brings her hands, imprisoned in his, to her lap. Acting on memory, he presses one of her hands down with his forearm and his fingers work at undoing the buttons of the glove on the other, a method he had once used to remove charm bracelets for the melancholy of reading engraved names not his own.

The pain he causes Mary is so excruciating that she gasps and bears down to keep for yelling. As he carefully turns the glove back from her throbbing flesh, she thinks clearly that their doctor should be here.

She feels the act to be the most intimate in which she has ever been involved. She feels it to be, all at the same time, violation, absolution, and genesis. She calls him, "My son," and he smiles, absorbed. It is, after all, easy; the pain she feels is only a token, a nod to the deeper pangs of deeper childbirth accomplished otherwise.

"What will we call you?" she says. "Help me find a good name."

His forehead is wrinkled with his effort not to hurt her.

"Glenn," he says.

"Oh," she murmurs, gazing with him at her bruised hands, swollen to the plumpness of youth. "I *like* that name. Glenn Lonergan. Yes. It has a lovely sound." He looks up at her, startled.

"Not Lonergan. It's Miller. Glenn Miller, the world-famous band leader." He claps a hand to his mouth, halfheartedly. She gives a little laugh, pushing inwardly at a feeling of claustrophobia.

"He's dead. He died in the war."

Johnny smiles at her, relieved and happy to be the bearer of such glad tidings. "Everybody thinks that—sure. I've let 'em think it. But, aw hell, I was getting tired anyway of nobody knowing who I was. They play my music every day in the mess hall and I just have to sit there like—like *anybody*. Like I was a dumb nobody. Like I was *before*." She tries to free her hands but he holds on, pressing them, sharing with her his triumph. "They don't know about the new clothes, see—just about the overcoats. They don't know about the tuxedos and the silk shirts and socks and five-dollar ties. And—listen!" He leans forward until his mouth is touching her ear. Softly, with the uncanny sound of a muted trombone, he plays for her "In the Mood." At the second chorus he stands up and pulls her into his arms. As they dance among the chairs and tables, he sings, " 'Mister Whatcha-callit, whatcha doing tonight, Hope you're in the mood because I'm feeling just right—' " Her feet follow his, never stumbling, until she grows tired of the lewdness of being held so closely by a stranger. During the war she had tried helping out at the USO in Anaheim, hoping to find a young man, an orphan, who would want what she had to offer, but her young face and body served her ill; she was forever being dragged onto the dance floor, and pawed, and sung to in just this fashion. That was why she had stopped going there, to the USO.

She pushes Glenn Miller aside, seeing from the corner of her eyes that they are being watched from the doorway. "Fool," she says, intending mere reprimand, but she is shaken by a terrible fury at the shapes of injustice crowding in upon her and she beats at the stranger with the flats of her hands, shouting words that she has only read before on dark walls.

The strange young man whom she is striking cries "Ma"; the wall of her madness is pierced by his need, and a needle point of hope before the young man runs to a disheveled weeping woman in the doorway and the hole in the wall seals over. She is left no fleck of irony to let her identify the sounds the attendant is making, as he walks slowly toward her, as those grown-ups make to soothe babies.

CITY SUNDAYS

Third Avenue looked clean as though somebody had washed all the storefronts and windows and scrubbed down the gutters in the night. Well, he said, this is preposterous, and examined the miracle and saw that the cleanness came from the light, which told him that it had to be, definitely, a satisfactory day. He breathed with some lessening of caution. Generally, as any New Yorker could tell you, Sunday mornings tended anyhow to look cleaner than other days because of a dearth of traffic, vehicular and human, and as this was an early Sunday morning with decent air, the combination of light and space put the shabbiness into a lower-than-usual profile.

In part, his days were spent assessing such phenomena, and in New York there were a lot of them: abrupt light changes, atmospheric shifts, both physical and psychical, and sometimes tremendous emotional effluences that affected blocks of people at a time, causing them to walk faster so that they looked like characters in a speeded-up film. The sense of well-being that could cause people to stroll and look really casual seemed to be confined to warm afternoons of brilliant sun and was rare in Eastern American cities he had visited.

He looked in windows at the junk: moldy furs, sagging rattan, tables and chairs that were as dejected, probably, as the people who had discarded them or had had to sell them for a few cents. An ornate birdcage in mint condition looked like a biological

sport in a degenerate family, the bright one who was also com-
pulsively clean.

Next door to the antique shop he saw a sign: Duck eggs, Irish
bacon and sausage. He passed the shop, then backed up. It seemed
like a good place to begin. As usual, the impulse came as a surprise.

The shop was cozy and dark with good smells. The proprietor, whom nobody would mistake for a mere clerk, was in his
sixties and when he came forward it was with a manner easily
described as courtly. He spoke in a rich rolling brogue. The cus-
tomer, who had decided on the name Jamie O'Donnell, responded in kind, speaking of the bright weather, the cold that
was not objectionable, interspersing the give-and-take with re-
quests for double-yolk duck eggs, Irish sausage, Irish soda bread.
He admitted that he would give a lot for a decent cup of Irish
tea, though he knew that it was impossible to achieve with New
York water. The proprietor told James that he had known, the
minute he saw the lad walk in the door, that he was Irish through
and through. And, he said emphatically, a gentleman to boot,
rare enough in these upper reaches, though his customers, the
Lord knew, were a good lot, by and large, for he had never been
robbed and seldom insulted. The element, however, was moving
down, as though to bear him out one of the element came in and
was asked to wait, if she didn't mind, while he finished convers-
ing with a relative new to the country, this said with a disarming
wink. But Jamie O'Donnell now felt some constraint and soon
enough he bid the proprietor good morning, saying he was sure
to return for he had found, so to speak, a home away from home.

He bought a paper, went home and breakfasted well, sharing
with his dog bits of soda bread dipped in sausage dripping. The
duck eggs were rich and gamy, like the old man's brogue, so that
talking to his dog he retained the lilt that had fallen so easily
onto his tongue from the air of the dark friendly little store.

He had meant to stay at home and work on his papers but just
after midmorning clouds rolled in from the west on a sharp wind
and the tone of the day altered drastically, making him restless.
He changed his tweed suit for something more amorphous,
wound on a drab scarf, and took a hat from the closet shelf that

contained, among other headgear, a tam-o'-shanter and a stocking cap and a ten-gallon Texas job that he had worn only once. He recalled with affection the dejected little chili joint where he had worn it. The hat he chose was dark felt with a versatile brim, which with no more than a flick of the finger could be made to reflect many an obscure longing.

Riding a bus, he did not know where he was headed other than downtown, until something informed him that he had arrived. He walked there with a stiffer gait, setting his chin down among the folds of the scarf and squaring off the hat brim. Stopping to gaze abstractedly into a window, when he was addressed through the cracked-open door he responded with no thought in the accents of the addressor and the two of them fell into a cautious and oblique exchange. Despite the indirection of the early colloquy there was emotion of a subtle nature, a bond of longing difficult to express. Chaim brought a younger viewpoint into the discussion and with it, hope, which lightened the atmosphere and sent the price of an Israeli paperweight down by fifty cents. When he left, the pressure of their hands contained a secret that only flesh could share with flesh. Words were murmured in an old language. Chaim did not promise to return but his face glowed in a way that made it implicit. Still, when he turned outside the shop for a last look, something in the way his friend stood with hands clasping his belly brought tears that ran down Chaim's cheeks. Another time he would have pantomimed the needlelike wind as the cause of the tears, and laughing would have shown apologetic palms.

Walking on, he felt as though nothing could console him, but like the sun emerging and striking him an admonitory blow on the ears he heard a spate of raucous language, coarse and revitalizing, and his hands flew up and gave the scarf a toss, rearranged the hat brim, turning it up fore and aft, and did something to his coat to give it a swagger. He thought that he had never been so hungry in his life as he headed into a shop that reeked with cheeses and herbs, salamis and olives. Like a kid's his eyes grew round. "Ahhhhh. *Va bene!*" Vincenzo ate, drank wine, boasted of his town, Melilli, and the women therein.

He went down into the subway with high spirits and a warmed

belly. It was twilight and his fine patient dog would be waiting for supper and a walk. Returning to his dog was always a pleasure keen enough to override most sudden depressions, which could strike him with great force when he was off guard, always at the close of such a day. And it had been an especially good day, one he would relive, he imagined, more often than others that gave him similar sustenance in the dark hours, augmenting the sane, warm presence of his dog by his side.

And yet, for a time, observing the riders whose lives he could never enter because of the accidents of fate that determined that some skins and hair should be beyond the competence of his mimicry, which was in truth assimilation, he felt lonely and deprived, though he tried to avoid the self-pity in that word and condition. Some would call what he felt "unaccountably sad." But those doubters were not city people, no matter where they lived, and knew nothing of a city's longings and possibilities, and the ineffability, for the believers, of its fulfillments.

THE SILVER SWANNE

The Silver Swanne who living had no Note
When Death approcht, unlockt her silent throat.
Leaning her breast against the reedie shore,
Thus sang her first and last, and sung no more;
Farewell all joyes, O death come close mine eyes,
More Geese than Swannes now live,
more fooles than wise.
—Seventeenth century anonymous

November the First, 1770

On Robert Vilet's sixteenth day in possession of the house there was explicated by the occupant of the neighboring farm the small but engaging mystery of why the house, long fallen into insuetude on its high seacliff, should have been called The Toll House. The old name was in fact The Tall House, which was assuredly, Vilet concurred, descriptive; when seen from the rocky beach below its several stories seemed immensely exaggerated; beneath its steeply pitched roof a lonely wanderer or spyer from a distant vessel could imagine conventicles of heretics thither drawn for the proximate escape route, in dire emergency, of the open sea; and its single spire, which contained a bell often restless when the wind sat in the Western board, muttering to itself like a great fettered creature, commanded the countryside.

Thus the small mystery lay solely in the pronunciation of the natives, which made of "water," "woder," and of "tall," it was apparent, "toll." Attending to his explanator with, as it were, new ears (the explanation of the name of the house was accom-

panied by gestures as if the man spoke to an idiot; "toll" he kept
repeating to Vilet, measuring from the ground greater and greater
distances, which Vilet, at first, took to be illustrative of the stacks
of money taken in at the toll house!), Vilet saw that he had not
understood a great deal of what had been said to him since his
arrival two weeks since, and settled another mystery with the
same linguistic yardstick, to his entire satisfaction.

When upon that first evening Mrs. Wince left him with the
instruction that "the bodder" was in the pantry, he imagined
that she referred to butter and was exceedingly annoyed when
he could not find it. Unwilling to sup without butter for his bread,
he made a thorough search of the house, convinced that the daft
woman could as easily have left butter, and churn as well, in the
spire under the bell. He found the coolly sweating crock at last
in an icy room, a subcellar through which water rapidly and deeply
coursed, a monstrously individual springhouse with labyrinths
radiating long fluvial veins of impenetrable murk beneath the
house and away, whence came the sighing sounds. This chthon-
ian temple, the pantry? Yet he supposed that it might be the
custom of the country to refer to the above stairs pantry as the
spence; or, given the cathedral-like aspect of the mansion, the
ambry!

On the following morning, searching the pantry (or spence or
ambry) for bacon for his breakfast (Mrs. Wince was to "do" for
him but two days in the week, to her perplexity, for which he
could offer no mitigant), he found a covered basin and in it a
mixture that smelt and tasted sweet with freshness; and upon
frying a bit of it he found that the good Mrs. Wince had left for
him the "makings," not of a seegar but of an excellent German
pancake, for in another basin by its side there was a well-sea-
soned decoction of apples and spices, a mellow "filling" for his
thin "pfannkuchen." By using the, as it were, linguistic yardstick,
he saw that what he had found was the "bodder" (batter) for
which he had been told to look in the *pondry!* But, he assured
himself, "pondry" had been translated smoothly and uncon-
sciously by his brain, for associative reasons: where else would
one find butter but in the pantry &c (the exception of his own
case nothwithstanding). The casualness of her reference—note,

he reminded himself, the "the"—aided his deduction, since proved blameless, that the apple pancake was "the" breakfast of this region.

He was sorry to let go the image of The Toll House functioning—as he had dreamed of it in early reveries—as a through station for drowned seafarers, wherein, consequent to payment of the proper toll in doubloons, they received tuition in haunting, and in dressing their garments in festoons of seaweed and shells; and, for those of more dramatic bent, inculcation in how impeccably to wear a slain albatross.

When he returned from his enlightening visit to the neighboring farm and entered the long tunnel of trees leading to Tall House (as he was determined to call it henceforth, omitting the extraneous article; there was no other like it), that tunnel so perfectly arched that one could discern in the interlocking branches far above the occult corbelling of lateral growth, his mare shied and danced down the dark aisle (which the romantic would be tempted to term "cryptlike") as though at some ferine presence, and in the distance he could hear the wild yapping of his terrier, penned in futile rage within the courtyard, for he had closed upon her the great solid gates, refusing, as punishment for an earlier prolonged absence, the romping cross-country jaunt for which she had guilefully pled.

Something, then, or a group or series of somethings, perhaps, had laid a trail of ferity that led from his terrier to his new quiet mare. Chin sunk in hand, surveying the twilight of the avenue before him, he mused that only he, least graced of the three known creatures momentarily concerned, could sense nothing with his inadequate nose, nor detect with his, in comparison, scarcely sufficient hearing, nor see with his truncated vision, aught of the alien presence. As though in mental concert with him, his mare pricked up her ears, then set them forward. In the distance, his terrier ceased her warning as abruptly as nightfall. Then, from the tenebrific shadows of tree boles cast before him under the falx moon, there stepped forth a young doe, the constellated marks of her youth agleam, as though preternaturally illumined.

November the Second, 1840

In reading over the beginning of my intended modern ghost story, set down just as I had envisaged it in the course of my white night, too weary to light a lamp and work for a while at my desk, but making mnemonic connections as elaborate as any I had yet devised so that no implication should be lost by morning, it occurs to me to question myself thusly: Am I belaborous on the subject (bodder, butter) of false comprehension? Yet I think I can be no less, and still expect the reader to receive the strong suggestion, at the onset, that the narrator is capable of, through a dreamy and curiously inattentive nature (of which he is partly aware, thus his dissertation that ends the section, concerning faulty senses)—that the narrator is capable of perceiving the truth while imagining he perceives another thing: in his search for the butter he stumbles on what should have been the object of the search, the batter. Perhaps a supernatural gift.

Well, of course these details can be altered as my own perception grows, of just what it is I wish to say, as it were, subliminally. I am amazed enough at this urge to write something so counter to my planned work: a ghost story, rather than the intended speculation, or extension upon the probable lies of his son, Sebastian, on John Cabot, like myself a transplanted Venetian. But the house does, as houses will, newly inhabited and mysteriously compelling, draw me to speculate upon *it,* and get to "know" it psychically; to decipher as well as I can the runes of its past, which, for all my supposed literary invention, may well be presented to me in some literalness. For example, the image and word "conventicle": in my two weeks of musings it had not once occurred to me to give the house any sort of religious, heretical or otherwise, connotation, and assuredly not of something I am so totally unversed in as the Protestantism of the past two centuries. Any yet there were both word and impression, springing, as one with the new fancy of the belled spire, like a cat out of the dark.

The cat. Occult occurrence number one, riding on the heels

of my invention of the doe. When I walked by Daisikins, the
autumnal sea yet calm below the cliff, whitely glowing as though
under a fine veil of snow, there appeared a cat. Perhaps an apparition, for Daisikins shied not, neither did she spin; her rum-
inative piss was accomplished at leisure, the while her eyes calmly
followed the cliff-stalking creature. And I thought: She believes
I cannot see it! And I wondered, not for the first time in this
place how much she sees that I do not, that with inaction she
shields me from, and if that is why she does not bound after the
imagined phantom. If, I say, "imagined," it is, for it seemed, like
the sea, to be whitely veiled, a bride-puss, the Tom dead or abandoning (how else?), trailing the tatters of her tragedy along my
cliff. More practically, if real, it had best be female, or, as my
erstwhile companions would have it, no dice. (To you, *gentlemen*,
maileçon, maileçon, may the Lady of Heaven forgive me!)

Then, observing my quiet bitch I saw that she too wore the
pale cerements and then that I myself was sepulchrally whited,
made false by the light's dissimulation which fell from no moon.
No, the sea itself engendered the rare glow, throwing at the high
cliff, as I gazed awestruck, the luminous phosphorical tide.

It was then, not an hour since, that I dredged from my memory, as a blind man may be caused to recall stars seen in sighted
babyhood, a similar sea, above which I lay secure in strong arms,
which I believe I felt as loving, and received instruction in the
numinal, spread out below: of organisms as countless as the stars,
rising to feed at the sea's surface, casting their light upon, for
the rare time, those fortunate watchers in the night. (Even here,
in this supreme privacy, of the first betrayer I can set down only
one word: father; and only within the walls of these parentheses.)

That was a Southern sea, a jasmine-scented summertime. I
must ask Mrs. Wince or my neighbor if this occurrence is not
recherché indeed in these chilly waters, nearly two months past
the autumnal equinox.

Now out with my candle to essay if, through wide windows
uncurtained, the phosphorus plankton may light the mound of
featherbed wherein Daisikins and I sleep in oft-submerged sy-
bariticness. The size of the bed, of this chamber, for two small

creatures! But more of the house anon, now that I have again taken pen in hand.

Nota bene: It is my conviction that Tall House, in my story, is a perfect name for the reality, and thus by candlelight and blissfully sleepy, I so Christian it, and let fact and fancy for once intertwine, sanctioned lovers in our littoral white night.

November, 1980

He is unsure of the date, not having left the place for over a week. Doorman ringing up, impertinent, asking if everything is o.k. No real concern, just thinking about tip time coming up. He asks the doorman if anybody has been looking for him and the doorman pauses, always that portentous pause, then says, "The Puerto Rican gentleman was here" pause "again." He thanks him for turning the Spic away, advises him to keep it up, voice hinting of bread to come. He thinks, timing, timing, balance, balance, thinks those words should have been tattooed on him at birth, as the tapping begins again. Thinks somebody should have castrated him at birth, thinks somebody should have left off piggy ruttishness for one night just one, and what was conceived another time even five minutes later would not have been him. And the tapping on the terrace door. A bird. A gull as far as he can tell. Tapping with her blunt beak, he can only see the head so she must be short. An hour ago when she first began that sly tapping he thought coolly that she was probably Death and wanted to let her in, let her beat somebody else to the game, but asked, How would a gull kill a man? and answered, Stab him with her beak. And she flies away or is gone, he thinks he sees her large-winged, amazingly white in the upspill of light from twenty-five floors below, flying over a street too quiet for the city at ten o'clock at night. Where, he asks himself, are the Spics and their bongos, where are the Wops and their voices, where are the Black ladies and gents of the night with transistors implanted in their chests? He is convinced these night-colored are given three implant operations in their lives: at birth, a mini-Sony; at puberty, a Panasonic Portable AM/FM Radio with Doze Control Alarm (for when they nod off); and on their eighteenth birthdays, a fucking BIG New World Monitor II with double superheterodyne circuit filters, bright digital frequency display showing frequencies to five digits, SW calibrater and RF control to minimize station drift, voltage switches for 120 and 220V use. Also picks up ham and CB bands. Mix playback, built-in condenser mike and all the volume of Gabriel's trumpet. Poem: Gabriel comes/he blows/nobody hears/over the radios. He also thinks, That gull is desperate for something and wishes she would go oh go away. Can she be calling him to come with her to the sea, or just down twenty-five floors to the street?

November the First, 1770

Vilet and the doe regarded each other. He believed that what he saw in her eyes was true intelligence of him and this occasioned him a moment of fright, for the notion of being inwardly perceived by a beast was against nature. And yet had not the beasts perceived the Divinity of Christ? A marvel of the descending gloom, in which now intermingled long fingers of brumous exhalation from the quickly chilling earth, was that Vilet thought he could divine around the doe the outlines of a crèche. If she had knelt at that moment and faced upward toward the moon and its attendant star he would not have felt an atom of his earlier fright at the thought of bestial perception. He thought humbly that the arms of the Church formed a crucible within which the Philosopher's Stone of Belief transformed all things.

And then as quickly as all had come to him—the doe, and the perception of the machinery of Grace, which worked as well on her behalf as on that of any mortal transgressor—all fled, the goodness of all fled, and where he had half-seen the arms of the crèche-church, he now saw the larder, the game-room of Tall House, and upon its rough table lay the doe, blood cold and dried among the constellations of her youngness, and golden fur half-flayed from her. Above her from the beams there hung the carcasses of all manner of her kin, from huge-eyed hare neatly slain to boar with near-severed head and long tusks dark red

with congealed gore. Beside her from hooks in walls was suspended a choir of pheasant, quail, snipe, doves. This, this, the
doe seemed to be piteously telling him, will be my fate. This is
why some of us are born, to welter in blood!

While the vision yet lingered, Vilet slid down from his mare
with a sense of immense weakness, as though he had witnessed
all of mortality after its sacrifice. He leaned against the flank of
his mare, his intention to advance, when he could, quietly and
with calm assurance, to the doe and lay his hand upon her. It
would be an act of triple intention, for he would with the gesture
claim her, soothe her, and ascertain for himself that she was not
a phantom. He had been inwardly informed that his hand upon
her would make her his. He did not wish to linger too long out
of her sight, taking strength from his mare's warm flank, lest the
doe believe that he plotted against her. With steady step and
gentle hand at the ready he walked around his mare and found
that the doe had gone.

Given a moment for recovery he tried out his laugh, perceiving that he had in some wise been made a fool of, and said to
himself, "Inwardly informed, indeed" and laughed again, then
sprang upon his mare enjoining her to gallop with him. They
flew up the avenue, his laughter ringing out, a hammer for the
night's frosty anvil, and his distant caged terrier, hearing his voice,
resumed her riotous barking.

The terrier had been given the name of Marguerite, for her
resemblance to the meadow flower, the aureole of silvery fur
about her small bright face, and the sprightly way she sprang
from the earth. He flung open the doors of her cage, amused at
the image of so large a cage for so small a creature, and he and
Marguerite effected under the falcial moon a touching reunion.
Together they tended the worthy mare, Marguerite sniffing the
careful hooves for their savor of the great world which, for her
naughtiness, had been denied her.

Grooming his mare, Vilet mused on punishment, questioning
himself as to the efficacy of retribution levied upon creatures
whose comprehension does not include such a conceit. The satisfaction, morbid at times, of having "punished" his animals was
his alone: Marguerite would run away again, knowing only *run*

and not *away*. His mare would shy again and throw him if he lacked tenacity. And would he lash her, or withhold her mash, or vindictively run her into a lather? Those were human techniques, the lathering, the lashing, the starving, to be used against other humans; men withheld and punished passions, the desire and the gratification; the only allowable passion being the love of God. And what was Marguerite's desire to run and explore and smell and chase save an holy and innocent ardor? She had asked him, pled with him, turning upon him the while her immense charm, to go *with* her; she had asked for them to be together, opposite to his experience of the world of men, of humanity. In that world the final laugh, if one sought vengeful laughter, was in the growth of "human" from "humane," an example of utter reverse; of linguistic apostasy.

Vilet detested himself for the inferences of his attempt to explicate the interchange and reciprocity of humans and beasts, and concluding his ministrations to his mare, having watered and fed her with unwonted and yearning tenderness—for her sister, the doe, clung delicately to his mind—he whistled to Marguerite, whose feistiness, it occurred to him, had not been in evidence around the stall for some time. He expected her to come bounding to his sharp whistle from her nap in a corner where she recuperated from her excess in trying to scale the walls of the courtyard in his absence. Instead, from without, she made an answer, a small, quivering, questioning whimper. He found her standing in the stableyard, her usually curly undocked tail at half-mast.

But she could not tell him what of the night had touched that chord within her and he smiled grimly to discover, upon rehearing in his mind the sound she had made, that it was remarkably like certain sounds of which the human voice is capable when caught upon a throe of sensual passion, the flesh impaled, bleeding as upon a thorn. For her, please God, not the hell of consequence.

Sacrificing the walk upon the seacliff he had promised her, he caught Marguerite up in his embrace and carried her through the looming doors of Tall House. Pausing only to light a candle, and in each room and echoing corridor to set alight the tapers in sconce and candelabrum, to banish the double gloom of night and night thoughts, he hurried through the labyrinth of stone-floored hallways and came at last to the larder. The heavy oaken door stuck and in tugging at it, and in its sudden giving way, a wind was raised which extinguished his candle. He entered in a darkness that slowly gave way to an eerie illumination from without. As far as Vilet could see, the landscape beyond the room was deep in snow. The larder was low and square, and a large low heavy-paned window lay above the thick table on which, at last cursory inspection, a hare or two had lain, with a brace of woodcock hung above. But something larger now was thrown upon the table. His heart came with a mighty jump into his throat even as the object stirred, and rose to its forelegs, in silhouette against the snowy landscape. He felt that he would swoon so deeply that a thanatometer could not attest to his life, while his soul curled from his body, prone across the gory table, and mingled with hers. Even as his vision sought to fail him, or provide surcease, he saw that the creature, now on its feet, stood *beyond* the window, quartered by the sashing and panes. She had made her couch upon a bank of earth that came to the window's ledge, its purpose being insulation of the death chambers. The doe, whitely lighted in the illusory snow, which, he now esteemed, was a combination of moon and starlight and frost-rime, had chosen to lie at the very gates of her destiny; had willfully made her abode within sight of the corpses from her kingdom.

Vilet lost control of himself and cried out to her, through the thick atmosphere redolent of blood, "What is the *import* of this?" Her eyes shone at him like those of a creature beatified. She appeared radiant with holy perception, all discernible in the rays from her eyes.

With Marguerite at his heels he retraced his steps to the courtyard. Within him the double vision, of abomination and resurrection, dwelled *pari passu;* and in the courtyard he perceived that what he had assumed to be stalks of burdock growing in the flagging's interstices was in truth passion-dock, withered witness that Tall House was or had been a Christian castle. Faith lay like a coal in his breast as he opened the gates and set them ajar for the visitation.

November the Third, 1840

I am exceedingly annoyed with myself for having allowed Vilet to indulge in misanthropy. This is not, I repeat is not, an auto-biography. The point, I presume, having no other, and still amazed at the urge to go against my very reason for letting this house, namely, to write the dissertation on Cabot—the point, as I say, to indulging *myself* in imagined pursuit of eidolons would seem to have been escape from such thoughts as Vilet has al-lowed himself, despite me, to express. In point of fact, I began today's "chronical" in a bad mood, having discovered, in reread-ing what I had found of yesterday worthy of chronicling, that I had used, for my housekeeper's name, the fictional "Mrs. Wince." This would hint at a lack of control which I must emphatically and in haste counter with all at my command. My physicians proclaimed me cured, and I will have none of relapses.

As though to calm me, Daisikins has lately stood beside my leg, inviting me with smiles and an enchanting bow, forelegs ex-tended, paws crossed, for all the world like the greeting of some Eastern personage, to accompany her on another spectral walk (we have returned only a moment since, the walk cut short so that I might come and vent my growing displeasure in these pages). No, my dearest companion, I must refuse you. I had promised myself that this night and no later I would set down, or begin to set down, for the record of my life and time, my "chronical" as indeed it is, the situation of this house as opposed (or coincident) to the fictional Tall House, and the circum-stances, such as can be told, of my presence here.

The house is large; indeed, one must say, quite large, and as square as a Grecian temple, which it much resembles from the sea, whence I obtained my first (and fatal) long gliding look, putting, as I did, into the next port, which happened to be the village that this house once held in feudality. To the rear there is another flavor, of gables, and wings, and courts, all contained within a sheath as solid as rock and oak and iron-clenching, and the most massive of window glass, can render it. Twenty sweeps could stand with room to spare in any of the fireplaces, and all together be hoist up the flues to the roof, on which there stands, not the belled spire of my invention, but another flat square structure, columned about its periphery, with, on its roof, a Curiosity: a large, concave rusting dishlike thing of which I can make neither head nor tail.

In the square building, amiably furnished with windows, reached interiorly by a modest concealed staircase, the same twenty sweeps plus twenty more, horrid thought, could find comfortable quarters, each with a chamber (quickly fetid) of his own. In vain have I asked Mrs. Wince to. Dammit. And to hell. In vain have I asked of Mrs. Hubbard the story of this dishlike apparatus. She retreats behind her uncomprehension based upon language, or some such. When I put the same question to my neighbor (who fictionally advised Vilet on the subject of his house's name), the man gave me one of those looks which are a feature of all the resiants of this country, looks compounded of insolence and idiotic blankness. Well, I care not what the foolish builder thought he had placed upon the roof; I shall call it "The Dish" and have done with the dammed thing.

I have just spoken, and now I write, "I am sorry." This apology is tendered to the house, my shelter, castle, great and beautiful carapace. I apologize for the misplaced tone of anger, aimed at the ugliness of the encroaching world which may edge up to but not break through our stout barriers. As I wrote so hatefully it seemed to me that I heard a note like a whimper, and it was the house's voice, the sound of something in want, something wounded. It is thus, if houses could feel, that it should have expressed its woundedness. For when I came here, as though in response to a call, it was in the barest nick of time, for plans were being set in motion to raze to the ground this ancient bulwark, this temple, with its splendid wide corridors of sane proportions, its terra cotta and marble floors, its carved lintels, soaring ceilings, deep embrasures, curve and sweep of staircases, of which I have found a dozen and suspect, from certain symmetries traceable on the outside, that there may be a dozen more. There is one particularly lovely oriel window that overhangs some interior court, which, from its placement, denotes that it faces inward upon yet another stair; but I have not discovered it within the house. This has troubled me obscurely as though some interior beauty of my own were made inaccessible to me. But tonight as I walked in the Park there was a light behind that window. As a matter of course, one must state that one knows there was no light there, that the illumination came from without, some lingering upward-bent terrestrial ray, for the window's prospect is of the Park, the woodland. Yet, the illusion was breathtaking and shamefully comforting, for I allowed myself to imagine that there was someone waiting for me. And now of this, no more.

Today Mrs. Hubbard came fetching things from the village shops to see me through another three days, driving her own dogcart, and I, observing that she was somewhat downcast, questioned her. It appears that she is subject to fearful attacks of "lumbogo" when the wind lies in the Eastern board, whence it could continue to blow, she assured me gloomily, with a kind of rude poetry, "til stroms post the winter solstiz destroys the alcyons' nests." Could she, she inquired, hands clasped in prayer, if the pain got "torrible" bad, send another to stand for her until she recovered? With some indifference, wanting for her a feeling of warmth, I told her that she could. In her relief, she promised for my luncheon on the morrow a "brod bird," by which I assume she means "brad," or roast. (This usage is no more odd in her than her word for sleep; when she leaves me after dark she wishes that I may "sloff good," thus there would appear to be Germanic roots in these peasants. Though how she comes by "bertie" to mean "pretty" I cannot surmise. But often the effort to comprehend her speech is like the attempt to read unknown characters carved on a rough stone!)

Returning to the matter of a substitute in case of her illness she tells me that "in foct" one of her sister's own, a "load," could do for me splendid and perhaps be more to my liking than she! At which she gave the first sound of laughter I have ever heard from her goiterous throat. I nodded my permission to having a "load," which I assume is a localism for hard worker, take her place.

As she was quitting the room I felt a great curiosity to know how the majority of the villagers earned subsistence. Though I had scarcely gone abroad, only to the neighboring farm, and planned no excursions for the future, I had seen enough to know that the farmlands were sparse, and the village hardly teeming with commerce. Thus I questioned her: "How is it that the villagers in the main employ themselves, or how are they employed, especially in the cold months?"—the latter phrase lending it the tone of an anthropological enquiry. I had not expected, following her laughter, yet more levity. But her response was "Grumbling," and when *I* laughed, it came her turn to throw me a glance of noncomprehension. Perhaps on account of this, I asked her, with mischievous loftiness, if she knew of "a cat deswarré," and gave a sea-lit description of the creature. Her response exasperated me further: she looked dazed, as though I had struck her! But in a while she said, "Thot cot is ombsus." I asked if that was its name; she repeated, "Ombsus, ombsus" and took her leave.

And to bed, having spun out too long for my patience the tale of Mrs. Whatever. The story of my affliction must wait but I repeat that I am cured, healed, entire. Hallucination is once more only a literary device to be used when I play, cat and mouse, with Vilet and his doe. And to bed. No phosphorus this night. It is black and deep beyond the casement, which I have cracked to the night, the crack to widen, once my light is doused, to let in the still tolerable air. Now bearing a current into my room of, can it be, jasmine. Jasmine! A southern scent! A current blown in high warm air all the way from Italy to my chamber. I could bathe in it. I could weep for joy.

November, 1980

No gull. Swan. He says, swan. On the terrace. He calls the SPCS (Society for Prevention of Cruelty to Swans) who advise him to call AA. He is having a drink instead. A swan.

November the Third, 1770

Vilet slept scarcely at all the night of November the third, seventeen hundred and seventy. He had chosen for his bedchamber one to the rear of the mansion, with a prospect of the Park. Mrs. Wince had advised him on the day of his arrival of the quarter of the prevailing wind, and further stated that those chambers fronting on the sea were nigh impossible to heat, for all the capaciousness of hearth and excellence of flue. She had chattered on and on, quite like a scold, as though it would be difficult to persuade him to house himself to the leeward, and yet that somehow, for the good of humanity, it must be done! He had seen the samphire growing on the rocks and wondered if she were one of those whose "dreadfull trade" it was to gather the herb.

For appearance's sake, for the seaward outlook was majestic, he feigned doubt as to her wisdom and then allowed himself to be persuaded, to her, he thought, imcomprehensible relief; though he had other and more than sufficient reason to prefer the quiet Park with its crescent of gleaming birches holding back the dark woodland.

Lying sleepless in the silent frosty night, he tried with his mind to coax the doe into the aegis of the Courtyard, which, he promised her, would be, from the first fall of her hooves therein, her own domain; which, with balsam branches and bales of fodder and the berries of the wood, he would make luxurious for her, giving to its appurtenancing a tenth of his time. The moonlight fell across his bed in a configuration that lacked stability as though figures moved within its rays, as inconstant as firelight or a restless sea; as though, indeed, branches, waving, intercepted its beams, although no tree grew nearer to his casement than the woodland, some two hundred yards distant. Helpless in a vise of some sort, he was caused to speculate that the fluctuation thrown upon his counterpane was a satanic projection of his inward turmoil concerning the doe; that it was the *process of the distillation of his passion* that he was forced to witness.

November the Fourth, 1840

Slept tolerably well, though the waves of jasmine brought me to the edge of melancholia; I awoke gibbering, "More wind for the miller!" having dreamt, I suppose, guiltily, of the dispersal of some of the heavy scent. I must question Mrs. Wince as to the possible source of this phenomenon. My skin exuded jasmine until I gave myself a good scrub, feeling in the process somehow disloyal. It was as though in the night, in some version of enfleurage, I had myself become the source of the odor, and that, seeking to rid myself of it, I was seeking to rid myself of *myself*.

Here a curiosity must be recorded. I lay in the waves of jasmine and at last fell asleep, or nearly, but could not quite cross the last threshold, for, though I was covered, wrapt, coddled, swathed, and all but smothered in featherbeds, my lower left extremity was like to have froze, and from the leadenness of its weight there occurred at length the following: Daisikin's grumbles could not stay me and I arose, stuck a light, took a lamp, and proceeded, as it were, at the direction of Something. In fine, I wandered, eventually coming into a chamber I had not yet visited, and there found that the window stood wide, so that a rime of frost had begun to form upon the sill and would, but for my intervention, have seized upon the bed curtain, which, blowing, had caught upon that sill. I made the window fast and only upon returning here and snuggling with my welcoming friend, did it occur to me that, if the bed had had an occupant, that creature would have been cold in the lower left extremity, for it was in that quarter that the curtain was rucked up, allowing the current of frigid air entry at that point! Now it is my fancy, conceived as I write the very words, that the chamber itself, in the symmetry of the house, corresponds to the lower left extremity of the human mansion. But this is once again the hour of fantasy, not of fact.

And having written those words I must pause to ask: roses? For the current which last night brought jasmine to my room tonight bears roses. And yet my window is fastened.

But to Whatever, or to Whomever: I will not question you, but thank you for your beneficence: for the gift restored.

This house, this mansion, contains some fifty rooms distributed among its principal three floors (thought this is hearsay, as I have neither viewed them nor counted those I have viewed), and that number does not include those that form, on the roof, the pedestal for The Dish. Let us say that those may number as many as thirty; therefore we are embedded, Daisikins and I, roughly, like raisins in a pudding, somewhere near the center of seventy-five or so chambers. I am told of wondrous apartments in the East Wing, which held Royalty and its entourage, and which, foolishly, in response to some inner directive of the kind that once had the power to frighten me (and others), my mind compares to *youth,* as though the Stages of Man might be contained in other wings, the house comprising the record of a lifetime. There is also a planetarium (I believe Mrs. Wince said there was; for all her dark voweling I believed myself to have extracted that word; though, for all of me, she could have said "*san*itarium," or "sonitorium"). There is said to be a great bath somewhere, a Roman extravagance of colonnades and whirlpools and waterfalls at the command of concealed levers. There is the extravagant count of seventy fountains hid within the hide of this manse! For myself, I have found a library of genuine distinction, and the mausoleum—but no, I have promised that I would not jest about this wondrous asylum, so recently endangered. To consider such a splendor no more! equivalent to the destruction of the world's Seven Wonders. My feeble half-jest was only a reference to the vastness of the bedchamber I share with Psyche, my soul, my Daisikins. We two are like segments of a circle. *Arco non è altro che una fortezza. cavsata da due debolezze, jpero chè l'arco negli edifiti è cōposto di 2 quarti. di circulo, i quali quarti circuli, ciascuno debolissimo per se, desiderā cadere, e opponē dosi alla ruina l'uno dell'altro de' due debolezze, si cōvertono in vni ca fortezza.*

A humble and vincible ignorance led me to omit that we are but segments, which, with *the house's* vast arc, comprise a secure and stormproof edifice.

And now it is as though the arc were spanning the centuries, audibly, the sound of its flight like riffled leaves of immense volumes on architecture; and falling from the leaves with measured beat, the sound of pebbles dropping to mark the Roman mile; pebbles to measure the retreat of treachery, punitive Syracusan pebbles!, medicine for the cat if, in her sea-lit boots, she continues (I hear her voice now, yowling upon the cliffs) to measure the way Daisikins and I are protected within our localumentum. I am warmed and chilled, exalted and afraid. Roses, celestial music, the machinery of time! What would become of me, if the author of my fortunes were to desert me now?

November, 1980

Effort to forget the waiting putting his nerves on edge. As pent up in here as that swan sitting on the terrace. If she had a way to get down wouldn't she go? Does he feed her? He watches her through the door and sees that she weaves her long neck back and forth, and thinks pretentiously, Like Penelope's shuttle. But the swan is waiting too. He wonders all of a sudden what she would do if he, the author of her fate, should just vanish, if God should just go. He tells himself that they used to be concerned about all the crap but no more. God, that hot idea in a terminally cool world.

That swan. When death approcht unlockt her silent throat. Death. He'd better feed her. What do swans eat? Does he give her a name? Why not Margharita? His mother's name.

To pass the time he is beginning to scribble, taking refuge in another century.

Note: Look up "feisty." May not belong to 19th Cent.

November the Third, 1770

Images of passion, coming as they did to Vilet, caused him, in terror, to snatch up into his arms the symbol of his purity, his little Marguerite, and fly sans light save that of the moon, inconstant within as without, for not all windows showed her in pursuit and though the night was cloudless she would not appear. Then as suddenly, as stealthily, she would resume the casting of her bizarities upon the floors, that in their patterns resembled rune staves, and as Vilet could not pause and read, nor read if he paused, it seemed as though whisperers in the arras interpreted for him. He came to a windowless passage, an abrupt claustral blackness, but though afraid, he did not slacken his pace; and underneath the soles of his bare feet he felt moss, and among the mossy tendrils, the sharpness of pine needles. The air here, contrary to his expectations, was ferny, and now and then brackish, and there brushed against his face light airy objects that he envisaged as aerial seeds, like the spinning oakseed, and spores, wet and dry, the moist ones often bursting against his skin in the fashion of soap bubbles, emitting tiny plopping sounds, leaving upon his face circlets of webby residue. Emerging again into shifting light, he found himself in a hall of mirrors; but as he feared what the residue of spores might cause his face to resemble, he avoided the mirrors, and flew onward, only tightening his hold upon his innocence, who napped in his arms as if the movement of headlong flight were only the lulling motion of his rocking torso as he sat and read to her. The foot of a stair, wearing a figured carpet slipper, emerged from the darkness ahead; he trod upon it, offering no apology, and plunged upward, and some mass of hanging material slowed his progress, so that he must claw and grope his way through and between its tatters, some strands of which felt warm, others cold, some desicated, some others appallingly fleshy, and these touches were accompanied by various odors characterized by rancidity, ancientness, squalor; and the last through which he plunged, gasping and retching, was the malodor of ruttishness.

He ran into a chamber so immense that it commanded all the sea, through an expanse of glass so unencumbered by mullions that it was, in itself, a veritable wonder. The chamber was flooded with the cold supernal light of the moon, which illuminated the darkest corners, save one; a murk in the far distance appeared to contain some bulk, amid which gleamed—but no longer. Vilet pressed himself to the cold vast pane; it was his illusion that he had lain himself upon the very bosom of the sea. Before he gave himself to the night's indulgence—thoughts he could no longer stay through flight—he placed his dearest possession, his little Marguerite, within a divan and laid upon her covers, and bade her sleep. In the interval that he faced into the room there again arose the sense, the instinct, that the far unlit corner contained something capable of volition.

He turned once more and lay upon the wind's eye, outstretched, without defenses.

There was for him an awfulness in the glare of a moonlit sea; and in the retreating sound of the tide across the shingle, there resided a forboding that could become despair. Once, to his undoing, so his thoughts ran, the transmogrification occurred; that was on the shores of another sea, in another time so distant that it and the sea could have belonged to some universe . . . denied, or which something had denied him. On that night, the essence of the moon on the wastes and the retreating tide had led him to the brink of some comprehension that he was instructed would be awesome and irreversible. He had thought that he stood upon an impossible precipice and was enjoined to look down.

He saw now that the chamber he had attained was the terminus of the house for he heard above him the restless mutter of the great bell, and a beating, as of wings.

That long ago he had been a young curé. The precipice, then, was of the imagination. Tonight he stood where it had been foretold that he should stand. Looking down with scaleless eyes he saw the samphire gatherers' crooked shapes upon the rocks, and under the pelagial, transparent surface he saw the upthrust snouts of mammals gray and blunt as teethed reefs.

On that long ago night he was told that if he cast his eyes downward he would comprehend. He had not looked. In his failure was the betrayal of the idea of God and the very concept of Belief, for what he had feared to see was no shimmer of eternal life but only the vacant sea upon which he now gazed; and what he had feared to hear was not the stars singing together but the abandoning tide across the shingle. And in his despair he had turned to someone. And afterwards, after the turning, the apostasy as it may have been, he had cried out. What had he cried? To whom? Something in the corner stirred. Marguerite? No, within the covers she was still. Walking towards the dark corner Vilet received the impression of creatures pressing against walls to allow him passage.

November the Fourth, 1840

At my desk I have found a mass of scribbled papers, ink overturned, dripping onto the carpet. That is what I found when I approached my night roost a moment ago. I believed the creature to have gone directly, following the dictates of my forcible instruction, but it is likely that "it" made its way here in error or in malice hoping to find something to smuggle away as a souvenir.

As briefly as possible, Mrs. Wince sent word that she was taken to her bed and that a relative would appear, as I had been forewarned; and the deliverer of the note, a child of amorphous gender, was given some coins and left. As though it had followed the child here, the cat of late-spectral propensity slunk about, although that is hardly the good word, such was the beast's assurance and insolence, as like to its fellow natives, human variety, as could be. Daisikins left no doubt as to its reality but sought to chase it from the courtyard. The cat would have none of it but proceeded to inaugurate, if you please, a courtship dance, presenting itself front and rear for inspection, arching its back fetchingly; and, to the bewilderment of my Daisikins, the cat sought to rub itself, flank and tail, against the chest of my little creature. I do not know why something in me, at that moment, chose to strike a light, but it did so with a loud report, as it were and may actually have been. I heard Mrs. Wince's voice saying "Ambsus" and in reply to my question about what the natives did in winter, her voice obligingly repeated "Grumbling." Except that it was vouchsafed me to hear, in the repetition, what the woman had actually been saying. "Grumbling," because of the curious sound, was in actuality "gombling," or "gambling"; and "Ambsus," which I took to be the cat's name, was "Ambsace"—the two aces, in gambling parlance, as I have the horrid right to know—ambsace, the veriest symbol of bad, of disastrous, of foul, of tragic luck! As though the cat read my mind, and my sudden, terrified cognizance of it, it sprang upon the newel of a gatepost where it showed itself to be a Tom; grinning down at my purity, who gazed back at the Tom in, I swear this, the dawning stage of comprehension, the cat exhibited lewdness. I was seized with violence, which nothing, no cautioning word could have assuaged; I took hold of a loose timber with one hand and a cobblestone with the other; letting fly with the cobblestone I followed upon its heels with the heavy board. All precisely as it had been in another time. In short, I killed again. There appeared, instantly, as far as I could ascertain, for my rage continued to expand after the murder—there appeared as once before there had appeared, a human creature, rosy-cheeked and mouth open in a great *O,* a grimace which I saw as a willful attempt to distort the features out of a *discernible gender.* I shrieked at this fantoccino, for the past was upon me; and if only I had shrieked *then;* I demanded to know what it wanted of me. It told me in a quavering voice that it was "standin" for Mrs. Wince. Suspicion did not *assail* me; it dwelled within and about me; it had taken possession of me. I rushed at the creature and demanded of it, *Show me your breasts.*

It fled, weeping and wailing. And, I propose, found its way here by some route known to it but not to me, some ingress hidden in weeds, some secret door; and here in my private chambers, in its haste to get at my valuables with which to compensate its master for wages denied, it defaced these papers and split this ink.

Rage has exhausted me. I will postpone for just another night the description of my house, my beloved and nearly-lost. And here again the sweetness of perfume, issuing from some secret, radiant duct, for such odors must, as well, be filled with light. Good night, beloved Mansion of my soul!

November, 1980

He thinks in the middle of the night that he hears the swan make a sound of distress. He gets up and does not turn on the light but pads through the hall in his bare feet. He passes the vestibule and hears a whispering sound, like somebody's thighs encased in leather rubbing against each other. Under the door he sees the feet. His senses direct him to concentrate near the lock of the door, and he knows that the sound is the insinuation of a credit card down the slit of the door. He says out loud, "Credit's almost run out," and watches while the boots go, but it is no hurried retreat they beat. He goes to the terrace and looks out at the swan. She is in a very awkward position, stretching up, craning her neck, pressing against the tall wide tub that contains his stand of bamboo behind which the fountain with the recirculating motor gurgles. Is she trying to get to the water, trying to get into the grotto? He has a feeling, totally inexplicable, of rage, so sudden and intense that there is foam on his lips. He senses that the swan is in great danger. He says, the philosopher, "Like all things out of their element." Then, projected over the city in a corridor of time unsuspected in the symmetries of a willfully and eternally new town, he sees a small dark man kneeling at the feet of a deer, and radially, like a tunnel connecting the images, there is another tube of time and within it is a great . . . bird. The images are so suffused with eroticism that he longs for someone, anyone, especially the Puerto Rican who, he can sense, is leaning against the wall in the hallway.

November the Third, 1770

When the doe stepped from the corner Vilet fell to his knees before her and the gesture was accompanied by the sound of winds rushing, that could have been stirred by great wings. And though he was mortally engaged in thanksgiving, some untouched part of his brain could see the winds destroying the smugness of motionless sea, the menace of mammal-fish, churning the abyssal waters and tossing waves higher and higher until they would reach and douse the cold and faithless light of the moon. He kissed the doe's hooves, which were of a surpassing nobility in shape and odor for they smelt of attar of roses, and the fetlocks breathed forth a ferny perfume as though hoof and fetlock together formed a bouquet. Her gentle eyes bent upon his head, bowed in worship, a forgiveness so profound that it burned the nape of his neck.

In time Vilet arose and with the utmost deference took into his hand the silken ribband around the doe's slender neck, and under the guidance of a now-altered moon, he led her back to his apartment, uttering her praises all the way. And to mark their passage, the great unfettered bell rang. The rush of wings in the air mingled with the sound of the risen, abluent wind.

Vilet lay upon his bed with the doe, humiliate as a nun of Blassoni, and as one presses one's lips to the Sacred Heart, he pressed his to that part of the doe's breast beyond which beat her own heart.

Toward sleep—for the doe had attained hers, attested to by the gently bellowsing sides—he had a moment that was like a return to earlier fear: he believed that he lacked something, or had misplaced something, or had betrayed or been betrayed by something, and he started up; but another fear, protective of the doe, caused him to clear his mind of doubt and lie down again in faith, between the doe's forelegs, and resume his adoration of the Sacred Heart.

November the Fifth, 1840

I am too fatigued to write more than this perfunctory entry, a fatigue born of excellence of spirits and health, which kept me too much "on the go" the livelong day. Bed will not seem at first so comforting, because Daisikins is not with me. I see that having made that statement I must at least offer a version of explanation, however truncated.

Expecting the agents of retribution (relatives of the wretched thief of yesterday, of whom I demanded a show of mammaries), I received today instead a genuine jewel: the arrival, and consequent performance, of the Perfect Servant. She is a lovely child, and as soon as, with the aid of sign language on her part (she is a mute; a not unwelcome "flaw" in a servant), we had reached our agreement, she set to work with such a will and such grace that I was smitten in the best way, with gratitude. And in the course of the day, altogether too short, even though it was prolonged, by the blissful child herself, past nightfall—in the course of the day we had occasion for many encounters, for she was here, there, everywhere, turning up unexpectedly on staircases, dodging out of closets, springing, like a Jill in the Box, out of chests; so that at one of these charming encounters I asked her if she was indeed following me, and the child blushed and gave me such a look! I do believe that I am to be, if indeed I am not already, the object of a tender and infinitely virginal little case of hero worship.

Nightfall came too soon and she asked, perfectly clearly with her brown hands, if, due to darkness &c, I might not spare her my Daisikins for company on the dark road home! I was startled and momentarily frightened at this expression of the hitherto unthinkable. But something allowed me to put myself in the place of the voiceless child, for whom, in the event of trouble, my little terrier could serve as clarisonous alarum, and I acquiesced. Yes, I could have taken the child in front of me on the mare; but something in me recoils at the idea of it, I become agitated, I cannot say why. My skin crawls as I write, at the image of myself astride the horse and the child between my legs, my arm pressing her to my chest. Gender does not absolve her. This will never be. Only Daisikins, my purity . . . A sound, like a cry, a whimper, something in distress. I have in my thoughtlessness hurt the sensibilities of my asylum.

Having thrown myself upon the floor in penance I feel somewhat forgiven and I am being, even as I continue to write, rewarded, for where there was fatigue there is now ease; where there was turmoil, a peace grows in my head like a white flower; and about me eddy soothingly faint odors; and of sounds, less a discernible melody than a vibration, more like the awareness of a coursing, as though I could follow the progress of my blood within my veins. It seems that daily, hourly, I learn, in my cloistered school; "If there is a heaven on earth, ease for any soul . . ."

I am most blessed of men, most blessed of houses.

Vilet awakes in the night and finds himself entwined with the laidure of a hairy Being. Crying out to the author of his fortunes he remembers what he has left, of what he has been bereft by his will and a satanic dazzlement: his little dog Marguerite, whose still form he has abandoned under covers in a divan so distant in space and time that he believes even she and the room in which she lies are manavilins from another Universe. He believes he has not only been abandoned by some Author as he has abandoned his pet, an Author to whom he himself has been briefly a pet, but that he had been cursed and condemned before his conception, the which was the idea made manifest of a damned creature. With all his sudden intelligence as sharp as a needle to the eye, he knows that the forelegs between which he lies belong to His Satanic Majesty. He thrusts his hand down among the fetor of the wakeful Being's hairy thighs and finds there the erect lingam and feels upon his naked instep the clawing of the cloven hoof. He springs from his bed and grasps with a hand that knows all manner of darkness his dagger.

I have just awakened in a sweat as profound as the termed desudation of my sickness, of which other symptoms were asnomia and malaena; and there were hallucinations involving the three major senses. I pause in my flight to set down, however heavy the sweat, that the fever has certainly broken and with it all illusion. I continue to write even as wings beat overhead. I can see clearly as though I had found the planetarium of this cursed mansion that some immense white bird, the swan of hell, is circling the house and will set down in the rusty dish and produce some monstrosity. That dish was built for her centuries ago; her journey from hell has spanned the centuries, a ceaseless flight, parallel to mine in the opposite direction, for I must kill again before the doors creak and yawn for me. In my thrall to the house, its perfumes, its melodies, its palpable heartbeats, I failed to see with eyes that besought my intelligence, eyes which I willfully blinded, and failed to smell with a nose that strove to inform me: *that child of yesterday, of my enamouredness, of my blindness, was no female. It feigned dumbness for its voice would have betrayed it. And its brown hands, that, observing my fascination with their beauty, it gloved thereafter, pantomiming some minor injury. And its gait. And its odour. And its symmetries. Those of my perdition. Mrs. Wince's "lod" after all.*

He opens the terrace door and hears the swan singing, a garbled song of geese and fools. He thinks that her voice is as rusty as charity and he stabs her to the heart with a feeling of great gladness. He returns, leaving the door open, for the faint dying song continues, the sound of blood singing. And he comes here to this blue instrument and types the words on this page and it is as though he is timing someone and he has been on the button, his timing for once flawless as each man's is once in his life. He hears now he is hearing the slither of the credit card down to the lock which willingly gives. He is hearing now the steps not stealthy but like those of an old lover returning. And he wants to call out a welcome, something on the order of Daddy Death I have been waiting for you so long.

It draws a sigh upon the air.
It draws a sigh upon the air.

It draws satisfaction.
It draws satisfaction.

It draws tired.
It draws tired.

And waits.
And waits.

The names of those to whom this work is dedicated are
concealed, like Vilet's little Marguerite, within
this "divan." In addition it is addressed
to High House and its phantoms, dead
and alive, of which Daisy and I,
dead or alive, are now two.

POSTSCRIPT
by Bradford Morrow

"Connected thought," Coleman wrote, having just finished his final redraft of "The Silver Swanne": "last night I broke a glass in my bathtub. I had had a drink on the rim and was drying myself and thus. The water had run out and there was glass everywhere. My first thought was, 'Who'd have dreamed the old man had so much blood in him!' which I thought was odd at first, but understood it to mean: that to comprehend the density of existence, of things, the fragments and shards and layers which compose the compact surface of things, it is necessary to 'break' them. Thinking along these lines, one understands the meaning of saying that a poem or book has 'great weight'—like a Black Hole, perhaps. That compact little glass, a small wine glass—but broken, it seemed to contain enough glass to make three, or four, that size." Engineer's Gate, far below the window of his writing room, sang with snowplows that "dark polluted morning" in February 1983. An aside in a letter, the incident, broken glass and an image of dissection reveal a paradigm of his aesthetic, his technique, and his vision.

Coleman called upon life to be romantically charged, each of its elements the key to a possible metaphysic. His manner of introducing into the objects around him a reckless mystery and magic was civilized and awesome and sometimes frightening. The passion of these conversions of the natural world—the glass, a swan improbably sheltered on a city balcony, houses on islands and in the mind, a Sunday afternoon that must be filled with mimicry—into a mysterious kingdom (one which our tired eyes and reluctant hearts are called to reconsider) is carried through the absolute and original beauty of his language.

A hundred pages into a new novel, *Eve of the Green Grass*, twice as far into his memoirs, tellingly entitled *A Dark Book*, Coleman declared to his friends that he was no longer a writer. His novel *White on Black on White* had enjoyed substantial critical praise without finding the popular audience he longed for; this depressed him profoundly. Writers by definition function in solitude, even isolation. But Coleman's youthful exposure to the world of New York theatre—come innocent, eager, a self-described Kentucky "hick"—may have given him an idea that literary success could have the same rewards: money, recognition, approval. In the fifties he had worked as songwriter/lyricist for the DuMont Television Network production *Once Upon a Tune*, which starred the then-unknown Bea Arthur, Elaine Stritch, Alice Ghostly, and Charlotte Rae, composing nearly a thousand works for weekly broadcast. In 1955, as a protégé of David Merrick, he worked with John LaTouche on a Broadway musical rendition of Eugene O'Neill's *Ah, Wilderness!* In the late fifties he adapted Carl Van Vechten's 1924 novel, *The Tattooed Countess*, which was produced at the Barbizon Plaza in May 1961. It closed, a disastrous flop, at the end of the first week. A year later he wrote a play called *Eve of the Green Grass* (whose theme of absolute evil the novel was also to study), staged at the Chelsea Art Theatre with Kim Hunter in the lead role. He free-lanced as a model, circulated among photographers, actors, producers, and so developed the rich, tapestried idea of what fame could mean for an artist. Seeing *Eve of the Green Grass* performed caused him to change his direction yet again; his skills were not in playwriting. He would write a novel.

But while his novels *One of the Children Is Crying, Mrs. October Was Here,* and the masterpiece *Island People* brought critical acclaim from voices as different as Tennessee Williams, John Hawkes, and Maurice Sendak, none of this could assuage his need for a popular readership. *Too Much Flesh and Jabez*, with its tone-perfect dialogue and its cunning tale-within-a-tale, only strengthened his reputation among fellow writers. A writers' writer—but it was as if he were marked, he averred.

Three of the stories which make up this volume—"Ham's Gift,"
"I Envy You Your Great Adventure," and "In the Mood"—were
written as early as 1961, before Coleman became a novelist. A
master of the possibilities of short fiction, he built the architec-
tures of his five novels to rise from foundation to clerestories in
intensely rendered narratives, short tales, all compounded by
psychological systems of mirrors, blind passages, and *faux fe-
nêtres*. The house—possessed of gender, spirit, fate—in essence
breaks itself, chipping away at itself to ambush the facades and
rooms. They bring forth the gauzy soul of conflict and obsession
so impossible directly to describe. The epigraph for *Island People*
carries the metaphor forward into absolute anthropopathy: "One
need not be a Chamber to be Haunted/ One need not be a House."
Goethe said, "My field is time." For Dowell it was the shattering
of time into constituent shards for psychological examination.
Since time is, in its passage, such a harrowing element, behind
whose razor-edge we irremediably trail, its study—the study of
its effect within a mind—is doubly harrowing when the exam-
iner believes in ghosts. Thus the impact of what is arguably his
greatest work of short fiction, "The Silver Swanne." Coleman
absolutely believed in ghosts. Ghosts deny death and abjure time.

This prose of intense "breakage" or analysis will not leave time
alone, will subscribe to no tenet about linearity of past-present-
future. As a consequence it subverts the more popular, "realist"
conventions of narrative sequencing such as flashback, nostalgia,
baroque sentiment. Consider "The Great Godalmighty Bird,"
whose impulse is domestic, a boy's remembrance of his grandmother, not so distinct in its form from so many mainstream
short stories. What occurs near the end, however, flies free, ex-
plodes, folds time like batter back in a layer over itself. There is
an almost electrical shift of vantage—subtle, abrupt—hurtling
the story you thought you were reading into a centrifuge. The
effect is sculptural. Suspecting the strictly linear mind of signi-
fying nothing that knows of the daily soul, Coleman developed
strategies that seem simultaneously centrifugal and centripe-
tal—Heraclitean and Parmenidian. Yet the work is so accessible

and readable! Empathy, love, courage, soulfulness—all the traits of the born storyteller—are present to such a degree that the powerful technique is rendered invisible. In "The Moon, the Owl, My Sister" our narrator, we may or may not come to learn, is a fieldmouse. In "Writings on a Cave Wall" he is a child who happens also to be a cannibal. A father *is* a river, a fox, a mountain lion.

The level of craft and breadth of emotions available to Dowell as a writer is dizzying, as is the range of scenarios—from the surreal, decadent Europe of Augustine and Omerie in "I Envy You Your Great Adventure" to Marriott's mother-dominated, memory-haunted room in "If Beggars Were Horses." The syntax, spun from Brontë as much as Faulkner, forges in the power of its obsession something beyond the recognized parameters of Southern fiction. Intolerant of spare simplicity—except when spare simplicity works best—it builds through layers, trusting language to shoot us deeper and deeper into the compound souls of Vilet and Wool Tea and the boy whose hunchbacked grandmother comes to embody physical and spiritual perfection in the grotesquerie of received norms.

Late in 1984 Coleman, often reclusive, gave dinner parties like mad—he was a master chef, as anyone who ever was fortunate enough to dine at the aerie table under the gaze of the shepherd in the old English painting would attest. He composed a new song, "He's Reaching Out," which he sang for us at the piano. He was going to take up photography. He did a few book reviews, but fiction was as a pariah, an unmentionable. Thinking it might rekindle his interest in writing, I urged him to assemble his stories. It would be a book, something he could produce without giving over to the high anxiety of composition. Not until the summer of 1985 did this idea finally take hold. One evening the last week in July, he presented *The Houses of Children* to me in finished typescript.

Coleman discussed suicide frankly, often, for years—all the years I knew him. "The balcony beckons me," he said to me so many times. It was a phrase I could only persistently counter

with: "Exhaust all other possible options." In the earliest minutes of Saturday morning, the third of August 1985, he leapt
from his balcony fifteen floors to his death. What we have lost in
that hauntingly American tragedy is immeasurable, as this mas-
terly, unique book of "great weight" will attest. I can think of
few contemporaries who combine in writing the formal angular-
ities, the sheer effulgence of word and phrasing, the Gothicism,
the tenacity—almost inhuman in its deliberate gaze upon what
we may consider so violent, so radically disturbing that we would
wish not to glimpse it at all—and the authority present in this
work. Possessed of their own logic, it is as if these stories are
jealous of their method of proposing and evolving character.
Their maker surely never encountered a better way than his own,
and so any sentence one could pull from its context nevertheless
would still reflect that method. Fractile: pertaining to fractions,
or breakage. The logic of shattering compels us to glimpse
the vision as a whole in the very fragments it might make. Like
all high art, this work is concerned with the pursuit of fresh
orderings.

New York
July 1986

About the Author

Coleman Dowell was born in Adairville, Kentucky, in 1925 and died sixty years later in New York City. After service in the Army Medical Corps during World War II, he settled in New York, where he worked as a writer and composer for the DuMont Television Network. During the late 1950s and early 1960s he authored several plays, including the musical *The Tattooed Countess,* based on the novel by his friend Carl Van Vechten. He published his first novel, *One of the Children Is Crying,* in 1968; it has now been reissued by Weidenfeld & Nicolson. This was followed by *Mrs. October Was Here, Island People, Too Much Flesh and Jabez,* and *White on Black on White.* His short stories, here collected for the first time in book form, have appeared in numerous literary magazines. At the time of his death, Coleman Dowell was working on a novel, *Eve of the Green Grass,* and a volume of memoirs to be entitled *A Dark Book.*

Bradford Morrow is the editor of *Conjunctions* magazine, in which many of these stories first appeared. He lives in New York City and has recently completed his first novel.